The Long Lie

The Long Lie

Simon Michael

SEVERN SH HOUSE

This first world edition published in Great Britain 1992 by
SEVERN HOUSE PUBLISHERS LTD of
35 Manor Road, Wallington, Surrey SM6 0BW
First published in the U.S.A. 1992 by
SEVERN HOUSE PUBLISHERS INC of
475 Fifth Avenue, New York, NY 10017–6220.

All situations in this publication are fictitious and
any resemblance to living persons is purely coincidental

British Library Cataloguing in Publication Data
Michael, Simon
  The Long Lie.
  I. Title
  823.914 [F]

ISBN 0–7278–4396–6

Typeset by Hewer Text Composition Services, Edinburgh
Printed and bound in Great Britain by
Dotesios Limited, Trowbridge, Wiltshire

To Elaine, for everything
With thanks to Dr Roger Ingram and David Swain
for their assistance

PROLOGUE

On the last morning of her life, Hilary Prentice rose feeling unaccountably happy. It was just another day, a Monday; Bob had to be packed off to work as usual and she had to clean the house and do some cooking, but for some reason the good humour of the weekend remained with her. They had held a dinner party on the Saturday night, their first for years, and it had gone well. Peter and Anne had stayed late and slept on the couch, and on Sunday they had all gone out for a pub lunch. It had been delightful. Hilary pulled on her dressing gown and gave Bob a shove to reawaken him.

"It's twenty to six. You'll miss your train," she said. He had a business meeting in Northampton that day, hence the early start. He did not respond, so she shoved him harder.

"Bob!" she hissed, keeping her voice down, forgetting momentarily that the twins, whose term had ended last week, had spent the night at the Bells' and were not due home until that afternoon. Her husband groaned, but turned over, opening a bleary eye.

"How can you be so perky at this ungodly hour?" he demanded, his voice hoarse.

She grinned. "Don't know." She sat on the edge of the bed next to him, and smoothed the tousled greying hair out of his eyes. "It was a lovely weekend, wasn't it?"

1

"Hmm?" Bob opened his eyes again with an effort. "What? Oh, yes, it was."

"Can we do it again?"

"Sure, if you like."

Hilary rose again. "I'll put the kettle on."

A small convoy of vehicles travelled into Coulsdon up the Brighton Road from the south. Two British Gas vans, and two expensive saloons. It was still dark, and they travelled with headlights on, the road surface sparkling with frost, passing shops decked out in their Christmas finery – only three more shopping days. The convoy slowed almost to a halt. The driver of the leading vehicle, a Jaguar, seemed to be looking for a landmark, for he peered ahead into the dark. Apparently satisfied, he pulled over onto the kerb where the Brighton Road met a side road, The Avenue. He swiftly opened the door and, leaning out from his seat, illuminated by the glare of the lights from the vehicle behind, he waved urgently to the other vehicles to pull in. The first British Gas van stopped immediately behind the Jaguar; the second continued past it and stopped in front. The yellow hazard lights on top of each vehicle began to revolve. The last car, a BMW, turned round neatly and came to a halt on the far side of the road, pointing in the direction from which the convoy had come.

Men decamped from all the vehicles and immediately set about their tasks. There was a sense of controlled urgency about them, as if they depended on one another, and each was practised in his part. One, wearing British Gas overalls, lifted a manhole cover in the centre of the road and unfolded a red and white striped screen around the hole. A second, also in British Gas overalls, ran back down the road and placed plastic cones at two-pace intervals so that the road was gradually closed off into one lane. Another man followed him, carrying a set of traffic lights mounted on a tripod. He placed them on the northbound

2

carriageway where the cones stopped. At the same time another team of two men carried out the same procedure in relation to the southbound carriageway. They had been fortunate, for no traffic had passed in either direction in the two minutes taken to complete their task. A line of cars then did approach from the south, and while one of the men began to wire the traffic lights, another directed the cars through. The driver of the Jaguar was the last to emerge on to the road. As he did so, he reached back into the car, and took something off the passenger seat. It was about two feet long and was wrapped in oilskin. He placed the object under his arm, walked to the rear of the second van and climbed into the back, pulling the doors closed behind him.

Bob Prentice saw flashing yellow lights through the obscured glass of the bathroom window as he shaved. He tried to open the window with one hand, his razor in the other, but his fingers were soapy and he could not get a good grip on the handle. He grunted, and continued with his shaving. He could see from his watch, propped on top of the cabinet against the toothmug, that he had only twelve minutes to leave the house, or he would miss his train to London, and thus his connection at Euston. He heard the toaster pop up downstairs in the kitchen, and Hilary's humming as she pottered about, but he doubted that he would have time to eat.

The volume of traffic on the Brighton Road was increasing. A small queue of vehicles was by now accumulating each time the traffic lights turned to red, particularly in the northbound direction, as early commuters attempted to beat the rush hour. They watched with irritation the activities of the two or three gas employees who appeared intent on the leak, or whatever it was, in the middle of the road.

*   *   *

3

Bob Prentice took a bite of toast and struggled into his coat, briefcase in hand. Hilary handed him his gloves and stood by the front door. He took another bite and placed the last of the uneaten slice on the hall table.

"Sorry," he said with a grin, spraying crumbs.

"It's okay. Have a nice day."

"I'll phone from Northampton as soon as I'm finished," he said, pulling on a glove.

"Bye," she said, leaning forward and kissing him briefly for the last time.

Hilary opened the door for him, the blast of cold air making her shiver, and he waved from the gate, turned, and walked off to the station. Hilary was about to close the door when she noticed the vans outside. She peered out to see what all the activity was for, but, apart from the flashing lights, she could see nothing. She had thought of going back to bed for an hour, but if they were going to start digging up the road, there was not much point. She closed the door behind her and picked up the toast, popping it into her mouth. She swept the crumbs into her hand, straightened the photo of the girls on the hall table – such a lovely picture, that one, taken when they were fifteen – and went back into the kitchen. The house was on a corner, and from where she stood by the sink she could see the road more clearly. For the first time she realised that it was gas men working outside. The thought suddenly occurred to her that if they were working on the main, they might have to turn the supply off. Damn, she thought, that's all I need! With half the baking for Christmas still to be done. She drew the curtains back and stared outside.

"What the fuck's she doing?"

"Dunno. Just watching, far as I can tell."

The men's voices echoed eerily around the inside of the van. The one first to speak joined the other and replaced him at a spy hole in the side of the van. He could see the middle-aged woman standing in her kitchen, the net curtain pulled to one side.

"What if she rings— " began the other.

"I know!" he shouted. He turned from the spy hole, looking grim. His long black hair was pulled back from his face and tied in a ponytail. A tiny shaft of light entered the dark interior of the van and fell across his face, picking out a scar that slanted down his forehead and cheek. His brow contracted in furious concentration, and his cold, dark eyes flashed. His companion watched him, waiting patiently for orders.

"Okay!" said the man with the scar. "Come with me. And bring the shooter."

Hilary had finished her now luke-warm cup of tea, and had decided to have a bath. She was climbing the stairs when the back door of the house opened, and two men with balaclava helmets pulled down over their faces crept into the kitchen. Hilary heard a noise, but thought that it was the catflap. She paused on the staircase and leaned over the balustrade.

"Billy?" she called.

The two men stormed into the hallway and ran at her. It was so fast and unexpected that Hilary did not even move. The first one grabbed her by her dressing-gown hem and dragged her down the steps on her bottom back into the hall. She cried out once, but could make no further sound as the second man clapped his gloved hand roughly across her mouth. One grabbed her feet and the other her shoulders, and they half-carried, half-dragged her into the dining room. They slung her on the floor with such force that the breath was knocked out of her. As she lay there gasping for air one of them sat astride her, pinning her hands to the floor on either side of her head. Hilary felt a ball of material shoved hard into her mouth, so far that

5

she almost gagged. She felt a draft of cold air around her buttocks and thighs, and realised that her dressing gown had been torn open. I'm going to be raped! she thought, and started writhing furiously.

"Grab her feet!" ordered the man on top of her.

Hilary started kicking even harder. She felt a sudden blow across her face.

"Pack that in!"

She looked up at the speaker. He released his right hand from her wrist, and reached into his jacket. He pulled out a gun and held it right in front of her face, almost touching her nose.

"You either lie there quietly while we tie you up, or I'll kill you here and now." Hilary went suddenly still and looked into the eyes of her attacker. He stared back at her, his chest heaving from the struggle, but his eyes calm and steady. She believed him.

"That's better. Now, if you're sensible, this'll all be over in ten minutes, and you'll be fine. If not . . ." He waggled the gun in his hand and shrugged.

Hilary felt the belt of her dressing gown being pulled from under her waist, and then her feet were being tied. The man astride her got off.

"Roll over on to your front," he ordered. Hilary complied, her nightie rucked up and her bottom showing. The man tying her ankles pulled her nightie down for her, and she felt a sudden wave of gratitude to him. He fastened her ankles, and brought the belt up to her back. Hilary felt her wrists being pulled down. He was trying to tie them with the end of the same belt but it was not quite long enough.

"For God's sake, give it to me!" ordered the other.

He yanked her feet up behind her. Hilary's body suddenly convulsed, her feet thrashing, one striking her attacker in the face. She was thrown on to her back again and the gun was pointed at her head. She seemed not to notice it. Her hands clutched at her breast and her eyes stared wildly. Her two attackers gaped at her, uncomprehending.

"What's she doing, Tony?" asked one. His voice was taught with fear. Tony brandished the gun again, putting it right to her forehead. He saw beads of perspiration starting from her brow, and her face, only seconds ago red and flushed from the struggle, was now a dull grey colour. He reached down with his free hand and pulled the gag from her mouth but it made no difference. She tried to sit up but only managed to raise her head a few inches above the carpet. Her torso shook once, twice, three times, and then with a gasp, her hands fell from her chest, and she sank back to the floor, completely still.

"Jesus Christ!"

"Shut up, Ray!" ordered Tony, leaning across Hilary's body, trying to locate a heartbeat.

"Jesus Christ!" repeated Ray.

"I said shut up!" hissed Tony savagely. He pressed his ear to her left breast. Nothing. He stood back and looked at her face again. The clammy whiteness of her skin was now tinged with blue, especially round her lips.

"Is she dead? Tony? Is she dead?" His voice rose an octave with each question.

"It fuckin' looks that way, don't it?"

"But how? How, Tony? We barely touched her."

"How the fuck do I know? I ain't no doctor. Heart attack, looked like."

"Oh Jesus— "

"If you say that once more, I'll fuckin' do you, I swear it."

"What're we gonna do?"

Tony paused. "Get her shoulders," he ordered, untying Hilary's ankles and stuffing the belt in his pocket. Ray stood there, his eyes vacant, his mouth open. "I said get her shoulders, you bastard!"

They carried her back to the hall. "Stand her up a minute," ordered Tony. Ray held her under the arms, panting with the exertion, while Tony rearranged her nightie and dressing gown. He threaded the belt back in its loops, and tied it again across her front. "Help me get her down there," he said, nodding at the foot of the stairs. They arranged her body so that her feet were pointing to the door, and her bottom was on the lowest stair, her head two or three above that.

"There," said Tony with some satisfaction. "The lady fell down the stairs and had a heart attack. Or the other way round." He examined her ankles. They had been lucky. The belt, made of towelling, had barely left a mark on her.

"You can see something there," pointed out Ray.

"Yeah, but you do get marks and so on if you fall down stairs, don't you? She's probably got a bruise on her bum too, where she fell, right?"

"Christ, Tony, I never expected this . . ." whined Ray.

"For God's sake, Ray, what d'you expect me to do? She's dead, right? There ain't nothing we can do about it." He looked at his watch. "Come on. The van'll be along any second."

Tony made for the back door. Ray hesitated, looking at Hilary's body. Tony returned to him and dragged him by the sleeve through the kitchen and back out into the cold dawn.

CHAPTER 1

"Will the foreman of the jury please rise?"

"Where the bloody hell is that girl from the CPS?" swore Bruce Withers QC under his breath. The case had been running for two weeks, and it seemed as if a different representative of the Crown Prosecution Service had attended every day. That was, of course, when they bothered to attend at all. He scanned the bench behind him where the CPS representative was supposed to sit, and looked in vain for the case file.

The clerk of the court addressed the foreman of the jury, a tired-looking middle-aged man in his shirtsleeves. "Please answer the next question either 'Yes' or 'No': have you reached a verdict on any of the counts on the indictment, in respect of which at least ten of you are agreed?"

A dishevelled young man appeared at the back of the court and scurried to the bench behind the prosecution barristers.

"Sorry I'm late," he whispered. "I didn't hear the tannoy."

"Why not?" asked Withers icily.

"I've been assigned to two courts in the building today. I was in the other one."

"And I don't suppose you've the faintest idea what this case is about, eh?" The young man looked glum. "As I thought. Well," hissed Withers with controlled irritation,

9

"this is the retrial of the Coulsdon Diamond Robbery; the jury are about to be discharged; and I am about to offer no evidence. I assume that that course would be in line with your instructions?" The young man shrugged. "Thank you," concluded Withers with icy sarcasm.

"And good night," added Withers's junior, who had listened to the conversation. He winked at the hapless clerk, and turned to face the Judge. The clerk sat back in his seat, his face burning, and looked around him. The courtroom looked like a television studio. Video monitors were dotted across the room, on the benches for the Judge, counsel and the jury, there was even a miniature screen perched on top of the witness box.

The foreman of the jury spoke wearily, his voice betraying the two days of argument in the jury room. "No, my Lord, we are still divided."

Mr Justice Griffith drew a long breath. The cost of the four-week trial was enormous. To discharge yet another jury . . .

"Is there no assistance that I might give you?" he asked hopefully. He had asked the same question on numerous occasions since the jury retired the day before.

"I don't think so, no, thank you, my Lord."

"Do you think," asked the Judge, "that you might break your deadlock if given further time?" The foreman spread his arms wide in eloquent answer. Several of the jury members shook their heads and glared at one or two of their number sitting at the end of the front row.

"As I have said before, if you think that you might be able to bring in a verdict, whether it be guilty or not guilty, on any one or more of the charges faced by Kenny, I shall ask you to retire further."

The foreman looked at the two ranks of faces for guidance. There were a few resigned shrugs, but most shook their heads again.

At the mention of the accused's name, the clerk looked

across at the dock. A large square-faced man sat looking at his feet. His lips were pursed together, and it was unclear whether he was stifling a grin or a yawn. He wore a dark blue pin-striped suit, a light blue shirt and a red silk tie. He might have been a banker or a stockbroker had it not been for his long black hair which swept up from his forehead and fell lank on to his shoulders. That, and a scar that disfigured his temple, starting in his hairline and slanting in towards his nose. The knife – or, perhaps, bottle – that had caused it must have just missed the eyeball, as the scar continued faintly on his cheek until it was lost in the crease of his nose. The pallor of his complexion betrayed a long period on remand.

"Mr Withers?" asked the Judge.

Withers rose slowly to his feet. He was in his early eighties now, but still a striking figure. Even with the hunch imposed on his spine by the years, he stood over six feet tall. His face was like weathered granite, but penetrating light blue eyes still spied like a bird's out of the network of lines carved between his features.

"With regret, Mr Withers, I feel that the time has come for me to discharge this jury. Has the Crown considered its position?"

"It has, my Lord."

"So be it. Members of the jury," said the Judge, turning to address them, "I now discharge you from giving a verdict in this case. I would like to thank you for the great amount of time and effort that you have put into your public duty, at a cost, I know, of great inconvenience to at least some of you. You will be pleased to know that your duty has now been discharged, and that you will not be required to sit on any other cases. I shall direct the jury bailiff to make a note that you should not be called again for jury service for a considerable period!" He smiled, and the relief among them was palpable. "You may stay and watch what happens now, or you may leave."

11

"Never use two words when ten will do," commented the junior barrister under his breath.

The Judge turned again to Withers.

"The jury having been unable to agree on two separate occasions," said the Queen's Counsel, "and bearing in mind the enormous public costs already thrown away by two inconclusive trials, the Crown takes the view that it would not be right for this defendant to be tried a third time. In all the circumstances, the Crown offers no further evidence against him."

"Do you have any comment, Mr Blackburne?"

"No, my Lord," replied the defence barrister.

"Very well. Stand up, Kenny." The accused man stood in the dock. "I formally record a verdict of Not Guilty against you. You may leave the dock. Are there any other matters, gentlemen? No? I shall rise."

"Court rise!" called an usher, and the Judge swept out.

The court relaxed, a parade permitted to stand at ease. There was a sudden clamour from the public gallery, and the reporters rushed out to file their stories.

Withers turned to the CPS clerk. "What's your name?" he demanded.

"Spencer, sir."

"Well, Spencer, don't go away yet. You'll be needed."

Kenny was taken by the arm by the dock officer. His hand rested on the rail on top of the dock for a moment, and he was about to descend the steps into the cells, when a man approached him. Spencer recognised him as a prominent defence solicitor. He did not speak, but instead patted Kenny's hand. Kenny nodded briefly in response. The solicitor turned away, and he did not see the look Kenny gave his departing back. It was not a look that Spencer would have liked directed at *his* back. Kenny then descended out of sight into the cells to collect his belongings.

Spencer turned to Withers and the junior who were busy collecting up their papers. A man was weaving his way across the court towards them. He was a stocky, heavy-jowled man in a grey suit. He looked uncomfortable, as if his shirt were a size too small, and he was sweating. His hair was cropped extremely short, so that light was reflected from his scalp. He resembled an unhappy bloodhound, which, in a sense, is exactly what he was.

"Do I have to give it back to him?" he scowled, addressing Withers. He lifted his right hand and revealed that the briefcase he carried was handcuffed to his wrist.

"Yes, Sergeant, you do. We have been through this already."

"But it's the proceeds of crime!" protested the policeman.

"That may very well be. However, Kenny called evidence to the contrary which we were unable to damage."

"But the handwriting evidence— " interrupted the sergeant.

"—was inconclusive."

"What about the Police Property Act, or whatever it's called?"

"Mr Smith," replied Withers, indicating his junior, "has written a very detailed Advice which deals with that, and I agree entirely with his conclusions. Come along," he said, cutting short any further argument.

The two barristers led Spencer and the sergeant out of court. Kenny, now released from the cells, stood outside, a broad grin on his disfigured face, conferring with his solicitor and barrister. There was a girl with them. She was blonde and cheap looking, but Spencer was still unable to take his eyes off her. She was well tanned, with large breasts only notionally covered by a diaphanous white blouse, and long brown legs that disappeared into the shortest of leather skirts at the last

13

permissible moment. She clung resolutely to Kenny's arm. She had watched every day of the trial from the public gallery. Now her man was free and about to become eighty thousand pounds better off, she was not about to let go.

"Mr Robeson," called Withers. Kenny's solicitor motioned for Kenny to stay where he was, and approached the QC. "Sergeant West here has the cash found at your client's home."

"Ah, yes," said Robeson with a smile and a mischievous twinkle in his eye. "Are you really going to waste everyone's time and money requiring us to make a formal application for it? Without, what was his name . . . Pritchard? Pilchard? Whatever. Without the teller, there's no way the company could even start to prove— "

"I can save you the trouble, Mr Robeson," interrupted Withers. "The matter has been considered at length, and I am authorised to return the money to your client. This young man here," he indicated Spencer, "and Sergeant West, will deal with it immediately. We shall require a receipt."

Robeson smiled. "Of course. Shall we go into the interview room over there?"

Robeson led the way. Kenny untangled the girl from his arm and followed him. Spencer and the disconsolate Sergeant West brought up the rear.

Spencer closed the door behind him. Without speaking, West unlocked the handcuffs and opened the combination locks of the briefcase. All eyes in the room fixed on the briefcase as it was opened.

"Eighty-four thousand, one hundred and fifty-five pounds," announced the sergeant. Spencer looked at the old ten pound notes held together with rubber bands in bundles inside the briefcase. It was more money – real money, not just noughts on a cheque – than he had ever seen in one place at one time. Sergeant West simply tipped the cash on to the table in front of him. Robeson looked at him quizzically.

"It's my briefcase," explained West. He produced a small pad from his jacket pocket. The top sheet was a formal Metropolitan Police receipt. It was already completed, and required only a signature. He handed it to Kenny with a pen. "Sign there," he said.

"What?" asked Kenny, his soft voice contrasting surprisingly with the scarred face and muscular build. "How do I know it's all there?"

"'Cos I say so."

"Well, I'm sorry, mate, but that ain't good enough— " began Kenny. He would have said more, but Robeson held up his hand to silence him.

"Sergeant, I'm sure that it's all there, every tenner of it— " Sergeant West nodded and breathed a sign of relief, which was cut short by the rest of Robeson's words, "—but I do think that it should still be counted, formally, so to speak. So there can never be any question about it in the future."

The sergeant glared at the solicitor, but the latter simply smiled at him benignly. He looked to Withers for guidance. The QC nodded.

"Okay, if you've got all day . . ." replied West, taking the band off the first bundle. "Ten . . . twenty . . . thirty . . ." His face was as black as thunder and his fury so great that he seemed about to strike Kenny. Kenny stood defiantly over the sergeant, ignoring the counting, and staring aggressively at the policeman's face, loving every second. It was scant revenge for over a year spent on remand, but it still tasted sweet.

"Funny things, juries," said Kenny, so quietly that it might have been to himself. "All that evidence too— " The sergeant dropped the bundle he was counting and turned on Kenny.

"That's enough!" commanded Withers. He took a step

towards Kenny. He drew himself up to his full height. Although only an inch or two taller than the scarred man, he seemed immense next to him. Kenny's smirk faded slightly.

"Now you look here, Mr Kenny," Withers said softly, but with polite menace. "Let me tell you something: I know you robbed that convoy. And you know it too. Well, you got off. That's your good fortune, and the sergeant's bad fortune. But don't push your luck. I'm warning you."

Kenny continued to smile, but Spencer could see that it was bravado. The old barrister had scared him.

"Now," continued Withers, "go and wait outside. Mr Robeson here will protect your interests, and your money."

Kenny nodded slowly, and backed away to the door. He looked at the group, nodded, and departed. Sergeant West resumed his counting. After a few minutes the barristers left, sweeping past Kenny in their black robes without a word.

The sergeant was clearly unused to counting large sums of money. He made a number of mistakes and had to go back and recount several bundles, and it was over an hour later that he came to the final bundle. So tired were his fingers that he knocked that bundle and the one before it on to the floor. At last he was finished. He nodded to Spencer, and the young man opened the door and called Kenny over and into the room.

"Sign here," the sergeant said to him, and this time Kenny took the proffered pen and made his mark on the receipt. Robeson began to gather the bundles together and put them in his briefcase.

"Here!" protested Kenny, placing Robeson's wrist in a vice-like grip. He leaned over and grabbed a couple of the bundles. "Pocket money," he said. "And I'll have a receipt from you too, Mr Robeson," he added, placing a strange emphasis on the "Mr". He turned to Sergeant West. "As for you: I'll be seeing you," he said with an unpleasant smile.

"That you will, sonny, that you will," replied the sergeant with feeling.

"Yeh, but not before I've got meself a suntan," said Kenny, with a broad smile, patting his pockets where the bundles of notes spoilt the line of his Italian suit.

The others watched him leave the room, collect the blonde and walk off, his hand resting lightly on the girl's buttocks. The sergeant stood, hands in pockets, watching Kenny's departing back. Then he smiled to himself as his fingers closed around the crumpled banknote that he had palmed from the bundle of spilled notes. The sleight of hand had been entirely opportunistic, and, at that moment, Sergeant West had not considered quite what he was going to do with the marked note. But "Don't get mad; get even" was a philosophy that had always appealed to him, and the tenner that now rustled slightly in his pocket would, he was sure, come in handy sooner or later.

CHAPTER 2

As Robeson emerged on to the pavement, a pester of reporters swarmed up to him. He ignored their pleas for a comment, and, squinting in the bright afternoon sun, peered about him for a taxi. One was just pulling up on the far side of the road, and he brushed his way through the questions without speaking, and trotted across the road. Two men were in the process of descending from the taxi's other door, and Robeson simply jumped into the door nearest to him while the second of them was still half in. Robeson pulled the window up tightly and locked it, and resolutely turned his head away from the newspapermen banging on the window. As the two previous occupants finished paying the cabbie, Robeson leaned forward to give his directions and the cab pulled away.

The two men just delivered to their destination walked into the Old Balley and placed their briefcases and barristers' robes on the conveyor belt of the X-ray machine.

"Charming," said the younger, referring to Robeson's capture of their cab. Charles Holroyd smiled and shrugged. He collected his case and bag from the end of the conveyor belt, and hurried after his ex-pupil. They entered the lift and Charles pressed the button that would take them to the barristers' robing room on the fourth floor. He was glad to be back in the Old Bailey, even on a relatively minor case such as this. It was a step in the right direction.

"Nice to be back," said Charles.

"Is it that long since you were last here?"

"Some months."

"Are things still slow?" asked the young barrister.

"They certainly are."

Peter Bateman looked at his friend with concern. Charles was about forty, but the bags under his eyes, and what was becoming an almost permanent worried frown, made him look older.

"I thought Barbara was beginning to get some work in," said Peter.

"Oh yes. I spent a fascinating month in Magistrates' Courts applying for adjournments, with the occasional careless driver thrown in for variety. So useful was the experience, that I am considering writing a definitive text to be entitled *Holroyd on Remands*, a two-volume book with a loose-leaf index."

Peter laughed. "That bad, huh?"

"That bad. As I finally persuaded our lovely clerk, I may have been virtually unemployed for the last year, but even I do not need that sort of exposure. If a man of sixteen years' call spends all his time prosecuting careless drivers, he can't be any good. So much for that nonsense about taking silk."

"It wasn't nonsense, Charles, and you know it. This time last year, you had more work – quality work too – than you could handle. And in Chambers where you were the odd man out, the only criminal practitioner."

"And now I'm in a specialist criminal set, and I can't get anyone to instruct me."

"What does Barbara say about it?" asked Peter.

"That depends on the day of the week, or the tides, or something. At first it was 'Things always take a while to get going after a move, sir.' Then there was 'It takes a while for our solicitors to get to know your name, sir,' which alternated with 'Your old firms haven't got used to the new address, sir.' Then she moved to 'It's often slack

at this time of year, sir.' That one lasted for nine months."
Peter laughed.

"The truth is, Peter, that barristers are not frequently
charged with the murder of their wives, but when they
are, it tends to cause an understandable reluctance on the
part of solicitors to instruct them."

The lift arrived at the fourth floor and the two men
walked into the robing room. They replaced their normal
collars and ties with wing collars and bands, and slipped
into their black barristers' robes.

"Let's hope, then," said Peter, "that today's case is the
first of many." The comment was made sympathetically,
but Charles bridled at it.

"As grateful as I am, Peter, that you were double-
booked today, I sincerely hope that the renaissance of
my practice does not depend on your returns. Accepting
returns from one's ex-pupil is rather humiliating."

They took the lift back down to the first floor and went
into court. An usher approached Charles.

"Hello, Mr Holroyd. How are you? Haven't seen you
here in ages."

"Hello. What are you doing here? Aren't you based at
Snaresbrook?"

"I was. But we moved further in, so I applied for a
transfer."

"And the Lord Chancellor said yes?"

"I persuaded him in the end," joked the usher. "Are
you in this plea?"

"Yes, with Mr Bateman here, who is also in Court 12
on another case."

"It's listed for two thirty," explained Peter with a frown,
"and will take about ten minutes. Am I going to be all
right?"

"You're in luck, sir," replied the usher. "We're going
to be a bit late starting, three at the earliest. The jury
in the case before's been discharged, and so all this

20

stuff has to be moved." The usher indicated the court behind him, which was strewn with cables and television monitors.

"Oh, so this is where the diamond retrial was?" asked Charles. "I wondered why Harry was rushing off."

"Harry?" asked Peter.

"Yes, the chap who pinched our cab. Harry Robeson. Don't you know Harry? My God, you make me feel old. I thought *everyone* knew Harry." Charles looked at his watch. "That means we have time for a coffee. Come on, Peter. I'll give you some gossip."

Harry Robeson stepped nimbly out of the taxi, handed the cabbie a fiver and crossed the road, dodging the traffic. He walked briskly down a side street until he came to a gold-coloured Mercedes. He looked behind him, but the quiet street was deserted. He inserted the key and got in. He started the engine, executed a smart three-point turn, and waited for a gap in the traffic to enable him to turn out into the main road. A blue Ford Escort pulled in almost immediately opposite the mouth of the junction. Robeson smiled grimly. The driver of the car was looking around frantically, up and down the thoroughfare. Robeson fought the impulse to sound his horn at the man. This was a game they had been playing for nearly a month now. So well had Robeson come to know the two men following him, this one and the one who drove the white Metro, that he had given names to them. The one in the Escort had a thin face and fairish hair. Robeson had seen him out of his car, when at a funeral three weeks before. He had turned round suddenly, and there he had been, pretending to be a mourner. He was tall, with skinny legs and a way of walking that reminded Robeson of an anglepoise lamp, angular and slightly bent. He had thus been christened "Filament", "Fil" for short. The other man appeared to be shorter, but as Robeson had not been able to catch sight of him outside of the Metro, he could not judge accurately. He had, however, ferocious bushy eyebrows, so Robeson had named him Denis, after Denis Healey.

At first, when Robeson had discovered their presence, he had been quite alarmed. But he learned within hours that Fil and Denis were not very expert at their task. Robeson knew well that to mount an effective, and undetectable, surveillance operation on someone, at least three, and preferably four men, were required. Even allowing for that, these two were pretty hopeless. That, and the shortage of manpower, meant that they were almost certainly policemen. That had been confirmed on the third day, when Robeson had had to attend a Magistrates' Court in north London. Fil had followed him into court and had been greeted by the court inspector. Robeson, to protect the other's feelings as much as anything else, had pretended not to hear, and had gone about his business as if unaware that he was being followed. From then on he had waited for something to happen. Nothing had.

Fil had obviously had difficulty in keeping up with the cabbie, partly, no doubt, because Robeson had offered the latter double fare if he could lose the blue Escort behind, a challenge which the cabbie had accepted with glee.

Robeson pulled out into the traffic and passed directly in front of the other car. Even then, Fil, who was looking behind him, almost missed the Mercedes, but he turned round just in time, and ducked down in his seat. Robeson waited a few seconds and then glanced into his rear-view mirror. The Escort was directly behind him, and Robeson chuckled at the palpable relief on Fil's face.

The Mercedes travelled slowly through the afternoon traffic towards Hampstead, the Escort one or two cars back. When he arrived outside the gates to his drive, Robeson decided to have some fun. Rather than entering the drive and parking the car in the garage as he usually did, he left it parked on the road. He deliberately looked furtive as he closed the door, and then he ran into the house as fast as he could. That should be enough to attract Fil's attention, thought Robeson, just in case he had thought of slipping off for a cup of tea. Once inside the house, Robeson raced upstairs and closed the curtains in the front bedroom. He threw off his court suit, delved into his wardrobe, and came up with an old pair of trousers, a soft cotton shirt, a brown cardigan with patched sleeves, and a cloth cap. He threw them on, and stood momentarily before the full-length mirror.

"Perfect!" he declared.

He ran back downstairs, and, pulling on a waterproof jacket, he slipped out of the front door. He put his head down, and plodded down the drive, emerging on to the pavement through the tradesmen's entrance, a small gate set into the hedge a few yards away from the main gates. The Escort was parked further up the road. Fil looked up initially at Robeson, but appeared to dismiss the grubby chap in the hat and transferred his gaze back to the gates of the house. Robeson could see that he had a radio in his hand, and he spoke into it like a ventriloquist, trying not to move his lips. Robeson had not wanted his disguise to be that effective, so he crossed the road directly in front of Fil's car, but studiously looking the other way. That was enough; Fil looked again at the gardener trudging up the hill away from him, spoke animatedly into his radio for a few seconds, and got out of the car.

Robeson led the policeman on a three-mile trek round the streets of Hampstead and Highgate, trying to look as suspicious and furtive as he could without actually getting himself arrested. After just over an hour, he executed the *coup de grâce*. He turned into a road that led towards Queen's Wood, and, almost immediately, entered an alleyway between two houses. Once hidden from view he raced to the other end, and entered a wooden gate set in a tall fence to his right. He was in a large garden. To the right was a substantial house, and to the left the garden was divided by green plastic fencing into long strips, suggesting, as was the case, that the house was in multiple occupation. Robeson walked to the furthest section, which was set out as a vegetable patch. To one side, leaning on a spade, was an elderly man, peering intently at something in the soil. He looked up as Robeson approached, and reached behind his ear to turn on a hearing aid.

"Hello there, Harry," he called. "I didn't expect you today. Why didn't you ring?"

Harry put his finger to his lips, and went over to the man, stepping carefully over the neat lines of vegetables.

"Hello, Pop. I'm playing hide and seek. I'll explain in a sec." He held up his hand for silence. He could hear the familiar crackle and click of a police radio from the other side of the fence. The fence was however over six feet tall, and close-boarded; Fil would have trouble seeing into the garden unless he started climbing. Robeson strained to hear what was being said, but could not hear the words. Fil's voice, however, betrayed urgency, and Robeson smiled in satisfaction.

"What's up, Harry?" asked Pop.

Robeson laughed. "It's nothing. I've got some idiot policeman following me, and I've been leading him a dance."

"You're not in trouble, are you?"

He laughed again. "No more than usual."

"You be careful, young man. Your dad would turn in his grave if he thought— "

"I know, I know, I know," interrupted Robeson. He cocked his head and strained to hear what was happening behind the fence. The sound of the radio faded, and he heard footsteps receding down the alley. "Come on, Pop, let's get back to your leeks. What've you done since I was here last?"

Robeson did not hear the conversation that occurred via the radio at the entrance to the alley as Fil began the long journey back to his car.

"Five-two-four? Five-two-four?"

"Five-two-four over," replied Fil.

"Repeat that address, will you?"

"Two Queenswood Lane, N6, over."

"Thought so. You've been had. It's his uncle's flat. Popeye Robeson, d.o.b. second Feb, 1910. No previous convictions according to CRO. He apparently used to have a fish stall in the East End. Now retired. West says Robeson's always there, helping the old bloke with his garden. So much for your 'undercover liaison'. Our Harry's been taking the piss."

Fil's reply, had it been transmitted, might have constituted an offence under the Obscene Publications Act.

Charles led the way back upstairs into the barristers' mess where he purchased two coffees. He could not shake off the tradition of the pupil-master paying for the pupil's snacks, notwithstanding the fact that Peter was no longer his pupil, and had in any event certainly earned twice as much as had Charles in the last quarter. The two men sat down at a table and took off their wigs.

"Robeson, Harold. About sixty, and as canny as they come. He became a solicitor the hard way – by being a clerk for umpteen years, just learning the trade as he went. Been at it for over forty years, I guess. He's got a one-man firm in south London somewhere, and represents all the major villains. Remember the Camden rapist last year, and . . . what was his name . . . Billingsworth, Billingsgate . . ."

"Billington, the Wandsworth Murderer," said Peter, the words rolling off his tongue with relish.

"That's the one. He likes that high-profile stuff – who doesn't? But in fact his meat and drink is the south London criminal fraternity, the top blaggers like Tony Kenny."

"How does a one-man band like that get such classy work?"

Charles laughed. "Because he gets results. It's mostly privately paid too, no legal aid for the Tony Kennys of this world."

"But isn't Blackburne representing him? He must charge the earth. And then there's the junior . . ."

"Sure. But then most professional criminals I've known regard it as a necessary business expense. I expect Kenny is paying out of the proceeds of his last job but one."

"Tax deductible," said Peter with a grin.

"Precisely. They say he's also got a very good way with his clients. He speaks their language."

"Like you."

Charles looked up at Peter to see if he was teasing, but the young man's face showed genuine admiration. Charles smiled. "I suppose so," he conceded. "Like me, Robeson grew up in the East End, working-class family. He understands how they think."

"I met a copper the other day at some Magistrates' Court who'd had to arrest two of his own cousins. He caught them red-handed burgling Tesco's. He reckoned that, really, he had had only one choice of career: villain or copper."

"There's some truth in that."

"So Robeson became a pillar of the establishment, then?"

"Not quite, though he'd love to be. He has a bit of a chip on his shoulder from what I hear. He's got a wonderful sense of humour, mind. I heard an after-dinner speech he gave once, and it was priceless. But I suspect that he feels that he's not quite accepted, you know? Never been to university, working-class background, all that crap. I can understand that, too. He tries too hard, though: does a lot of charity work, and he's a Rotarian, maybe even a Mason."

Peter looked up sharply. He was Catholic, and disapproved of what he considered to be the corruption of Freemasonry. "Is he straight?" he asked.

"Honest, you mean? Yes, I think so. He's so anxious to be accepted that I doubt he'd ever do anything to jeopardise that. Oh, you get the rumours, of course. That can't be helped when you defend major-league villains. I don't know any solicitor in that position who hasn't been accused once or twice. But in his case there's nothing in it."

"Sour grapes by the police?"

"Exactly."

Peter sipped his coffee thoughtfully. Charles could guess what the young barrister was thinking: what wouldn't he give for work like that? Peter's next question seemed to confirm his suspicions.

"Have you ever been instructed by him?"

"No," replied Charles shortly. He sat in silence for a moment, and then shook himself out of his reverie. "Come on," he said, knocking back the last of his coffee, "can't let his Lordship wait, can we?"

"CID Office."

"Is Jack there?"

"No, I'm afraid not."

"When's he due back?"

"He's on leave today. He'll be in the day after tomorrow. Can I help?"

"Are any of the Compass Team there?"

"No, I'm sorry. Can you give me your name, sir?"

"No." Pause. "Look, just tell Jack that it's been

27

arranged for Friday, right? If he wants to know more, he'll have to get in touch with me before then."

"And who's the message from?"

"Just tell him 'Stinker'."

"Does he know how to get— " but the line was cut.

CHAPTER 3

Charles opened the door to his tiny flat in New Fetter Lane and tossed on to the sofa his briefcase and the red cloth bag in which he carried his robes (a relic of former glories: the bag had been given to him years before by a leader to mark his good work on a murder case). He walked to the kitchen and poured himself a drink. He had last worked three days before, and he was reluctantly coming to the conclusion that unless things turned round soon, he would have to find a job, a real job, one that paid a salary every month. The insurance company had eventually decided that Charles had not murdered his wife, and had paid out on Henrietta's life policy. That, the sale of their heavily mortgaged home in Buckinghamshire, and the backlog of unpaid fees, had ensured that he had had a few months' grace. But only the week before he had received a Please-note-that-your-current-balance-is letter from his bank manager, and that boded ill. He had started to scan the legal appointments in the paper every Tuesday, only out of interest, he told himself. He had had little difficulty in finding a reason to reject as completely unsuitable every appointment he had seen thus far, but the excuses were beginning to sound hollow even to himself.

He wandered into the cupboard that posed as a bathroom, taking his whisky with him, and peered at himself in the mirror. He was no more than average height, but extremely broad. He had come to accept as a fact of life the increase in suit size with his increase in age. Was it his imagination, or did his jacket appear to hang rather more loosely on his shoulders than usual? His face certainly did look rather thin. He examined his temples. His curly hair was its expected black, with just a little grey creeping in. At least no change there. He returned to the living room and opened his case. He should be getting ready to go out, but he could not face doing anything for a while, so he took out his crumpled newspaper and looked at what he would be missing on television that evening. No television at his parents' house on Friday nights.

His telephone rang, and he reached for it in anticipation. Barbara with a late return for Monday? There was that distinctive click of connection that signified a long-distance call, and then a woman's voice.

"Charles?"

"Rachel?"

"Yes. God, I can hardly hear anything. Can you hear me?"

"Just about. How are you? Hang on, isn't it the middle of the night over there?" There was a long pause.

"No, yes, well . . . what I mean is, it's early morning, but I haven't been to bed yet. The night is still young, as they say."

Charles's impression was that the last comment was not meant for him. There was a lot of noise on the line, but much of it came from what sounded like a party in progress at the other end.

"I gather you're having a good time?" asked Charles dryly.

"Wonderful!" she replied, a very slight but detectable slur in her speech.

"And when do you suppose these dismal shores will once more be illuminated by your presence?"

"What? You'll have to shout, Charles, there's a lot of noise at this end."

"I said, when are you coming home, darling?"

Before Charles had met her, Rachel had been a dancer. The year before Charles had persuaded her to take it up again. She had done so, more in an attempt to occupy the evenings than to revive a career she thought had ended. Two months ago she had received an unexpected call from an old friend who was the director of a small dance company. He desperately needed a replacement for one of his dancers who had fallen pregnant, and did Rachel know of anyone? They would be required for a three-week engagement in the United States and had to be ready to start rehearsals immediately. When Rachel told him nervously that she had started dancing again, he instantly offered her the place. Charles had insisted that she go. He would be perfectly able to look after himself, and he could flat- and cat-sit for her. She had now been away for five weeks.

"Well, that's why I'm ringing. We've been asked to stay on. It's fantastic, Charles, but we're sold out! You don't mind, do you?"

"Of course not— " he started to say, but was interrupted by her.

"I tried – sorry? What did you say, Charles?"

Charles realised that there was one of those infuriating delays on the line which made sensible conversation almost impossible. They would both speak at the same time, and then both wait for the other.

Rachel was trying again. "I tried ringing the flat most of last week and I could never get you— "

"Yes, I'm sorry— "

"Sorry?"

"I said I'm sorry you've not been able to get me. I decided to move back into my place. I pop over to Dalston every day or two to keep an eye on things, but all my books are here, and I can make as much mess as I like. It's also much nearer the Temple, and

I'm not embarrassed to use the phone. I brought Moggie with me, so don't worry."

"Charles, her name is Philomena."

"Whatever you say. When are you likely to be back, Ray?"

"I really don't know. A week or two, maybe a bit longer. You really don't mind, do you? It's a wonderful opportunity— "

"No, I really don't mind," said Charles, minding quite a lot but trying hard to sound as though he didn't.

"Look, I can't hear you, and I have to go anyway. Don't work too hard, will you? I'll call again at the end of the week. I love— " she began, but the line was cut.

Charles replaced the handset, more miserable than ever. The open bottle of Scotch beckoned from the table where he had left it. The idea of spending the evening getting very drunk was infinitely more appealing than the prospect of Sabbath supper with his parents. Reluctantly, but firmly, he screwed the lid of the bottle in place, knocked back the last of his drink and went to the bathroom to wash.

By contrast, the sounds of a very jolly Friday night celebration rang out over Greenwich. Tony Kenny, late of Her Majesty's Prison Pentonville, was holding court at the Victory public house, a pub that had been chosen at least partly for its apt name. It also had the advantage of an upstairs room that could be hired out for private parties, as was this one. Kenny and a few close associates had been drinking there since three o'clock, but as the afternoon wore on, the room had begun to fill up, and now there was quite a crowd. As the numbers had increased, so had the noise, and with that the concern of the landlord, a nice man who pulled pints downstairs and looked worriedly every few minutes at the trembling lights and undulating ceiling of the saloon bar where he was serving.

Harry Robeson, bound for the Victory, was as unenthusiastic about his evening's prospective entertainment as was Charles. He had, however, decided that it would be politic to accept Kenny's invitation, and so he would put in an early appearance and leave after an hour or so. He peered through the windscreen of his Mercedes and reached for the cassette player's volume control to turn Beethoven down. He could not concentrate with the music at full volume, and he was not sure of his way. He turned left slowly, and saw the public house ahead of him on his right. He pulled into the car park and parked in one of the few remaining spaces, next to the toilet block, the pungent presence of which he was unable to avoid as he got out of his car.

At the same time, approximately six miles away, an old battered Transit van pulled up outside a terraced house in Leyton. The van bore the legend "Terry Cooper, Plumbing Contractor". A young man in stained overalls climbed out of the van carrying a bag of tools, slammed the door closed behind him and raced inside.

"Is that you, Terry?"

"Yes, Mum." He put the bag of tools down in the hall, and met his mother on the threshold of the kitchen. He kissed her briefly on the cheek.

"Don't leave them there," she remonstrated with him, pointing at the tools. He turned and picked them up and set off upstairs. His mother returned to the kitchen, from whence emanated the smell of Terry's favourite tea, lamb hotpot, made with Guinness. Mrs Cooper shouted up to her son. "You're back late."

"Yeah," he called from upstairs. "Had a problem on that job in Hainault."

"You back there tomorrow, then?"

"No, got it all sorted. Just took longer than I expected. Have you had a call from the overflow in Stratford?"

"No, dear, no one's called. Don't be long, Tel, your tea's ready."

"I can't stay, Mum, I told you."

Mrs Cooper came to the foot of the stairs. "Oh, you're joking, Terry. I've made hotpot."

He came to the top of the stairs. He was naked to the waist and was towelling himself down from his wash. "I'm sorry, Mum, but I did tell you. It's the darts match over Greenwich way."

A sudden catarrhal cough from the front room revealed that there was a third person in the house. It was followed by a gurgling laugh. "You remember, Enid, the boy's been challenged by that girl's team. Eh, boy? Ain't that right?"

"Yes, Dad," called Terry, without enthusiasm. His father had been ribbing him about it for weeks. Terry was the captain of the darts team of his local, the Rising Sun. Their last match had been at home against the Victory. The visiting team had arrived two hours late, having gone to the wrong venue, by which time Terry and the rest of the Rising Sun team had assumed that they had won by default. By the time the match had started, the home team had had rather too much to drink, and they were thrashed. So heavily were they defeated, that the girlfriends of the visitors had even suggested that they could take on the Rising Sun first team. His male ego rather bruised, Terry had issued a drunken challenge to the girls, which was instantly accepted. Only weeks later was Terry told that the Victory's women's team were the current Southern Region ladies champions. Tonight was the night of the big match. Not only was Terry's male pride at stake, but probably his position as captain.

"I'd give a week's wages to watch this one," said Terry's father, his laughter tailing off into coughing.

"Well, that wouldn't come to much, would it?" retorted Mrs Cooper, "seeing's you ain't worked in four years!"

Terry came downstairs, pulling on a clean shirt. "What time you off?" asked Mrs Cooper.

"Right now."

"Can't you even stop for a sandwich?" asked his mother, wondering if the last of the ham had gone the day before.

"No, sorry, Mum. I'm picking up Roy and Adam in five minutes. Anyway, I'm feelin' a bit off," he said, rubbing his stomach speculatively.

"Why? What d'you have for lunch?" interrogated Mrs Cooper, eying him carefully.

"A pork pie from the newsagent's next door to the job."

Mrs Cooper shook her head. "Serves you right, then. Shall I keep the hotpot for you?"

"Yeah. I'll see how I feel when I get in. Ta-ra," he said, and kissed her again. He put his head round the door to where his father sat, a rug over his knees, watching the television. "See you, Dad."

"Cheers, boy. You better win," he called out after his son, "or they'll never let you in the Sun again," but Terry had closed the front door and was striding to his van.

His two team-mates were waiting for him as he came round the green, and they both squeezed into the front seat. Terry eyed their clothes.

"A bit posh for a darts match, aren't we?"

"Well, Tel," replied Adam, "the evening has interesting possibilities, don't you think?"

"Yeah," agreed the third member of the party, Roy. "It was you who said you only accepted the challenge so's to get your leg over that Sandra."

35

Terry groaned. "Did I?" He was feeling worse by the minute.

As the darts team drove to Greenwich, another car with three occupants drove into the car park of the Victory. It crawled up the aisles of parked cars, passing more than one empty space. The men inside appeared to be looking for something or someone. As the car was about to turn to go round again, one of the occupants, the rear-seat passenger, suddenly pointed to a gold-coloured car in the corner, next to the toilets. The driver stopped and reversed out on to the road, parking the car. The three men – all large and muscular – got out and walked towards the public house. They conferred briefly at the door to the lounge bar. One of them positioned himself by the entrance to the car park. The others entered the bar.

Charles walked across Fleet Street to the Temple where he parked his car. He still drove the battered old MG, despite the fact that what had been the family's principal car, the Jaguar, was still locked in a garage in Buckinghamshire. He did not really know why. Perhaps because it reminded him too sharply of Henrietta, who used to drive it most; perhaps because with his present practice he could not afford to run it, but at the same time he avoided confronting the logic of selling it – that would involve the admission that his practice really had failed. So the Jaguar gathered dust at a cost of £6 per week, and Charles drove a draughty, damp, unreliable car, suitable for a man half his age.

He moved out into the heavy rush-hour traffic and headed north towards Hendon, where his parents had moved the year before. His mother, Millie Horowitz, considered the move to have been a betrayal of their East End roots; she had been born, schooled, married and had given birth to her sons, all within a mile of

36

her parents' home in Stepney, and the wider roads and gardens of suburban Hendon were alien to her. To what it was she was being disloyal was not clear even to her husband, Harry; most of their friends had moved out years before, replaced by the new generation of immigrants, the Asians; minicab offices, pungent restaurants, shops open on Saturdays – the place of Charles's birth had altered beyond recognition. But still Millie pined for a way of life that no longer existed, and could not settle in suburbia.

Charles stopped briefly to buy his mother some flowers, and drove the last mile to his parents' home. He sat outside in the car for a few minutes, steeling himself. Then, with a sigh, he got out of the car and walked up the path that divided the neat garden in two, to the front door. He rang the bell. Harry Horowitz opened the door.

"Hello, Charles," he said softly, and hugged him, kissing him on the cheek. There had been little demonstration of affection between them before Charles had married; a gruff handshake or a pat on the back were the only clues to the almost unbearable love and pride Harry had for his firstborn son, the lawyer. Harry more than anyone else had been devastated by Charles's decision to change his name, and then, to commit the ultimate sin, to "marry out". He had sat *shiva* for Charles – torn his clothes and mourned for five days, as if bereaved. Thereafter Charles had ceased to exist, and part of Harry had died too. But when, against all expectation, Charles had returned, hounded and bereaved himself, Harry's emotional floodgates had opened. Even now, a year later, Charles sometimes caught his father looking at him from across the room, a smile on his lips and tears glistening in his eyes.

"How are you, Dad?" asked Charles.

"Not bad," replied Harry. "Go in. Your mother's waiting."

Charles resolutely fixed a smile to his face and went

into the dining room. The table was laid for Sabbath dinner, laden with the foods Charles associated with his youth, chopped liver, pickled and salted herring, and an enormous loaf of crusty bread. In the middle of the table were the cup of wine and the unlit candles. Charles's brother David sat at the far side of the table, in intimate conversation with his recent bride, Sonia. Their heads were bent together, and Charles could see David's hand in Sonia's lap, gently caressing her arm as he spoke. David looked up as Charles entered.

"Charles," he said, standing and holding out his hand across the table. Charles took his hand and shook it warmly.

"Hello, Davie. How are you, Sonia?"

She was young, twenty-three perhaps, and ten years David's junior. She was not so much pretty as handsome, with a full figure and long lustrous hair. Charles liked her open, frank face, and her serious eyes which missed nothing. She stood and leaned over the table, kissing Charles on the cheek.

"I'm very well, thanks, Charles."

Millie Horowitz entered the room from the kitchen, a large box of matches in her hand. Charles firmed up his smile.

"Good Shabas, Mum," he said, approaching her, holding out the flowers.

"Why is it always *you* who has to be late?" she said, brushing past him. "I was about to light the candles without you."

Terry and the team from the Rising Sun had arrived to find the Victory's car park full. They too parked on the street and went inside. The ladies' team was already there with a large number of good-natured but partisan supporters. The lads from Leyton received a boisterous, though not unfriendly, welcome. Terry and Roy began

38

practising while Adam bought some drinks. He watched with apprehension from the bar as the ladies also took some extremely accurate practice shots. Unnoticed among the noisy young people were the two large men who had entered earlier. They wore casual clothes, but they did not appear to be relaxed. They sat at a table from which they could see the staircase that led to the upstairs bar. They spoke little, looked frequently at their watches, and appeared to survey the room periodically. Every now and then, one of them would get up and peer up the staircase, and then return to his seat. A careful observer might have seen that their jacket pockets bulged. After a few minutes, the third man who had waited outside came in and sat beside them. He whispered something in the ear of one of them and the listener nodded slowly. The listener then put down his pint and went outside with the third man.

The match was about to start. Terry, as captain, was to play first, against the ladies' captain, Sandra, over whom he had rashly promised to get his leg. He was, however, feeling very ill indeed. He usually had a stomach like cast iron, but he was certain he was going to be sick. He took a swig from his pint in an effort to calm his queasy stomach, but it had just the opposite effect. There was nothing for it: he was going to have to excuse himself. To hearty catcalls ("Lost your bottle, mate?" "He's scared shitless!") and stinging laughter, he asked where the gents was located, and rushed out, impervious to the embarrassed protests of Adam and Roy.

Terry reached the toilet block. However, once there he found the only cubicle occupied. The smell of the place was dreadful. He returned as far as the door, made it into the shadow of a large gold car and parted company with his lunch.

"Don't you agree, Sonia?" asked Millie.

Sonia stood at the table, intent on ladling chicken soup.

It was a tricky job, as the soup contained *kreplach*, triangular dumplings filled with cooked meat, and they tended to fall into the soup bowls with a splash, making the white lace tablecloth. Sonia looked guiltily towards the kitchen where Millie Horowitz was slicing bread, but her transgression had not been noticed. She caught the eye of her father-in-law sitting patiently at the head of the table, and he winked at her. David entered the room from the hall, having removed his jacket now that the candles were alight, and the blessings over bread and wine completed. As he passed behind his wife he pinched her lightly on the buttock. Sonia responded with a gentle smile and continued to serve the soup.

Millie Horowitz entered from the kitchen, in her hand a breadboard piled high with the bread she had just sliced.

"Don't you agree?" she repeated. "It's like a criminal, hiding behind a false name." This was a favourite subject. Charles had been foolish enough to tell the family an anecdote about an incident in court which included a reference to his anglicised name. The ritual of the Sabbath meal seemed to goad Millie, and, like a terrier with an old rag, every week she would worry at the frayed edges of Charles's relationship with his religion.

"I don't know, Mum," Sonia replied uncomfortably, without looking up. "I can see it from Charles's point of view too."

"Well, I can't. It's nothing to be ashamed about, having a Jewish name."

"I never said it was," protested Charles. "Plenty of people anglicise their names. What about those friends of yours . . . Betty and Robert . . ." Charles groped in vain for their surname.

"Green," assisted David, regretting it the instant his mother's glare landed on him.

"Yes, thank you," said Charles. "They were Greenbaum

40

for forty years, and then all of a sudden they lost the 'Baum'."

"They should be ashamed too," replied Millie, putting the breadboard down too hard on the table.

"Mum," said Charles gently, "it's just assimilation. Look at any period in Jewish history, when there's been no persecution— "

"I don't need a history lesson from you."

"Look where you live, and who your friends are now. Compared with a generation ago . . ." Charles's voice faltered as he saw, too late, his father's expression of warning. "Look, Mum, let's change the subject, eh? Please let's not argue this time."

Millie hesitated, about to speak, but thought better of it.

For a while there was silence except for the clink of soup spoons against the bowls. Charles watched his father's bowed head as he ate. The ever-thinning silver hair, and the almost imperceptible tremble in his hand as it lifted the spoon to his lips, reminded Charles suddenly that his father was grown old, and he felt as if it was his fault. Ever since Charles had returned to the family, Harry had had to endure weekly internecine warfare between the two people he loved most. Whereas the two combatants recovered each week so as to be able to rejoin battle the succeeding Friday, Harry was left exhausted and despairing. Charles vowed again, as he did every week, that he would not allow himself to be drawn into more rows.

"Aren't these lovely dishes?" said Sonia, replacing her spoon in her empty soup bowl.

"Thank you, darling," said Harry. "They came from my grandmother."

"By the way," said Millie, everyone else round the table held their breath, "that reminds me." It was said in a conversational tone that allayed suspicion. "I've

41

got something for you two," and she nodded to David and Sonia.

"What, more?" asked David. "Every time we come here you give us something."

"It's just some fish knives, that's all. They were your grandmother's, and I never use them. You might as well have them now as when I die. I'm just delighted I have someone to give them to," she concluded.

The implication that the widowed Charles could not, in the circumstances, be the recipient of fish knives was not missed by anyone in the room.

"I've got an announcement," interjected David, trying again to divert the attack from his brother.

"I've been waiting for one of you— "

"Mum!" protested David, demanding his mother's attention.

"Yes? Harry, would you put this on the sideboard?" she said, handing to him a plate, now empty, that had contained pickled herring.

David shook his head in exasperation. "If anyone's interested— "

"I'm interested," replied Charles.

"So am I," said his father. "So give us your announcement."

"Well," said David, looking at his wife, who returned his glance with a smile, "I've been promoted. I am now a managing consultant."

"*Muzeltov!*" cried Harry and Millie together. "And what's a managing consultant?" asked Harry.

"It's a consultant who manages the team which services the client; it's one step above senior consultant, and, most importantly, it's one step below associate, which means," and David paused dramatically so that even his mother stopped fussing with the cruet and watched him, "which means, that there's a real prospect of partnership in the next few years."

"So, you see," crowed Millie, triumphantly, "you *can* succeed with a Jewish name."

David threw his hands up in mock horror and shrugged to Charles.

"For heaven's sake, Mum, it's hardly the same thing. Half the partners in David's consultancy are Jewish!"

"Sure, and they've done even better than Davie. They're partners already," she concluded with impeccable logic.

The cutlery jangled as Charles's fist thumped the table top. His mother ignored him and swallowed a mouthful of soup. Charles took a deep breath, and tried to remain calm.

"Look," he said softly, attempting conciliation. He took his mother's hand in his own and squeezed it gently. "Maybe you're right. Maybe I shouldn't have changed my name. And maybe if I had my time again, I wouldn't do it. There's a lot of things I wouldn't do. But it's done now. My entire career is based on that name. It's the one that I'm known by. It's too late to change back now – I've been Charles Holroyd for over twenty years."

Millie should not have answered. She should have accepted the proffered olive branch. She should have bitten her tongue and offered her new daughter-in-law some more bread. Instead she answered with venom: "And a fat lot of good the name's doing you now, eh? Now you're the Jewish barrister with the English name, the one who was charged with murdering his *shiksa* wife. And a great help *that* must be to your career."

Charles shook his head. "Nothing I can possibly say will make this right, will it? Whatever I say, whatever I do, you're going to punish me? Well, Mum, I've had a depressing day to end a depressing week, and, if you don't mind, I can do without this tonight!" Charles rose, threw his napkin to the table. "I'm sorry, Dad," he said, and stormed out.

*   *   *

Terry Cooper wanted to die. He had emptied the contents of his stomach over the rear wheel of the gold-coloured car, but he was still retching, and bringing nothing up. His eyes watered, his legs felt like jelly, and his insides hurt like hell. He heard, but paid no attention to, footsteps tentatively approaching the corner of the car park where he crouched. He was, however, quite startled to hear someone fiddling with something at the rear of the very car behind which he was hiding. Oh, Jesus, he thought, that's all I need! The boot sprung open. Terry kept his head down. The owner was not likely to be pleased at the mess Terry's pork pie had made of the wheel and paintwork and Terry, never a coward when in control of his insides, did not feel able to deal at that moment with an irate and probably wealthy driver. Terry succeeded in suppressing the spasms while the owner closed the boot again, and the footsteps receded in the direction of the pub.

Inside the pub the two large men returned to their colleague. He knocked back the last of his pint, and stood. The three of them navigated their way through the crowd around the dartsboard, where, to the evident delight of the home supporters, it appeared that a ladies' team was giving its male opponents quite a thrashing. One of them remained at the foot of the stairs, took a radio out of his pocket and spoke into it quietly. The other two made their way upstairs to the private room. At the head of the stairs they were confronted by a couple of even larger men, who had been guarding the entrance to the party, but who, surprisingly, gave way to the newcomers immediately.

There was a bar at the far end of the room, but it could hardly be seen through the crush of people inside. Tony Kenny was sitting at a table quite close to the door, and he saw the entrants almost immediately. He put up a hand to halt the conversation at his table, and, like ripples spreading outwards from a stone dropped in a pond, silence gradually worked its way to the margins of the party. All eyes in the room fixed on the two newcomers.

Kenny rose, the noise of his chair scraping on the floor sharp and loud. "Well, well," he said. "Sergeant West. I don't remember inviting any of Her Majesty's constabulary."

The policeman raised his voice so as to be heard at the back of the room. "Now, we don't want any trouble, ladies and gentlemen. There is someone here with whom we should like to speak, and then we shall be on our way. Will Mr Harry Robeson step forward please?"

There was movement at the back of the room, and the guests parted to allow Robeson to the front.

"Yes, Sergeant?" he said as he arrived before the two men. He was a good-looking man and, although sixty, was in good shape. He had clear grey eyes surrounded by tiny wrinkles, indicating, as was the case, that their owner smiled a lot. He was smiling now, an open, curious smile.

"We've had a report that a gold-coloured Mercedes parked in the car park has been tampered with," said Sergeant West.

Robeson's eyes narrowed slightly. The sergeant's head glistened through his cropped hair. He must get through buckets of anti-perspirant, thought Robeson. "Two detectives to investigate interference with a motor vehicle? I'm impressed, Sergeant."

"Would you like to come down, sir?"

"If you like," replied Robeson.

They trooped down the stairs, collecting the third policeman en route, and pushed their way through the bar and into the car park. Robeson walked around his car slowly, looking at each of the doors, and peering through the windows. He was careful not to touch any of the door handles.

"Looks fine to me, Sergeant," he said. He caught a worried glance passing between the two other policemen. "Except," he added, pointing to the rear nearside wheel, "that someone's been throwing up all over this wheel."

"Did you have anything of value in the boot?" asked West.

"Yes, there's the car phone. I put it there when I leave the car unattended." Robeson fished in his pockets for the key, and opened the boot. The sergeant looked over his shoulder, and then pushed past him. He leaned into the boot, and stood up. There was a shotgun in his hand.

"Is this yours, sir?"

"No, it is not," said Robeson very calmly. "As I suspect you know very well, *Officer*, I have never seen it before."

West turned to the others with a triumphant smile. He then turned back to Robeson. "Harry Robeson: you are under arrest on suspicion of unlawful possession of a firearm. You need not say anything unless you wish to do so, but anything you say will be taken down and given in evidence. Handcuff him, Walker."

CHAPTER 4

The last four weeks had seen Charles's position progress from bad to worse. The day before he had received the most polite of summonses to the room of his head of Chambers. Huw Evans QC was a friendly man, with a gentle Welsh accent and a sharp sense of humour, but the request to be in his room at six o'clock that evening had still made Charles feel like a schoolboy going to see the head for a caning.

The interview had been amiable and inconsequential. They had chatted over Chambers business and the case on which Evans was engaged. Only as Evans was rising at the end of twenty minutes did the real purpose of the meeting become evident. He reminded Charles, in the most charming way, that his rent was almost a quarter in arrears, and that the previous quarter had eventually been paid seven weeks late. There was no threat and the discussion was entirely amicable, but he made the position quite clear. It was not really fair for other members of Chambers to support one member – "We all have our overdrafts to manage, don't we, Charles?" joked Evans. He was sure that Charles did not want to embarrass any of his colleagues. He was also sure that Charles would make certain that the rent was paid within the next fourteen days. If that were not possible, although Chambers would obviously try to be as flexible as it could – "We all have bad patches, don't we?" – some

47

other arrangement would have to be made. He was sure Charles understood.

Charles understood. Red bills from British Telecom and the City of London had sat unopened on his desk at the flat for the last two weeks. He had exceeded his overdraft by six thousand pounds and had been asked to return his cash card.

Today he had appeared at West London Magistrates' Court to act on behalf of a client summonsed for exceeding the permitted area for the display of goods in a street market. The brief, originally destined for one of the Chambers pupils, had been marked with the princely sum of £25. It was now six o'clock, Barbara was turning off the photocopying machine in preparation for locking up for the night, and Charles was, again, unemployed on the morrow. He dug into his pockets, and came up with three pounds odd in change. He had some whisky left at the flat, but he did not want to be alone, so he turned right out of Chambers and walked across the Temple towards the Witness Box. It was not a pub he used often, but it was right outside the eastern gate of the Inner Temple and there was generally a friendly atmosphere in both bars. There was a private party in progress upstairs, and so he went down to the basement, bought himself a pint and sat at a small table.

"Hello, Mr Holroyd," said a woman's voice from the table behind him. Charles turned in his seat. Two young women were just finishing their drinks.

"Well, hello, Sally."

Sally had been the junior clerk at Chancery Court, Charles's old chambers. She had started there as an office girl cum typist, but had soon been promoted. Last Christmas, however, Stanley, the senior clerk for twenty years, had suffered a stroke, and although still technically in charge, he only came in three days a week, and even then would often leave early. Thus Sally found herself in charge of the set on a daily basis and, from what Charles had heard, was making quite a success of it.

She was now in her late twenties, but her petite figure and child-like face made her seem like an innocent schoolgirl. That is, until she opened her perfect rosebud mouth. Sally was from Romford, and although not a true Cockney, sounded just like one. She was the one person from his old set whom Charles really missed.

"How you doin', sir?" she asked.

"I'm all right," he said, pleased to see her. "Can I get you and your friend a drink?" he asked, forgetting the fact that he had only a few pence in his pocket and nothing in his wallet.

Sally's companion, a girl of about her age, answered. "No, thanks. I've got to go, Sal. See you tomorrow, eh?" she said, getting up and putting on a raincoat. She collected her bags and departed with a wave.

"Will you join me?" asked Charles.

"All right," said Sally, "just for a quick one. I've got me train to get. But I'll get them: I ain't seen you for ages. Lager?" she asked, pointing at his glass and moving off to the bar before he could object. Charles watched her departing rear and wondered, not for the first time, what it would look like naked. She returned with a pint of lager and a glass of wine for herself and sat opposite Charles.

"Well, then, Mr Holroyd, how's the new set?"

Charles grimaced. "Look, I'm not sure of the protocol here, Sally, but I really would prefer you to call me Charles, not Mr Holroyd. And for heaven's sake, not 'sir'! Particularly outside office hours; you're not my clerk any more."

"We never meet outside office hours," she replied with a coy smile.

"That can be remedied," he said, grinning.

"Chance would be a fine thing," she said with feeling. "Anyway, if you don't mind, I'll call you 'Charlie'."

"Good."

He had half-expected her to decline the familiarity, and was pleased she had not. He was also strangely pleased that she preferred 'Charlie' to 'Charles'. No one else called him Charlie.

"I've always thought of you as 'Charlie' ever since that . . . incident, you know?"

Charles remembered. He had been in Chambers late one night when she had appeared at his door dishevelled and distraught, having been molested by another member of Chambers the worse for drink. Charles had been her "knight in shining armour" – he had even saved her job by somehow getting the barrister responsible to resign. She had never known how he had accomplished that and she had never asked, but ever since then Charles had held a special place in her affections. She had called him Charlie that night and, briefly, had held his hand. When she thought of the events of that night, which she still did every now and then, she was always surprised to find that her principal feeling was not one of fear at the thought of how close she had come to being raped, but of that moment of intimacy with Charles.

"Charlie will be fine," he said softly, savouring the echoes of that evening.

"So, I gather from what you say that you're busy in Chambers?" he asked.

"No, it's not that. It's me mum. Since Tracey got married – she's my youngest sister – Mum's health has been terrible."

"What's wrong with her?"

"Hah. You name it, she's got it. She's even got a few that ain't got no names! She's a woman who they says enjoys ill health." She said it with feeling, but not unkindly.

Charles grinned. "You be careful, Sally," he cautioned. He reached over and picked up her left hand, and looked

50

pointedly at her bare ring finger. "With both your sisters married and gone now, you're all your mum has. There must be a temptation to hang on to you."

"I know it, Charlie, I know it. Both Tracey and Michelle keep telling me to move out now while Mum can still cope, but then as soon as she has one of her spells, they're always too busy with their husbands or kids or whatever to deal with her. The truth is, they prefer me to be there so they know Mum's being looked after and they needn't worry. Anyway, that's enough of my problems. How are you? Busy?"

That was always the first greeting in the Temple, or so it now seemed to Charles, since he had been unable breezily to respond with his customary: "Submerged!" He took a deep breath. He did not know quite how to answer. The Temple was a hothouse of intrigue and gossip, particularly among a particular group of the criminal lawyers who appeared to have nothing to do after five o'clock except drink and chat. He did not want the fact of his failed practice to be common knowledge; that would certainly have been the kiss of death. At the same time, he did not want to lie to Sally. She saved him the problem of further deliberation.

"I hear things ain't too good," she said simply. Charles had been a favourite topic of conversation round the Temple ever since Henrietta's murder. Everyone knew that his career had taken a nosedive.

He nodded grimly. "Not great," he confirmed.

"What you gonna do?" she asked.

He shrugged. "To be honest, I haven't a clue. It's not the Chambers themselves; they've so much work they don't know what to do with it. Anyway, I wouldn't exactly be attractive to another set. At least when I left Chancery Court I was the young flier who'd murdered his wife. Now I'm the one with no practice who was cleared of murdering his wife."

51

"Are things really a dead loss there, then?"

"As dead a loss as you could imagine."

Sally looked at Charles, her big brown eyes full of sympathy. It wasn't fair, she thought to herself. He was one of the best barristers she had seen and, unlike most clerks, she did actually take the trouble to see her guv'nors in action every now and then, so that she could talk of their abilities with authority when asked by solicitors. She had slipped into court on three or four occasions while Charles was in her Chambers and watched him conduct cases. He was good. What's more, she thought, he's such a nice man.

"I think it's rotten, what's happened to you, Charlie," she said softly.

"I agree, Sally. It's perfectly rotten. But it's no good moping about it. I won't be the first barrister to give up because of bad breaks, but I've come to the conclusion that I'm going to have to find a job. In fact, I've decided to start looking tomorrow."

Sally frowned and thought to herself. She desperately wanted to help him in some way, but there was little she could do personally. Most clerks had an excess of work at times, and usually "returned" briefs first to the Chambers where their friends were clerks, but Sally's set did civil work, and so even when there was an excess of work at Chancery Court, it would be of no use to Charles. She was, however, a popular girl in the Temple and she knew most of the clerks. She would have a word with a couple in criminal sets and see if something could be put Charlie's way. There was another route she could try also.

Charles broke into her reverie. "Where are you off to now?"

"Crikey!" she exclaimed, looking at her watch. "I've gotta go," she said, standing and picking up her bag again. "There'll be hell to pay if I miss that train," she laughed. She bent down to kiss him on the cheek. Charles turned his head towards her and her lips landed on his. Her eyes registered surprise, but she did not pull away. Her mouth softened, and her hand touched the back of his head lightly. She straightened up again and looked at Charles in silence for a second.

"Keep smiling," she said softly. "Something'll turn up."

She rushed off, turning to give him a wave as she ran up the stairs. Charles sat down with the dregs of his pint, noting that his heartbeat had quickened.

Charles arrived at Chambers the next morning only to be sent off to a Magistrates' Court where he spent the entire day waiting for his case to be called on, and so his decision to find a "real" job was deferred for a further day. Nonetheless, the next day he was again unemployed, and he went into the Temple bright and early to start his search in earnest. As usual, he was the first to arrive. On the mat inside the door was a manila envelope marked "To the Clerk to Mr Charles Holroyd." Charles tore open the envelope. Inside was a brief. It was headed "In the Central Criminal Court". Charles gave a little whoop of pleasure and took the papers into his room to read them.

The Queen
v.
Harold Joseph Robeson

Brief for the defendant

Enclosures:

1 Certificate on committal
2 Full bundle of prosecution depositions
3 Copy charge sheet
4 Copy custody record

Counsel is instructed on behalf of Harold Joseph Robeson, who is charged with conspiracy to rob. An indictment has yet to be received from the Central Criminal Court, but Instructing Solicitors enclose as Item 3 herewith a copy of the charge before the Magistrates' Court. It is not expected that the count on the Indictment will differ significantly from the original charge.

Instructing Solicitors do not propose to set out in detail the facts alleged by the Crown as they will be apparent from the prosecution depositions, but Counsel will see that it is alleged that Mr Robeson conspired with Anthony Kenny, Peter Simons, Raymond Papier and persons unknown to rob the South African Gem Corporation of a quantity of diamonds worth £1 million. Counsel may be aware that two years ago Simons and various others were convicted of their respective parts in the robbery, a man named Goldstein was convicted of handling the diamonds, and Kenny was acquitted, following two trials at which the juries could not agree. Mr Robeson is, as Counsel will be aware, a solicitor of the Supreme Court of forty years' standing, and acted for a number of the Defendants in these trials.

Instructing Solicitors apologise for the lack of a Proof of Evidence from the Defendant. Mr Robeson is presently in custody, but arrangements have been made for a Proof to be prepared and for comments on the depositions to be obtained as soon as possible. The Defendant will however be pleading not guilty to the charge (and indeed any charge that may appear on the indictment). Instructing Solicitors appreciate that the evidence against the Defendant is very substantial, but the Defendant strenuously denies any criminality, and asserts that he has been "framed" by certain police officers in response to Kenny's acquittal. In particular, he asserts that the gun found in his car (see Bundle 1) was "planted" there.

Instructing Solicitors anticipate instructing Counsel shortly to make an application for bail on Mr Robeson's behalf, and details of sureties and other relevant matters will be forwarded to Counsel in due course. For the present Counsel is instructed to represent the Defendant at the Old Bailey at his trial.

Robeson & Co.

"Well I'll be damned," said Charles to himself. Why Robeson should have chosen to instruct him was a mystery. He had his own select coterie of barristers with whom he worked regularly, some of them among the very best in the profession. Why he should chose to be represented on the most important trial of his life – his own – by a junior, who was not only unknown to him, but was also plainly on the way out, was completely inexplicable. Charles turned the brief over again to the backsheet to make sure that it was indeed intended for him, but there were his name and address in the clearest of capitals.

He pushed his chair back and, backsheet in hand, walked into the clerks' room. Barbara had just arrived.

"Look at this," said Charles, putting it on the desk before her.

The clerk picked it up, and frowned. She turned it over once or twice in her hands, and handed it back. "You'll have to give it back to me so I can enter it on to the computer," she said simply.

"But why have I got it?"

"I don't know, sir."

"But I've never worked for him in my life! It doesn't make sense."

"I agree."

"I mean, this is classy work. Why hasn't it gone to Fifer, or Blackburne, or one of his other regulars?"

"I really don't know, Mr Holroyd. Don't you?"

"Me?"

"Yes. These came in late last night, just before I left. I haven't had time to deal with them yet, but I've glanced through them."

She swivelled round in her chair and reached to the filing cabinet behind her. She grabbed a bundle of briefs tied together with string and threw them down on the desk before Charles.

"They're all for you too."

"What?" exclaimed Charles. He reached over and undid the string. Four small briefs fell out on to the desk. The names of the defendants and the courts were all different, but the name of the Instructing Solicitor was the same in each case: Robeson & Co. Barbara swept back the long red hair that was always falling in her eyes, folded her arms and looked carefully at Charles as she spoke.

"All for you, all from Robeson. All minor matters at the Crown Court and, you will note, not one of them Legal Aid. The first one's this afternoon, a traffic matter at St Albans. It's marked at £500."

"Jesus Christ!"

"Quite. The next one's in a week's time. It appears to be a theft by a company director. It's listed as a fixture for two days. There's a grand on the brief and three-fifty refresher. One thousand three hundred pounds for two days' work. Not bad."

"Not bad? It's wonderful! It appears I have a guardian angel after all!"

"I quite agree. But aren't you curious as to why?"

"But that's the whole point. I haven't a clue."

"Do you want to do them?"

Charles threw his arms wide. "Are you kidding?" Then he thought for a moment. "Look," he said, lowering his voice, "what's going on, Barbara? Why this sudden influx? Is there anything to suggest that there's something wrong with them?"

She shrugged. "I don't know. I've not been through them. They appear all right."

"Well, then? What about the cab-rank rule? They're in a field in which I purport to practise, I'm available – I assume I'm available?" The clerk nodded with wry grin. "And if I'm available, I *have* to take them. Isn't that one of our important constitutional safeguards on which the Bar Council places so much reliance when justifying our exclusive rights of audience?"

"Mr Holroyd," she said gently, holding up her hand to stop him. "I can see nothing wrong with any of these briefs and no good reason why you should not act in them, particularly in view of the trouble we've had getting you restarted since your move. It's just that you and I both know that a sudden influx like this *is* rather unusual. But it does happen. Maybe he's had a row with Mr Blackburne's Chambers, but I would have expected to hear of something like that on the grapevine."

"And?"

"Nothing." She shrugged.

"Maybe he can't get anyone to represent him on his own trial, and is using the others as a sweetener?" wondered Charles.

"Maybe," replied Barbara. "But the Robeson trial will be very high profile. I wouldn't have thought he'd have trouble placing the brief." She paused in thought. "Perhaps he's heard that you were very quiet and decided to help out."

Charles looked at his clerk, unable to decide if she was joking. "Charity's one thing. Risking your own liberty on a junior who's on the way out is something else altogether."

"I agree, although I wouldn't have said you were on your way out," said Barbara.

"You ought to talk to my bank manager."

"But," continued Barbara, "if you are professionally obliged to do the work, as long as you're not asked to do anything improper, you might as well take the money and be happy. You can't really afford to turn it away, can you?"

"You know very well that I can't."

Barbara shrugged again in reply.

"Right then. I'll start on Robeson's own trial first. When you've booked the others in, perhaps you'll let me know."

Charles returned to his room via the kitchen and sat down with a cup of coffee to read the case of *The Queen* v. *Harold Joseph Robeson*.

CHAPTER 5

Michael O'Connor took one last look around the tiny room that had been his home for the last eight months. He had never liked the place. It was too small and frequently too noisy, especially in the mornings when they wanted him up, and all he wanted to do was sleep and not allow himself to remember where he was, and why he was there. Still, he would miss it. It was safe and it was familiar. And when he had bad days, when the pain came surging back, or when he fell a lot, there was always someone there to cheer him up or tell him off for being self-obsessed.

That was what Patty called him when he was down: self-obsessed. Big, blonde, Geordie Patty, with her crisp manner and crisp uniform. A girl he would once have fancied. A girl he would once have "pulled" with no difficulty. He'd been something of a ladies' man, with his green Irish eyes and ready smile. Now it was all different. Now all he could do was imagine. On his better days, he'd still have a laugh, flirt with her, just like he used to, but it wasn't any good. It always stopped short of the point where he would say: "Would you fancy a drink tonight when you're off?" or "Have you seen the new film at ABC?" He couldn't ask – well, what was the point? So he lay in bed in the dark, staring at the ceiling, his insensate erection making a tent of the sheets.

He spun the wheelchair around. "Let's go," he

commanded the porter, his lips pale and thin. "I can't wait to get outta this place!"

They drove him to his adapted flat, where the social worker and the district nurse awaited him. He said nothing as they showed him round the low work-surfaces in the kitchen, the cupboard handles all within reach, the widened doorways. He nodded without comment at the newly installed lift, the modified bath and the lavatory. They asked him when his sister would arrive and he lied, saying that she'd be there within the hour. So they left him for a while to find his way round, with promises to return later. Only then, once alone, did he slacken the firm grip he had maintained all day and weep bitter, angry tears for his useless legs.

Statement of Michael O'Connor
Age: Over 21
Occupation: Security Guard
Address: Care of Stoke Mandeville Hospital.

This statement consisting of three pages each signed by me is true to the best of my knowledge and belief and I make it knowing that, if it is tendered in evidence, I shall be liable to prosecution if I have wilfully stated anything in it which I know to be false or do not believe to be true. I have read this statement.

I am a security guard employed by Securicor. On 20th December 1987 I was employed as part of a team to escort a consignment of uncut jewels from Gatwick Airport, where they had arrived on a special flight from South Africa, to a bank in London. I was the driver of the transport, and occupied the front cab with one other guard, Leon Curtis. Two other members of the team, Roger and Steven Woodleigh travelled in the van with the consignment.

At approximately 5.20 a.m. we left the airport and

proceeded towards London on the M23. We reached Coulsdon without incident at about 6.10 a.m. At the junction of the Brighton Road and The Avenue there were what appeared to be roadworks. There were two British Gas lorries parked on the west side of Brighton Road, and a set of traffic lights had been installed, with traffic on the Brighton Road narrowed to a single lane, and alternating in each direction. I noticed at the time that there was a Jaguar motor car parked by the side of the road between the two lorries, as I felt sorry for the owner who would have trouble getting out in the morning.

The lights were green as we approached. I drove into the part of the road controlled by cones and I noticed in my wing mirror that the lights changed to red as we went through. Before we reached the end of the coned area a British Gas van pulled out from the pavement directly into our path. There was a sudden series of bangs, perhaps five or six, and the van seemed to jolt on each one. I realised that we were under fire. I put the van into reverse, but from the steering I realised that all of its tyres had been shot. Another Gas van appeared behind us, preventing us from moving further.

Five or six men surrounded the transport. They were wearing balaclava helmets and identical boilersuits. One man, who appeared taller than the rest, positioned himself in front of the van, slightly to the passenger side, and demanded that we get out. He was carrying a gun. From the width of the barrel and the stock it appeared to be a double-barrelled shotgun with the front part of the barrels sawn off. Another of the men, who was shorter and broader than the first man, also had a gun. It was a short pistol, black in colour, with a barrel about five inches long. He held it with both hands, his arms outstretched, and pointed it directly at my head from his position just outside my door. The leader again shouted at us to get out and pointed his shotgun at the front windscreen. At the same time I felt the van jerk upwards at the side. I could also hear a "ratchet" sound beneath us, and I realised that the van was being jacked up at the side. I was forced to my left, on top of my co-driver. There was then the sound of a drill cutting into the metal of the underside of the van. That lasted for about two minutes. The van was jacked up so far on that side that I feared that it would topple on to its side. The man at the front then told us that there was a grenade placed through the armour on the underside of the van, and that he was giving us twenty seconds to get out. I did not believe him, but we were in any event preparing to get out, although the angle of the van made it difficult to open the door. There was then a huge explosion. I remember being forced back on to Leon, and the sensation of flying, rather like when you drive over a hump-backed bridge at speed.

I remember nothing more of the events. I awoke in hospital. I suffered a broken back in the explosion and I am paralysed from the lower chest downwards. I have been in hospital from the date of the robbery until now, and I am told that I shall remain here or in a different hospital for several months longer so that I may receive training. It was my impression at the time that the leader did not really care whether we got out of the van or not. He certainly did not wait for us to try to get out, despite the fact that it must have been obvious that that was what we were doing.

Signed Michael O'Connor. Signature witnessed by DC Russell 913

*   *   *

62

"And, of course, with that model you get the air conditioning."

"How much did you say it was?" asked the woman.

"To buy outright, eleven five, and, as I say, it's well underpriced, only because of the left-hand drive. But, of course, if as you say you're going round Europe in it, well, you're getting the benefit, aren't you? But, let me repeat: we offer very competitive finance deals. Basically, we can tailor one exactly to your needs, based on what you can afford monthly."

The young couple looked at each other. He was already sold. He had always loved Range Rovers and this was the day he had dreamed of for years. She was much less sure. The caravanette they had seen the day before was only a third of the price and much more suitable. They could sleep in it and save on hotel bills. As far as she was concerned, she would as soon fly to Greece again as go on this long and very expensive drive round Italy, but if they really had to go, a caravanette was so much more practical. *Her* friends didn't drive about in Porches and Range Rovers, whatever Stewart's new colleagues did. A caravan had been good enough for her parents for all those years at Canvey Island, and it would be good enough for her.

"Erm, Mr . . .?" she said tentatively.

"Rattle, but like I said, call me Rodney, everyone does."

"Yes, well, how many miles does it do to the gallon? See, we have a long journey to do . . ." she tailed off.

"I'd say twenty-eight to thirty, on a run," said Rodney confidently.

"Really? My dad thought nearer to eighteen or twenty. . ." said the woman.

Rodney gritted his teeth and smiled. "Well, it's true that they used to be very poor on fuel consumption, but over the last few years they solved that problem. No. I can't guarantee it, mind, but I'd be very surprised if you got less than thirty." He turned back to the man. Rodney Rattle had been in the used-car business for almost twenty years, since he was sixteen, and he could smell a sale at a hundred paces. Mister was almost hooked, whatever Missus might say. If I can just get him talking figures, he thought.

"How were you thinking of paying? Let's assume the vehicle's all right for a minute, how were you going to pay? Cash? Finance? Have you got a vehicle in part-exchange?"

"Well, we've got enough for quite a bit of it— " Mister started, but felt his wife's hand on his arm.

"Look: come inside, and I'll show you the tables. You'd be amazed at how reasonable the monthly repayments are. And frankly," and here he dropped his voice conspiratorially, "we might even be able to do something about the interest rates, eh? I know the chap at the finance company and, well, with a bit of arm-twisting, I might even be able to get him down a point or two— "

Rodney was cut short by a hand on his arm. He turned to see a tall young man dressed in a dark suit. He was holding up a card. A Metropolitan Police warrant card. Rodney contained his anger and smiled. The last thing he wanted was a copper nosing around just when he had punters in the yard.

"Mr Rattle?"

"Yes?"

"I'm Detective Constable McMillan. Mr Beeman, your boss, suggested that you could help me. We need the records relating to a car you sold a while back."

"There was no problem with it, was there?" said Rodney, glancing at his punters, who were looking far from happy.

"Oh, no, sir. It wasn't stolen or anything."

Rodney smiled nervously at Mr and Mrs Punter. "Look," he said to the policeman, "I'm a bit tied up at the present. Could you come back later, tomorrow maybe?"

"No, I'm sorry sir, but this is an important inquiry."

Rodney looked around. He could see Beeman talking to his secretary in the office, but everyone else was out on road tests or at lunch.

"What records are you after, Officer?"

"The bill of sale, an H.P. form, any document that might bear the handwriting of the purchaser."

"Oh, I don't think we keep anything of that sort— "

"Look, Mr Rattle, I've already been through this with your boss. Your company keeps all the records. I've even seen the filing cabinet. What neither Mr Beeman nor I know is where the hell you filed them! Now stop messing me about, and dig them out for me. It'll only take ten seconds."

Rattle doubted that. Filing was not his strong suit. He looked anxiously at Mr and Mrs Punter. "Would you excuse me for just a second? I'll be right back. Oh, you're welcome to some coffee, if you like. Shall I ask Joanne to bring you some out?"

Mister was about to accept the offer, but again Missus intervened. "No, thanks," she said, smiling, but looking at her watch.

Rodney fretted for another few seconds, knowing that if he left now he might well lose the sale. Then, seeing the officer's face, he scampered off to the office, the policeman at his heels explaining what it was he required. Rodney dived into the filing cabinet, throwing out files on to the desk, keeping one eye on the Punters outside. They were deep in conversation, with Missus making the running. Hold on, son, he willed Mr Punter. I'll be right out, just hang on in there! If he could only find the blasted file and get back there, he would make the sale. He knew it. The pile of files on the desk grew and one or two fell to the floor, to be joined by others as Rodney took his eyes off what he was doing to look through the window. As he watched, he saw Mister's resistance grow ever weaker. He was barely answering back now, just feebly gesticulating with his hands, trying to stem his wife's flow of words.

Finally, with a triumphant "Here!" Rodney found the relevant file and thrust it into the policemen's hand. Rodney charged outside again, but in the seconds it took to race down the corridor, during which Mr and Mrs Punter were out of sight, Mister had finally surrendered unconditionally. The yard was bare.

"Shit!" swore Rodney,

Statement of Rodney Baxter Rattle
Age: Over 21
Occupation: Car Dealer
Address: Performance Motors, 88 Kingsland St, London E8.

This statement consisting of one page signed by me is true to the best of my knowledge and belief and I make it knowing that, if it is tendered in evidence, I shall be liable to prosecution if I have wilfully stated anything in it which I know to be false or do not believe to be true. I have read this statement.

I am a car salesman employed by Performance Motors of Kingsland Street, E8. On 12th December 1987 a man came in and asked about a Jaguar XJ 12, 5.3 litre motor car, registration number A226 DBB, that we had for sale on the forecourt at £15,950. He asked about the car, and gave it a very thorough mechanical check. He was so expert that I took him to be a dealer or a mechanic, but I could not understand why he was prepared to pay retail prices if that were so. He took the car on a road test. When he came back, he paid the full asking price in £50 notes without haggling. He paid in cash and therefore filled in no forms at all. I produce the invoice as exhibit RBR 1.

I would describe the man as white, in his thirties, with short fair hair and a moustache. He was about five foot eight in height and of slender build.

Signed Rodney Baxter Rattle. Signature witnessed by DC McMillan.

Charles put the bundle down and made some notes. Then he picked it up again and flicked through it, looking for something. There! Three statements further on, another car dealer, only two days later, this time a BMW. Cost: £9,500. That made over £25,000 on transport alone. Whoever set up this job, two things were clear. Firstly, they took no chances. Many would have simply stolen two cars and put on false plates. By buying legitimately, for cash, there was absolutely no risk of being traced through the vehicles, nor of being caught while trying to steal them. Secondly, money clearly was not a problem. They were playing for high stakes, and someone had a lot of money to play with. Charles took a sip of now-cold coffee, grimaced, and started to read again.

May Charlotte Barlow pulled back her net curtains for the thirtieth time that morning and peered out of the front window of her Surrey cottage at the village green. It had been a quiet morning. The Jacksons opposite had had their milk and post delivered as normal, and then, at teatime (around quarter to eleven if May did not go to the shops, and half past if she did) someone had arrived to deliver a parcel. Mrs Jackson was out at the time, and May was about to go over and offer to take it in when Mrs Titherleigh from next door had appeared and signed for it. Mrs Titherleigh had been in her garden cutting her privet hedge, and May had heard the click-click of her shears all morning. It was reassuring, that sound. May did not like to be alone. The village was so isolated, and anything could happen. The nice lady from Social Services had helped get a telephone put in the winter before, just in case May needed to be in touch in an emergency.

May heard the sound of a vehicle approaching, and she craned her old neck round to see who it was. It was the plumber for number 21. He had been there the night before. May understood from Mrs Smith that their toilet had blocked again. I expect it's the baby putting things down it again, thought May. Last time it had blocked, Mrs Smith had told her, the plumber had pulled out of the U-bend the top half of an Action-Man and his opened parachute. It was the parachute apparently which stopped the toy from being washed down.

May watched as the plumber got out of his van and walked up the garden path. Steve, his name was. They lived in the next village, and she'd known his aunt at the WI, before she had to stop going. She really wasn't up to it any more, not since her last fall. Steve knocked on the door of number 21 and was allowed in by the eldest girl, Julia. My goodness, don't they grow up fast? thought May. She watched Steve all the way in until the door closed. You can't be too careful, she often said to her daughter. Her daughter, Ellen, lived near Guildford, but she still popped in at least twice a week. A good girl, was Ellen, and May counted herself lucky. Mrs Bolley up the road at number 1 had no one, not even on Christmas Day.

Ellen always teased her mother about her nosiness, but it wasn't nosiness really. Even the police approved of people keeping an eye open, didn't they? That's what the Neighbourhood Watch was all about. And, thought May, where would they have been without her being nosey, eh? That's what she asked Ellen when she poked fun. If she'd not kept her eyes open, they would never have caught those awful criminals. And, for once, May was quite right.

Statement of May Charlotte Barlow
Age: Over 21
Occupation: Housewife
Address: Lime Tree Cottage, Orchard Lane, Lower
Barnsthorne, Surrey.

This statement consisting of two pages each signed by
me is true to the best of my knowledge and belief, and
I make it knowing that, if it is tendered in evidence, I
shall be liable to prosecution if I have wilfully stated in
it anything which I know to be false or do not believe
to be true. I have read this statement.

I live at the above address and have done so for
the last thirty years. The house next door to mine,
called 'Staplecroft' is owned by a Professor Wilson
who is presently away in America. Since he has been
away the house has been let out to various people,
mainly teachers from the University. On Friday 18th
December 1987 a new set of tenants moved in. I know
it was that day because the previous tenants had been
students and they made a lot of noise the night before
with a party. The first new tenant to arrive was a man
in his thirties, tall, dark, and with his hair tied back
in a ponytail. I spoke to him, and he said that he and
some friends were moving in for a week or so on a
business course at the University. I was surprised, as
it was so near Christmas, but he said that that was why
the course was held then, when the University was
otherwise empty. A day later two other men arrived.
One was shortish, with fair hair. I only saw him briefly
and so I could not estimate his age. The third man
was very dark-skinned, not like an Indian, but more
like someone with a very good tan. He appeared
younger than the others, in his twenties, and very fit
and muscular. I think there were one or two others,
as I heard their voices, but I did not see them.

The men had two cars. One was a black car. I do not know much about cars, but I am sure it was just like the one driven by my daughter's husband. I have been shown some pictures and I picked out a car like that one. I am told that it is a BMW. The other car I do remember. It was a Jaguar, and its registration number was A226 DBB. The reason I remember it so well is that it has the initials of my sister-in-law, Dilly Beatrice Barlow.

About a week after the men arrived next door, I saw a report on the television of a robbery, and of a car being found abandoned. I saw then that the registration number of that car was the same as the number of the Jaguar driven by the men next door. I reported the fact to the police.

Signed May Charlotte Barlow. Signature witnessed by DC Walker

Before Charles could pick up the next statement, his telephone rang.

"Mrs Horowitz, sir," said Philip, the junior clerk, and he put the call through.

"Hello, Mum?" asked Charles, quite surprised. He had not spoken to her since the last row, weeks before. "Everything all right?"

"Does there have to be something wrong before I can ring my son at work?"

"No, of course not," he replied with a sigh. Less than ten words spoken, and already he was smoothing ruffled feelings. "How are you?"

"I'm fine." She paused. Charles sensed that something was indeed wrong.

"And Dad?" he asked.

"He's okay. You know how he is. He won't take things easy."

70

"Why? What's happened?"

"Nothing's *happened* . . ." she said, implying the contrary.

"But?" prompted Charles.

"He's been having one of his morbid patches. Talking about his Will, how he couldn't bear to die with his family fighting, that sort of thing. You know how he is. He wants you to come to supper." She paused again, struggling with what she had to say. "And he wants me to apologise."

Now Charles was certain something was wrong. He could not remember the last time his mother had apologised for anything.

"Mum, will you please tell me if he's all right?"

"He's okay. He's had another of his 'turns'."

Harry Horowitz had suffered from "turns" for some years. It was not unusual after such an attack for his mortality to weigh heavily with him. He refused to see a doctor for fear of confirmation.

"A bad one?" asked Charles.

"As bad as I can remember," said his mother, at last her voice betraying how worried she really was.

"Do you want me to come over?" he asked, looking at his watch. He was due in Court that afternoon on the first of Robeson's cases, but he calculated quickly and decided that he just had time to pop into his parents' home en route.

"No, it's not that bad. The doctor's been, and your father's got to stay in bed for the next while, that's all."

"Are David and Sonia coming on Friday?"

"I expect so."

"Shall I come too?"

"Yes, please. He wants to see you."

"Fine. I'll phone tonight and see how he is."

After he had finished speaking to his mother, Charles bundled up the Robeson papers. He would have to read the rest later when he got back from Court. Before he left

71

Chambers, however, he picked up the telephone again and dialled a London number.

"Newsdesk, please," he said when the call was answered.

"Staton," announced the person to whom he had been put through.

"Jeff," said Charles.

"Charles?"

"Yes. How are you?"

"I'm fine, mate. How are you, and that lovely dancer of yours?"

"I'm very well. As for Rachel, at the last report she was, as a rival rag would have put it, rather tired and emotional. I gather, however, that she was having a wonderful, if inebriated, time of it."

Jeff laughed. "Yes, of course, she's away at the moment, isn't she? You'll have to come round for a meal some time. Can't have you starving while she's away. I know Lucy'd love to see you. Is this a social call, or can I do something for you?"

"Well, you could lend me a hand actually. Ever heard of Harry Robeson?"

Charles waited while his friend's encylopaedic mind processed the name. "Yeah," he replied eventually. "Solicitor, isn't he? Quite prominent. Does a lot of dirty crime, and in his spare time is on a couple of charitable boards. Theatres too. Isn't it the Old Vic?"

"I haven't a clue. That snippet of information was new to me. But that's why I called. I guess you've got a file on him somewhere."

"Not me personally, but— "

"But the paper will, right? Any chance that I could see what there is?"

"Can I ask why?"

"You know he's been committed to stand trial on conspiracy charges?"

"Yes."

"I'm representing him. I just want to know a bit about the man I'm dealing with."

"Congratulations, Charles. It'll be a good case. Yeah, I expect I can help out an ex-employee. Didn't you once read for libel here?"

"Yes," laughed Charles. "In my young and carefree days."

Charles, like young many barristers struggling to make a living, used to spend a couple of nights every week reading the next day's issue of the newspaper before it went to press, in an attempt to ensure that no one was libelled by its contents. He had long since given up the job, although he had in fact thought more than once recently of applying again.

"Do you want to come and browse?"

"I'm afraid I can't; it's a bit too urgent."

"Okay. I'll see what I can dig up. I'll pop a few bits and pieces in an envelope and post it to you. Actually, come to think of it, you're only in New Fetter Lane, aren't you? I'll drop it in tonight after work. I'm going to the Aldwych Theatre this evening anyway."

"That's terrific, Jeff. Thanks a lot. I owe you one."

"When you come for dinner, you can bring an especially good plonk, okay?"

"Agreed. Must run. Love to Lucy. Bye."

"Bye."

Charles collected his robes, picked up the brief from Barbara, and rushed off to St Albans Crown Court.

CHAPTER 6

The woman tied her scarf more tightly round her head, seized the hand of a child in each of hers and joined the back of the queue. It was a damp and miserable day and the wind swirled around her, seeking out the gaps in her thin clothing and chilling her bones. There were more visitors today than she had seen before and she despaired of keeping the boys occupied for what would be a long wait before they were allowed in. Two men in suits carrying briefcases walked to the door, ignoring the queue of mainly women and children. They knocked on the door, spoke a few words to the man who opened it, and were allowed in. Legal visits, I suppose, thought the woman; they don't have to wait. Look what you get to know about, she thought to herself. Never did I expect to be an expert in prison procedure.

Her youngest son, Raphael, began struggling, trying to twist his hand out of hers. She gripped tighter.

"Keep still, Rafi, please," she said without looking down. The boy quietened for a few seconds and then aimed a kick at his older brother who was standing on the other side of her.

"Stop that!" she hissed.

"He kicked me first," complained the child.

The woman looked at the boy on her right. He was studiously examining his shoes, strong evidence that he had provoked the kick.

"Please, Hershel, be a good boy," she begged. He did not respond, but looked at her out of the corner of his eye. He had become so sullen, so sly. He would goad the others, particularly Rafi, the youngest, until he prompted retaliation, and then he would run and tell tales, or worse, hurt them out of all proportion to the retaliation. That formed another entry in the account of bitterness she kept awaiting the day of her husband's release. They had never had a moment's trouble with the children until the day Avraam threw away his sanity and his good name and landed himself in prison. Now they were all wild, even the two girls whom she had persuaded her mother to care for for the day. She simply could not manage the trip to the Isle of Wight with four children – even assuming she could have afforded it – so she took them two at a time, alternating boys and girls. This month was the turn of the boys to see their father, the criminal.

"Can we go and sit down over there, Mama?" asked Hershel, pointing to a patch of grass.

"Will you be good, and play with Rafi?"

"Yes," he replied.

"Go on, then."

She watched the two boys run over and begin chasing each other. It was likely to end with one or both of them crying, but for the moment she hadn't enough energy to stop them. A number of heads among the waiting families turned and watched them. The boys' scullcaps, strange clothes and the long curled locks at the side of their heads always attracted attention at the prison. Then the woman would feel herself the object of scrutiny and her face would burn. A Jew – one of the "pious ones", a *chasid* no less – a common criminal. At those moments she would hate Avraam, with an intensity that surprised her, for having brought such shame upon them.

As always, when, finally, she faced her husband over the table in that disgusting room filled with the smell of

75

institutional cooking, she did her best to put on a brave face. She knew that he lived only for her monthly visits, and tried to blot out the days in between. When, last month, the eldest girl, Naomi, had developed mumps and had forced the visit to be cancelled at the last minute, Avraam had sent a letter so piteous that Ruth had cried for a week. She knew too that however bad it was for her and the children – the ostracism of her friends and relatives, the endless self-vindication of his parents – for him, the last two years had been hell, sheer, living hell. And she knew finally that thoughts of suicide were his constant companion. The knowledge that he had available that means of escape (and he claimed, to her distress, that he had contrived at least two certain methods of accomplishing it) was his only refuge from total despair.

They talked for a while about the home, her mother's health, and Hershel's school work, but in the silence that followed, the false cheer slipped from her grasp as it did every month, and tears again welled in her eyes and ran down her plain cheeks to land in two puddles on the table. Rafi clung to her skirts and began to cry. Avraam picked up her hand, bent his bearded head towards it and kissed it repeatedly.

"Razel, Razel," he whispered her pet name sofly, "please do not do this!"

"I can't help it, Avraam. You don't understand . . ." she sobbed, shaking her head.

He stared at the table between them, stroking her hand. "Listen, my love, I have good news."

She did not hear him through her sobs until he repeated himself.

"Ruth, I have good news."

"What news?"

He bent forward and lowered his voice. "There's a possibility of parole soon," he said.

"How?" she replied incredulously. "You told me at least another year."

"Things have changed."

"What things?" She eyed him carefully. She knew his face so well, but it was a moment or two before she recognised his expression, so unexpected was it: he looked guilty. "What have you done, Avraam? What have you done now?"

"I would have told you last month, but you didn't come. Razel, you must understand: I can't bear it in here. I cannot tell you what it is like. For *them*, the *goyim*, I suppose it isn't so bad, but for me . . . it's unspeakable."

"What have you done?" she repeated.

Statement of Avraam Shimon Goldstein
Age: Over 21
Occupation: Jeweller
Address: H.M. Prison Camphill

This statement consisting of four pages each signed by me is true to the best of my knowledge and belief and I make it knowing that, if it is tendered in evidence, I shall be liable to prosecution if I have wilfully stated anything in it which I know to be false or do not believe to be true. I have read this statement.

I am a jeweller with premises in Hatton Garden, London, and I am expert in the valuation of diamonds. Through the course of my business I met a man I knew as Tony Kenny. He started coming into my shop to buy jewellery about five years ago. At that time I thought that he was a successful businessman. He came in infrequently, but when he did, he would spend up to £5,000 at a time.

One day, in the middle of 1987, he came in and brought a small pendant. He told me that he was owed a large sum of money by a business associate, who was unable to pay. He had been offered payment by way of certain jewellery, but he did not know if it was real, or, if so, whether or not it was worth the amount of the debt. He asked me if I would be prepared to value the jewellery. At that stage I did not realise that anything might be illegal about the transaction, and I agreed. I am often asked, by people in the trade and by others, to give valuations.

I heard nothing more for some months and had entirely forgotten about it until one night just before Christmas he arrived at my shop with another man just as I was about to close for the night. He asked me to go with them to value the jewellery. I said that I had to go home, and invited them to return the next day. Kenny became very upset and said that I had made a deal, and that he stood to lose the chance to take this jewellery unless it was valued that night. He offered me £5,000 to do the valuation, but I still refused. He then became angry and said that he would hold me personally responsible if he lost his chance to recover his debt. I began to realise that the story of the debt was not true, and I suspected that he was doing something dishonest. However, he was very insistent, and I was quite frightened. He and the other man were very powerful and I was alone in the shop. He then offered me £10,000 for what he said was only a couple of hours' work, £1,500 in advance in cash. I agreed, and he gave me the £1,500 which I put immediately in the safe.

I was taken to a Jaguar car parked outside my shop and I got in the rear with Kenny. The other man, who did not speak at all throughout the evening, drove. After we got out of the centre of London, Kenny asked to blindfold me. He said that the location of the meeting was a secret, and that it would be better for me if I did not know where it was being held. I thought it was a strange request, but I did not feel as if I could protest. We travelled for nearly an hour. Much of the middle part of the journey was on a fast road like a motorway, as I could feel that we were travelling at speed and there were no stops at all for some miles. We arrived at a house that I think was in the country, as I could hear very little traffic and there was the sound of wind blowing in a lot of trees.

I was taken to a room upstairs and the blindfold was taken off me. I was shown to a desk on which there was a lamp, and asked to look at a total of thirty-five cut and polished diamonds. The diamonds were among the largest and most beautiful I had ever seen. Together, I valued them at £1,150,000. While I was at the house I only saw one other person. He was a middle-aged man, wearing expensive clothes. He stayed at the back of the room out of the light, and watched me while I worked. He did not speak while I was there. I saw him quite clearly as I stood up to leave. I believe I would recognise him again.

I was then returned, blindfolded, to my shop in Hatton Garden and had to make my own way home. Tony Kenny had also watched me working and, as I was getting out of the car, he gave me a diamond that I had valued at £9,000. He told me to keep the change.

On 4th June 1991 a police officer came to H.M. Prison Camphill with an album of photographs. One of the photographs was of the man who was in the bedroom of the house where I did the valuation, and I pointed this person out to the officer.

Signed Avraam Shimon Goldstein. Signature witnessed by D.S. West.

Charles picked up his pen and made some further notes. The cross-examination of Goldstein would be one of the critical parts of the case. There were a number of ways in which he could be impugned, not least of which was the fact that by giving evidence for the Crown, he obviously hoped to improve his chances of parole. Charles was also curious about the diamond: had Goldstein returned it? The statement made no mention of it. Charles made a further note to ask the solicitors to check whether Goldstein had ever been in trouble with the police before this incident. In a case like this, where his client was a man of "good character" – without previous convictions – any dirt Charles could throw at the prosecution witnesses would be invaluable.

He returned to the bundle of prosecution statements and leafed ahead. It appeared at a glance that the rest of the witnesses were policemen or Home Office experts. The next statement was by an Inspector Bathington, and he confirmed that he had shown an album of unnamed photographs to Goldstein, and that Goldstein had, as Charles expected, picked out the photograph of Robeson as the man at the house. Charles grimaced as he read on to discover that Inspector Bathington had had nothing whatsoever to do with the primary investigation itself; he had simply been asked to show the album to a witness and record his reaction. There was therefore very little prospect of suggesting that he had done anything improper. If

Goldstein had been "primed" to pick out the right man, it had happened in advance of the identification. Charles went back to Goldstein's statement. It was dated the same day as the identification, 4th June, the day after Kenny's second acquittal. Charles scribbled a few further comments and read on.

He got no further than finding his page when the telephone rang.

"Yes?" he asked.

"Mr Holroyd? It's Barbara. I have Robeson & Co. on the telephone. They want you to go on a conference at Brixton *this afternoon*."

"Oh, come on! I'm working on something. Why can't they make an appointment like anyone else?"

"I've told them all that. But the client they want you to meet is Robeson himself."

"Oh. I see. I wonder what all the rush is. But I haven't finished the papers yet."

"I told them that too, but they don't mind. They realised you've only had them for a couple of days, but the client is very anxious to meet you before you come to any conclusions. They've set the conference up for two o'clock. You'd have to leave almost immediately. If you really can't make it, they'll cancel, but— "

"No. Don't cancel. I'll do it. Do they want to speak to me?"

"No, I'll just tell them you're on your way. Oh, by the way, they've paid you for the St Albans case yesterday."

"What?" asked Charles, utterly astonished. The average time barristers await for payment from solicitors is measured in years, not days. He had hundreds of cases on his records that had been unpaid for ten years and more, and his position was no different to that of any other barrister. To be paid by the next day was almost unheard of.

"I know. But they just *happened* to receive funds from

81

the client yesterday, and they just *happened* to have a clerk from their office near Chambers, and so they thought they'd drop it in by hand."

"My God."

"So you can have the cheque on the way out— " for which Charles silently thanked Barbara, as it usually took three days to go through the account system before it reached the barrister concerned – "and you'd better be very nice to them this afternoon."

Charles hung up, a broad smile on his face. If this was seduction, he could grow to like it. He returned to the papers. He only had a few minutes, so he skimmed the last few statements. The first two, almost identical, were from the police officers who found the gun in the boot of Robeson's car. The third was in standard form, and was the statement of a ballistics expert, confirming that the gun was one that had been fired at the robbery. The last was from the police officer who had interviewed Robeson under caution, although the solicitor had wisely declined to answer any of the questions. Altogether a strong, but not impossible, case, thought Charles. Goldstein was clearly a flawed witness. Given the two acquittals of Kenny, it would not be wholly incredible to suggest to a jury that a frustrated policeman had overstepped the bounds of propriety and "assisted" the evidence by planting the gun.

Charles retied his brief in its pink ribbon, grabbed a new notebook and set off for Brixton Prison.

CHAPTER 7

Charles parked his car in a side road off Brixton Hill, in the certain belief that it would not be there, or at least intact, when he returned. His certainty was not in the least based on experience – he had parked his car there on each of the dozen or so occasions that he had had to visit clients at Brixton Prison and it had never apparently been touched – but on the fact that the area itself seemed so villainous. To what extent that feeling was prompted unconsciously by the knowledge that at any time a quarter of London's less successful male criminals were housed in the rambling brick buildings across the road, he had not considered.

He walked down the long access road to the prison entrance, wondering, as he did on every visit, why the complex looked so much like a council estate, and identified himself to the officer on guard at the entrance. He walked through the security procedures, the frisking, the emptying of pockets and the electronic scanning, with only half his mind on what was happening. He was thinking of Harry Robeson, solicitor of the Supreme Court. What must he be going through now, thought Charles, whether guilty or not? This was no old lag for whom prison was no more than a business risk, inconvenient, but, with experience and patience, endurable; according to the newspaper clippings that Jeff had posted through Charles's door, this was a civilised man, a *bon vivant*; a man reputed to be expert in wine, architecture and the history of Italian opera; a man whose knowledge of the classics – self-taught, too – it was said would rival that of a don. Charles was curious to see what incarceration would do to such a man, incarceration, indeed, with men who must have been as foreign to Robeson as if they had been Tibetan. A few hours in police custody was the worst Charles had ever endured, and that had been enough. Imprisonment had always held a particular terror for him.

He was shown to a tiny interview room and awaited Robeson's arrival. Footsteps sounded along the corridor and Robeson entered. As a prisoner on remand he was entitled to wear his own clothes and, possibly because he had never seen him in anything else, Charles, foolishly, had expected him to be wearing a suit. In fact Robeson was wearing comfortable slacks and a lambswool pullover. His greying hair was combed neatly and he smelled slightly of aftershave – aftershave which, curiously enough, Charles recognised, as he used the same one himself. Robeson greeted Charles warmly.

"Charles," he said, extending a hand. "Delighted to meet you. I hope you don't mind the use of your first name."

Charles did mind. It always irritated him when strangers used his first name without prior permission, but he none the less smiled, shrugged and shook the other's hand. Robeson had a firm grip and he looked Charles straight in the eye for a few seconds, as if evaluating him. Charles returned the look with equal steadiness. Although he had never actually been introduced to the solicitor before, Charles had the odd sensation of recognising something in the other man. It was a sort of openness, a frankness in the wide grey eyes and the bluff, square face that made Charles feel comfortable. Robeson reminded him, for some inexplicable reason, of a Yorkshire cricketer.

"Charles will do," replied Charles, offering the solicitor a seat.

"Good," said Robeson with approval as he sat down, "I don't know why, but I would rather call you Charles. I thought about it, and decided that if I were not the client, I would call you 'Mr Holroyd', and be quite miffed if the client didn't do likewise. Strange, eh? Anyway, I don't think I could bear it if you kept calling me 'Mr Robeson', so let's start as we mean to go on, okay?"

"Fair enough," said Charles, smiling. "I must warn you, Harry, that I haven't been through the papers in detail. I've read them once, but— "

"Forget it, forget it," replied Robeson quickly with a wave of his hand. "You've only had them a minute. I gather you had a result yesterday."

Charles raised his eyebrows in surprise. The man was facing a life sentence if convicted, in prison for the first time in his life, and he looked for all the world as if he was relaxing after a round of golf. Now he was asking Charles about yesterday's case, a relatively trival matter of reckless driving. Charles looked hard at Robeson, trying to judge whether this was just bravado, but the solicitor regarded him steadily and with what appeared to be genuine interest.

"We did all right," replied Charles. "He pleaded to careless driving."

"Well done. Bernice was duly impressed with you," said Robeson, referring to the clerk who had attended at court on the firm's behalf. "But then, the opinion of an eighteen-year-old typist with two 'O' levels and a month's experience of the law might not be much of a testimonial."

He said it with a completely straight face and a twinkle in his eye, and Charles could not help but grin. One of the particular applications of Sod's Law to practise at the Bar was that one's greatest forensic triumphs were always achieved before an audience consisting of a legally aided client, a part-time Judge, and the instructing solicitors' temporary secretary, none of whom could affect one's future practice in the slightest, however impressed they might have been with one's brilliance. On the other hand, when things went wrong, one's cock-up was always witnessed by a High Court Judge at the least, a very substantial litigious client, who could, if impressed, guarantee a barrister's income for life, and the senior partner of a prestigious firm of City solicitors. It was an insight into practice that had occurred to many a barrister, but was one which Charles would not have attributed to a solicitor.

Charles undid the ribbon on his brief and opened his new notebook.

"Don't worry about that," said Robeson. "Have you got a light?" He produced a cigar and held it up. "Do you?" he asked, offering another to Charles.

"I don't, thank you," declined Charles, "but I do have light. Standard equipment on prison visits."

Charles lit Robeson's cigar and the solicitor leaned forward on the table.

"We both know there's no point in a con if you haven't read the papers properly. I didn't ask to see you to discuss the case, anyway. At least, not the evidence."

"What, then?" asked Charles with some irritation.

"Don't fret, Charles," chided Robeson gently, "you'll be paid for the con, whether we talk about the case or the weather. And paid handsomely too. I want to get to know you," he explained.

Charles shrugged and pushed his papers to one side. There was a knock on the door and a man in blue prison uniform put his head round the door. "Tea or coffee, gents?" he asked.

Robeson raised his eyebrows at Charles. "Coffee, please," said Charles. "Milk, no sugar."

"Twice, please, Spike," said Robeson. The trustee

disappeared for a few seconds and then returned with the drinks, for which Charles paid.

"An ex-client," commented Robeson after he had departed.

"Presumably a dissatisfied one, then."

"No. We represented him throughout his career until his last job. Then he was recommended to a firm in Islington with potted ferns and smoked-glass windows. Got two years."

"How are you finding it?" asked Charles.

"What, in here?" He paused, wreathed in cigar smoke. Charles watched him ponder the question. "It's funny what you miss. Not what you'd have thought at all. I miss my car." Robeson glanced at Charles, slightly embarrassed at the confession. "It's got this lovely smell of leather and polished wood. I look forward to getting into it every morning. Had it two years now, and I still feel exactly the same about it as on the day I took delivery. I had a background like yours, you know? East End. No money. Worked my way up the hard way. Always wanted a Merc."

"What do you know of my background?" asked Charles, surprised.

Robeson just smiled. "I didn't just stick a pin in the Bar List, you know."

"All right. If this is a getting-to-know-you session, I'd like to ask you a question. What's more, it's one I've never asked a solicitor before, just in case I prompted him to ask it of himself: why did you choose me? You've never instructed me before. I'm not a silk. You could have chosen a dozen barristers more experienced than me. So: why?"

"Are you a good barrister?"

"Yes, I think so."

"So do others to whom I've spoken. Are you available to do the case?"

"Yes."

"Do you think it's winnable?"

"How often do you give guarantees to your clients, Harry?" asked Charles with a smile.

Robeson did not smile in reply. His voice was low and very serious. "Agreed. But I'm not asking for any guarantees. I asked if it's 'winnable', not whether you will win."

"In that case, yes, it is winnable. As you know, anything can, and often does, happen, but the Crown's case is far from watertight. But that still doesn't answer my question. There are many very competent barristers who would be available."

"Well," replied Robeson slowly. "I'm afraid I can't give you any better answer than that for the present. If you like, you can ask me again at the end of the trial. I don't promise that I'll give any further answer then, though."

Charles shrugged. This was certainly an unusual conference, but he was rather enjoying it. The usual format was that the barrister would ask questions about the evidence, the client would ask if he was likely to be convicted and, if so, how long he would get, and the barrister would leave. Charles realised that he was waiting for Robeson to speak, and that he had surrendered the initiative. He wondered if this had been Robeson's policy, to see how he would react.

Robeson regarded Charles for a long moment and then nodded slowly as if satisfied.

"Now I have a more difficult question for you. Do you believe I did it?"

"That's not my job, Harry. It's irrelevant what I believe. I'm not the jury. All that matters is that I convince them to believe you. You know all this very well."

"Yes, Charles, I know all that. The number of times I have said exactly the same thing to my clients and thought them dense for not understanding. But they're not being dense. I realise that now. What they're doing when they ask the question – what I suppose I'm doing – is making sure there's someone, anyone, who will believe in them. This is incredibly lonely, you know? Not just for me, but any accused, particularly on remand. We stand alone against the combined might of the Metropolitan Police, the Crown Prosecution Service and an able barrister, not to mention, very likely, an unsympathetic, prosecution-minded judge. All of them are fervently striving for our conviction. When you sit in that cell, hour after hour, it comes home to you how alone you are, and how the odds are stacked against you, no matter how flawed the Crown's case may be." Robseon stood and began to pace up and down the interview room, trailing cigar smoke behind him.

"I understand."

"No, you don't!" Robeson almost shouted, wheeling on Charles. "You don't," he repeated more softly. Charles began to wonder whether under the urbane exterior Robeson was frightened. "My whole life has been governed by this system. I believe in it. Sure, we all gripe from time to time; I'm not pretending that it's perfect – we all know it isn't. But I've always believed that it's the best there is."

He paused for a while and sat down again, a frown creasing his brow.

"And?" prompted Charles.

"And now I'm on the receiving end, I'm not so sure. You try telling an innocent man who's just been convicted that, statistically, this happens less here than in other jurisdictions! What if I'm convicted? I'm innocent, you understand; I didn't do it. And yet I know that I may still be convicted. To you it's just another job – all right, maybe a good one, an important one, but a job all the same. For me," and as he spoke, Robeson thumped himself on the chest for emphasis, "this is my life! I can't just hand the case over to someone who may or may not believe in me, to whom it is just a job. Can you understand?"

"I can."

"Well? I repeat: do you believe I'm innocent?" He leaned forward again, his face only inches from Charles's, staring directly into Charles's eyes.

Charles wondered if this question were an even more direct test. How could the man expect him to answer?

"Harry," he answered slowly, "if you were any old client, I could bullshit you, and say 'Yes, of course I believe you.' But the truth is, firstly, I haven't heard the evidence and secondly, even if I had, I still wouldn't know whether you did it. I wasn't there, and I'm not God. All I can say is, I'll fight as hard as I can to have you acquitted. So far as my *opinion* is concerned, it's irrelevant."

"What if I *demand* your opinion?"

"I can't and won't give it to you. But I'll do a deal with you: just as you did, I'll say that you can ask me again at the end of the trial. But I don't promise – any more than you did – to answer differently then."

Robeson threw back his head and laughed. "Touché! All right, Charles Holroyd, you'll do! I think you're straight, and I'll accept that for now."

Robeson took another lungful of cigar smoke, and sat back in his chair. The tension in the room had gone and Robeson was as relaxed as when he first entered.

"Is that what all this was for, Harry? For you to decide if I'm 'straight'?"

"Now, now, don't be offended, Charles. I am genuinely up against it here. And I wouldn't put much past Jack West. I had to know whether or not he could get to you."

He saw Charles frown and realised he did not know who Jack West was. "Sergeant Jack West. The principal investigating officer in my case. Unlike you and I, he doesn't believe in our system of justice – or at least, if he does, he believes it needs a leg-up every now and then. He's been fighting his own little crusade for some years now. I started to keep a file on that man in 1986. Since then I have accumulated over thirty statements, various clients and witnesses, unrelated cases. Many involving people who, in truth, had never done anything worse than park on a yellow line."

Robeson paused, and spoke slowly, emphasising each word. "Every one of them alleging that he's planted evidence, fabricated confessions and bullied suspects. On two occasions he's even bribed witnesses. Presumably with his own money, so I guess he believes in what he's doing. I won't bore you with the details – you're welcome to see the file if you like – the point is, if West thought he could get round you, he'd do it."

"I see. And you reckon he planted the gun?"

Robeson shrugged and raised his arms. "How do I know? 'I wasn't there, and I'm not God,'" he quoted. "All I know is that *I* didn't put it there. I know too that West's been after me for years. He's lost too many cases against me. The Kenny retrial was just the last straw. You know the score: if you defend important cases and if you're any good, the time will come, sooner or later, when certain police officers start being sore losers. From then on, you're fair game."

"You realise that it's not going to be possible to prove it," warned Charles. "Your dossier on Sergeant West isn't admissible in this case: it's only relevant so far as his creditworthiness is concerned. I can't go behind the answers he gives me in cross-examination."

"I realise. I just want you to appreciate the situation. Thirty witnesses. They they can't *all* be lying." Robeson leaned forward once more, his face suddenly serious again. "I was set up, Charles. And whether you believe me or not, I wanted to tell you, face to face, not just in some statement that my staff have prepared, but man to man.

91

Maybe that's part of the reason I chose you. You were charged with murder, right? You were entirely innocent, but all the evidence seemed to point at you. You know as well as I do that the system didn't save you. The system would have had you locked up for life by now. You had your back to the wall – just as mine is now – and you had to get yourself out of it. So, of all the barristers I know, you probably understand better than any how I feel at this moment."

Robeson rose. "Anyway, Charles, I shan't take up any more of your time. You've got some work to do," he said, indicating the brief. He offered his hand. "I'll get the office to arrange a proper con in a few weeks. I'm going to ask you to make a bail application before then, for what good it will do, so I'll see you at Court."

Charles watched the solicitor walk off down the corridor. Then he packed his papers back into his briefcase, smiled to himself and left.

CHAPTER 8

Charles arrived back in Chambers just after six o'clock. Barbara had already left, but there, in his pigeonhole, was another brief. It was from a firm of solicitors who had instructed him regularly at Chancery Court. He had long since given up hope of further work from them. Maybe my luck's really changed, he thought excitedly. There was a note under the ribbon from Barbara: "Better late than never, I suppose. Warned for next week. Con arranged for Friday 4.30 p.m. Clear tomorrow." Even the last sentence did not deflate him. On an impulse, he picked up the telephone in the clerks' room and dialled a number he knew well.

"Chancery Court," announced Sally.

"Hello Sally, it's Charles."

"Hi," she replied, the official tone leaving her voice.

"I'm glad I caught you."

"Yes."

Charles thought of the kiss, knowing that she was thinking of it too. It was as if they both knew that a line was about to be crossed and both held their breath, savouring the moment.

"Have you time for a drink? I've something to celebrate."

"Yes, I think so," she answered. "I'll have to make a phone call first. Charlie?"

"Yes?"

"Will I be quite late?"

"Yes."

They met in the same pub. Charles arrived a minute or two before Sally. They kissed as soon as she walked in, this time with no hesitation. Thereafter they did not touch again except by accident. They talked for the duration of a drink, and Charles told her briefly about Robeson and the sudden influx of work, but neither of them paid much attention. A mutual decision had already been made, and both were impatient. They left after fifteen minutes. Sally faced Charles as they emerged on to the pavement.

"Charlie, I missed lunch and I'm really hungry. I'm sorry, but can we grab a quick bite first?"

"Sure," he said, laughing. "We've waited ten years or more; another couple of hours won't matter."

"It will to me," she said, squeezing his hand. "I reckon I could wait half an hour at best!"

Charles entered the flat and put on the light. He took Sally's coat and hung it up, and she disappeared into the bathroom. Charles took two glasses and what was left of his Scotch into the bedroom, checking briefly that it was not too untidy. He threw some socks into the washing basket and Rachel's cat into the lounge. He smiled wryly at the irony and wondered briefly why he did not feel guilty. He slipped out of his shoes and socks. There was a light tap on the door and Sally appeared in the doorway. She had untied her hair, which she normally wore pulled back off her face, and it fell like a dark curtain to her shoulders. She was wearing Charles's dressing gown which had been hanging in the bathroom. It was enormous on her, and made her look even more like a child. Then she stepped towards Charles and let the front of the dressing gown fall open and she was no longer child-like. Charles's eyes travelled down her body. She was very slim, but with much larger breasts than he had imagined, and small, nut-brown nipples. She stood before him and, without speaking, helped him out of his jacket. While he took off his shirt and tie, she put his jacket neatly over the arm of a chair. Then she turned back to him and undid his trousers, pulling them and his pants down at the same time. Her face brushed him as she stood up. She looked down again and laid his penis on her open palm, watching with a smile as it became erect, rising in little jerks with his heartbeat. He looked down too, his breath catching in his throat. He felt his entire body pulse. Then she looked up at his face and grinned.

"I never knew you cared, Charlie."

"Oh yes you did."

"Hmmm," she purred, looking coy. "P'raps I did."

He laughed, and slipped his arms inside the gown and held her slim body against his. He luxuriated in the warm softness of her and drank in her perfume. He wanted to take things slowly, but his body was screaming to let go. His hands travelled down the velvet depression of her spine to reach her bottom. He cupped her buttocks, and they fitted neatly in his huge palms just as he had always imagined they would. Her nipples hardened against his chest, and he lowered his head to take one of them in his lips. She sighed deeply and gave an involuntary shudder. He lifted his head and, moving his hands down so that they were under her thighs, lifted her clear off the ground. Her legs parted, and she straddled his waist. Her arms went round his neck and she pulled his face to hers and kissed him deeply. Charles carried her, lips still joined, until his knees struck the side of the bed, and then he lowered her to the mattress.

Their breathing subsided gradually. Her fingers traced a light pattern on his back.

"That," he mumbled into the duvet, "was amazing."

"Yeah. It was nice. Why did we wait so long to do it?"

"God knows. But now we've finally managed it, we can make up for lost time."

"Not tonight, Charlie. I told Mum ten thirty at the latest."

Charles raised himself with an effort and peered over to his alarm clock. "But it's only eight o'clock. Plenty of time for at least once more."

"The way you was going at it, there's time for about thirty more!"

"Yes, well, sorry about that. Put it down to lack of practice and over-stimulation. I used to be quite good at this sort of thing."

"Oh, yeah," she challenged. "And how do you know?"

"Applause, mainly." She laughed. "Still," he continued, "I was rather hoping to take it a bit easier next time."

"That'd be nice. I love quickies, but there ain't nothing like a long slow fuck, is there?"

They dressed at nine-thirty. Charles threw on some jeans and a sweater. He had offered to drive her home, but she declined. "It'll only set Mum off, asking questions, you know."

"But I can't let you just get on a train."

"Yes you can. You can take me to the station if you like."

Sally gathered her things and stood by the door waiting for Charles. He opened the door and turned the light off, and then the telephone rang.

"Damn," he said.

"Well, go on, answer it," she said. "There's plenty of time."

Charles put the light back on and picked up the receiver.

"Charles?" It was Rachel.

"Hello."

"How are you?"

96

"I'm fine. Where are you?"

"I'm in America. Remember?"

"No, I meant where exactly."

"At a friend's house, just outside Los Angeles." She sounded puzzled.

"Right."

There was a pause. "Charles, is there anything wrong?"

"No, why?"

"Well, you sound very strange." There was another pause. "Have I called at a inconvenient time?"

"No, it's perfectly all right. I'm sorry." He looked across at Sally. She smiled and slipped out into the hall. He could hear her footsteps as she walked to the lift.

"Charles, look, I've got something to say. I'm sorry it has to be over the telephone. I meant to write, but never got round to it and now I have to make a quick decision." She stopped, clearly finding the conversation difficult. "Look, I've been offered full-time work over here as a member of the company."

"Oh. I thought you didn't want to dance full-time again."

"I don't. They want me as a choreographer cum dancer. The work's really interesting and the others in the group are fantastic."

"I see. What are you going to do?"

"Well, that's what I wanted to discuss with you."

"It sounds to me, Ray, as if you've made up your mind already."

"I suppose I have. But there's something else."

"And that is?"

"Kieran, that's the theatre director, he's been trying for the past month to get me a work permit, but they're being very tight about it— "

"For the past month! You mean that you knew a month ago— "

"Don't interrupt me, Charles," she pleaded, "or I'll

never say it. Where was I? Yes . . . the only way I can get a permit . . . is if I marry an American."

"So?"

"So Kieran's offered to marry me."

"I see. I thought they checked up on that sort of thing. They don't approve of marriages of convenience."

"Yes . . . but . . . it wouldn't be entirely a marriage of convenience."

The pit of Charles's stomach suddenly felt hollow. "What are you saying? Are you having an affair with this chap?"

"Sort of." She paused for so long that Charles thought that the connection had been broken. "Charles, I'm in love with him. That doesn't mean," she added quickly, "that I don't love you too, it's just that . . . well . . . I'm very happy over here, and, much as I care about you, I'm not sure I really want to come back, at least for the moment. I'm so sorry, Charles."

"It's okay, Rachel. You don't owe me any explanations."

"I do, I do. I've known for a while, you see, but I sort of just hoped the problem would go away. For a while I thought it was just a holiday romance, you know? And that I'd get bored with it. But it hasn't happened like that."

"Rachel, you really don't have to say any of this. We made no commitment. You have the right to your career, and if you're happy there and . . . attached to this bloke, you'd better stay there."

"Oh, Charles, please don't be so reasonable! Why don't you shout at me or something?"

"Would it do any good?"

"Not really, no."

"Well then."

"Do you really understand?"

"I do," he lied.

He felt chilled and empty. A scene from a thousand

westerns flashed into his mind: a desolate ghost town, dust and tumbleweed carried on a howling wind through deserted streets – that was how he felt. The sensation so captivated him that he almost told Rachel. It was the sort of thing he used to tell her.

The implications – if there were any – of the evening's passion with Sally he had not considered. All he knew at that moment was that he and Rachel had lived together for a year, one of the most contented he could remember, and although they had never spoken about it, as the months had elapsed, the prospect of a future apart seemed to become less and less likely. He felt immensely lonely.

"I must go now, Charles." Her voice was broken and Charles guessed that she was weeping.

"Yes."

"I'll write to you. Please look after yourself. Oh, and can you deal with Philomena for while? I'll have to come back and sort out the flat and so on, but not for a couple of months I should think. I guess she's more attached to you by now anyway. Got to run. Bye, Charles." She broke the connection.

He listened to the dialling tone for a moment then hung up, turned off the light and closed the front door behind him. He joined Sally at the end of the corridor. She was in the lift, with her finger on the button preventing the door from closing. She raised her eyebrows in interrogation, but he shook his head and pressed the button for the ground floor. Sally looked up at him as the lift descended, a slight frown on her face. She took his huge paw in her delicate hand.

"Charlie?" she said softly. She had to repeat it before he looked at her.

"Sorry, Sally. I was miles away."

"Yeah, well, when you get back, you know where I am, right? If you need me?"

She looked up at him with her wide brown eyes, and her impish grin. He bent down and kissed her nose. "Thanks, mate," he said.

"My pleasure, mate."

CHAPTER 9

The sound of the telephone gradually percolated into Charles's deep sleep. He groaned and reached out blindly to lift the receiver and still the noise.

"Charles?"

"Yes? Hang on a sec, I can't find the light." Charles fumbled with the switch on the bedside lamp, trying to turn the thing on. He eventually managed it.

"Davie? Is that you? What time is it?" Charles looked across to the bedside table to see the clock. For a moment he thought that he had overslept for court. Why was David telling him, though?

"Charles, wake up and listen to me. It's Dad. He's been taken ill."

"What? What's wrong? Is he okay?" Fear, like freezing water, suddenly filled Charles.

"It looks like a heart attack. That's all I know. He was alive when he left here."

"Oh no." For a split second, a vision so powerful that it blotted out what David was saying, swam before Charles's eyes. He saw himself and David standing before a coffin, reciting in unison the *Kaddish*, the prayer for the dead. It was a scene he had always known would come one day. He took control of himself, and attended to his brother.

"I'm at home, that is, Mum and Dad's home. Mum called us over while waiting for the ambulance, and Sonia's gone with her and Dad. I'm on my way there now. The Royal free"

"Okay. I'll meet you there. It's off Haverstock Hill, isn't it?"

"Yes. See you soon."

"Twenty minutes."

Charles leapt out of bed, and ran to the wardrobe, catching his little toe painfully on the corner of the bed as he went. Yelping with pain, but not stopping, he struggled into his jeans. He tore the wardrobe apart looking for a clean shirt, shouting with frustration, and then gave up and rummaged through the washing basket to come up with the one he had worn the night before. As he raced around the tiny apartment he urged himself on under his breath: "Come on . . . come on . . . come on . . ." like a punter willing a horse to the finishing line.

"Shoe . . . shoes . . . shoes . . ." he repeated as he turned the bedroom upside down in the search for them, not realising that they were next to the bed and covered by the edge of the duvet. Eventually dressed, he grabbed the car keys from the kitchen table and raced into the cold night.

Once on the road, the vision of his dead father returned to him. "Please God, don't let him die . . . don't let him die . . ."

Charles arrived at the hospital thirty minutes later. The roads had been clear, but he had been caught by every red light between Grays Inn Road and Haverstock Hill. Sonia was just inside the door to Casualty, an overcoat covering her nightclothes, and immediately took Charles to where David was being spoken to by a doctor.

"Doctor, this is my brother Charles," said David, with an apparent calmness Charles envied. "Can you start again please so that he can hear it too?" asked David.

"Yes, certainly. I'm Doctor Patel, the registrar on call." Charles shook his hand. "Your father is in no danger. He has almost certainly had a bad angina attack. Your brother was telling me that your father has not apparently suffered from any similar attacks before, indeed, that he seemed to be in relatively good health before this."

"Yes, that's right. I mean, he's almost seventy, and he has the usual aches and pains, but nothing serious."

"According to Mrs Horowitz— "

"Where is she?" interrupted Charles.

"Sonia's with her," answered David. "She was lying down in one of the cubicles. She was very shaken up by Dad's attack."

"Sorry, Doctor. Please continue."

"According to Mrs Horowitz, Mr Horowitz was running up the stairs when the attack started."

"What, at three in the morning?" asked Charles, astonished.

"Mum wanted a glass of water," explained David.

The doctor continued. "We've had him on the ECG, and his heart rate seems perfectly all right. He was given some GTN, which is a very effective drug for angina, and he responded immediately."

"What will happen now?" asked David.

"In the circumstances, I think we shall keep your father in for the rest of the night, but I expect he will be fit to go home tomorrow morning."

"And then?"

"With the drugs, there is no reason why we can't avoid any further attacks like this. He will, however, have to take greater care with strenuous activity. In view of the severity of the attack, it may be necessary for your father to have an investigation carried out, called a coronary angiography. That will be for the consultant to decide."

"What is it?"

"We thread a wire up through the artery towards the heart, and inject some dye which can be seen under X-ray. We are then able to discover if there is a blockage in the artery. It is a simple procedure, carried out while the patient is conscious."

"What if there is a blockage?"

"Well, that depends on where it is, how serious it is, and so on. Drugs may sometimes clear it. Sometimes the investigation itself can clear it. Sometimes surgery is indicated."

"Will you be doing this test tomorrow before Dad is sent home?" asked David.

"That's unlikely. There is quite a waiting list and your father is not in any immediate danger, as I have explained."

"How long's the waiting list?" asked Charles.

"Between four and six weeks. Now gentlemen, I really must get back to work."

"Of course. May we see him?"

"He was asleep when I left him. I suggest that you leave it until the morning."

"Thank you, Doctor," said David. The doctor left the two brothers in the corridor. "What now?" asked David.

"Let's find Mum and Sonia. I suggest we take Mum home."

"What about collecting Dad tomorrow?" asked David, worriedly. "I'm supposed to be in Birmingham by ten a.m."

"Erm . . . okay. I should be able to do it. Let's worry about that later."

Millie and Sonia were in the canteen. Millie's eyes were red and puffy. She sat nursing a mug of tea. Charles and David went over to her and Charles crouched beside her, putting his arm round her shoulder. She turned to him and began crying again.

"Oh, Charles!"

"It's all right, Mum, he's going to be fine." She sobbed into his chest, her tea still in her hands, and Charles folded

104

his arms round her. She felt unfamilar, and he realised that he could not remember the last time he had hugged her.

"Shhhh, it's okay . . ." he soothed. "Dad's comfortable, and he's asleep. He's in no danger. It wasn't a heart attack at all, just angina." Millie nodded and said something incomprehensible. Charles looked at Sonia.

"We know," she explained. "A nurse from the ward came down to tell us that he was all right."

"Mum," said David, "I think we should go home." Millie began to protest, but he cut her short. "We can't do any good here. Dad's asleep. They're going to release him tomorrow morning," he looked at his watch, "probably in five hours or so, and it won't help anyone if you've been sitting here all night."

"He's right, Mum," confirmed Charles. "You should try and get some sleep. In the morning you'll have to get the house ready, as I expect Dad'll not feel up to much for the next day or so. Davie and I will sort out how to get him home."

Millie brightened up a little at the prospect of being able to do something. David winked at Charles over her head. Millie looked at Sonia for confirmation, and she nodded her agreement. "Yes, Mum. It might be an idea to make up the bed in the downstairs back room for a while," she said.

"Okay," said Millie. "Take me home."

Charles got back to bed by six-thirty, just as dawn was breaking. He could not sleep, so he got up and tidied the flat. He was due at the Old Bailey at ten fifteen to make a bail application on behalf of Robeson. At eight o'clock he rang Barbara at home and asked her to contact the court when it opened, explain the situation and ask for the case to be kept back in the list until he arrived. At nine o'clock he returned to the hospital in a taxi. His father was waiting for him.

"I gather I gave everyone a bit of a scare last night."

"You could say that," said Charles, hugging him. The two men stood holding one another for a long moment. Then Charles held his father at arm's length, and looked at him. "I love you, Dad," he said, his vision blurring with tears.

"I know," replied his father, struggling equally hard not to cry.

"Right. So, don't do that again, you old bugger."

Charles took his arm, and took escorted him to the taxi. Millie and Sonia were waiting at the house, and Charles took the taxi straight to the Old Bailey. He arrived just after eleven and went directly to see Robeson.

Charles stood outside the door to the cells in the basement of the court building and pressed the bell. One of the Old Bailey's original oak doors had been preserved and was retained opposite the new door to the cell area. While he waited for the officer to admit him, Charles looked at the old weathered oak, wondering how many men has passed by it on their way to a life sentence, or even the gallows. Eventually he heard the jangle of heavy keys, an interior door clanged open and closed and the wicket in the outer door opened.

"Good morning," said Charles, "counsel for Mr Harry Robeson."

The wicket clanged shut, another key was selected, and the door opened to admit him. The familiar smell of frying bacon greeted Charles. It was always breakfast time in court kitchens, whatever the time of day. Charles realised that he had had nothing to eat and was hungry. The prison officer closed the outer door and then opened the inner door, this one made of steel bars. Charles gave his name to another officer who, between reading THE *Sun* and drinking a cup of tea, noted the arrival and departure of legal visitors, and Charles was directed to a cell.

He rose as Robeson entered. "Harry, I'm dreadfully sorry that you've been kept waiting this long. I don't know if anyone got a message to you— "

"Yes, Charles, don't even mention it. One of my clerks is upstairs and he came down and told me. Tell me, is your father all right?"

"I think so. He gave us all quite a scare, but it appears to have been a severe angina attack rather than a heart attack. He has to have some investigations carried out, when the NHS can get round to it," he said with some bitterness, "but he should be all right."

"There's a waiting list?"

"Isn't there always?"

"Can't you do it on your health insurance?" asked Robeson.

"I'm afraid that that was one of the first casualties of the last year's doldrums. I had cover for both my parents and myself, but I cancelled my subscription."

"Oh. Bad luck."

"Yes. Anyway, let's concentrate on your problems."

"Are you all right?" asked Robeson with genuine concern. "You look like death. Sorry," he said, appreciating his lack of tact.

"That's okay, Harry. No, I didn't get much sleep last night, but I'm fine. It'll hit me this afternoon. So, let's get to work. I received the extra instructions, thank you," said Charles. "I think you have a reasonable chance of bail, albeit on strict conditions. The real problem will be persuading the court that you won't skip the country. You're not in the same position as most villains, who wouldn't have anywhere to go. I gather you've connections in Italy and France."

"Afraid so."

"I suggest, Harry, that in addition to offering conditions such as reporting to a police station, surrender of passport, and sureties, you offer a very substantial security."

"What do you call 'very substantial'?"

"Substantial enough to make it inconceivable that you'd risk forfeiting it. I like to offer even more than the client is alleged to have made from the job, but here the Crown aren't suggesting any particular figure. What about a hundred thousand pounds? Can you get that sort of cash to deposit?"

"The value of the jewels was over a million, right?"

"Correct."

"Let's offer two hundred and fifty grand."

Charles whistled. "You can get hold of that much in cash?"

"Given an hour or two."

"Well, let's go for it."

An hour later Charles again waited for Robeson to appear in the cell beneath the courts.

"Well done, Charles!" he said as he entered.

"Thank you. How long will it take?"

"Bernice is on her way with a banker's draft. I should be out in less than an hour."

"Look, Harry, would you mind terribly if I left? I'd like to pop over to Mile End to see my father."

"Sure. Mile End? I thought your parents lived in Hendon."

"Good God, you're right. For a moment I completely forgot that they'd moved."

"You're tired. Whereabouts in Mile End did they live?"

"British Street."

"What d'you know? I grew up in Eric Street; it's only a couple of streets away. Anyway, you get off. I'll give you a call in Chambers in the next few days. Sergeant West came down to see me just before you arrived. He was looking too happy by far. He says there's a nasty surprise for us in the post."

CHAPTER 10

It was early the next week that Charles discovered the nature of Sergeant West's surprise.

In the Central Criminal Court   91/8021

The Queen v. *Harold Robeson*

NOTICE OF ADDITIONAL EVIDENCE

Take notice that in addition to the evidence given in the Magistrates' Court, further evidence, the effect of which is set out herein, may be given at the trial. Unless you serve notice on me within seven days of receipt of this Notice objecting to this course I propose that the evidence of the witnesses listed below in Column A shall be tendered in accordance with s.9 Criminal Justice Act 1967.

Chief Crown Prosecutor

"A"

Peter Millard
Declan Mahoney
Roger William Duncan

Statement of Peter Millard
Age: Over 21

Occupation: Estate Agent
Address: 13 High Street, Windlesham, Surrey.

This statement consisting of two pages each signed by me is true to the best of my knowledge and belief and I make it knowing that, if it is tendered in evidence, I shall be liable to prosecution if I have wilfully stated anything in it which I know to be false or do not believe to be true. I have read this statement.

I am an estate agent trading from the above address. My firm's principal business relates to the sale and purchase of residential properties, but we do have a letting service also. One of the properties on our books is called "Staplecroft", Orchard Lane, Lower Barnsthorne, Surrey. It used to be owned by a Professor Wilson, but it was recently acquired for a company called Overbrooke (GB) Limited. We were asked to continue handling the house for the new owner. I was told that Overbrooke (GB) Limited owned a number of similar properties.

Just before Christmas 1987 I received an enquiry relating to the property from a Mr Smith. I think that this was after the company purchased the house, but I am not certain of that as we did not act on the purchase. I showed Mr Smith round the property, which he said he required for himself and a few colleagues while they attended a course at Surrey University. He decided to rent the house and paid in full on that day in cash and took the keys. I did not see him again. I deal with so many people that I am afraid that I could not describe Mr Smith, except to say that he had long dark hair and a scar across his forehead and cheek. I might recognise him again.

I have spoken on the telephone to a Mr Carlysle who is, I understand, a director of Overbrooke (GB)

Limited, but I have never met him nor any other officer of that company.

Signed Peter Millard. Signature witnessed by D.S. West.

Statement of Declan Mahoney
Age: Over 21
Occupation: Clerk
Address: c/o Companies House, 55 City Road, London EC1.

This statement consisting of two pages each signed by me is true to the best of my knowledge and belief and I make it knowing that, if it is tendered in evidence, I shall be liable to prosecution if I have wilfully stated anything in it which I know to be false or do not believe to be true. I have read this statement.

I am a clerk employed at Companies House by the Registrar of Companies. The Registrar is required by law to keep records relating to all companies incorporated under the Companies Act 1985. I have been asked to make a search in relation to a company called Overbrooke (GB) Limited. I can say that this company was incorporated on 1st June 1986. According to its Memorandum of Association, its principal object was to buy and sell residential and commercial properties. The identity of its directors has changed a number of times, but in December 1987 they were Robert Milton Carlysle, Jennifer Angela Carlysle and Frederick Costen. The company has an issued share capital of £100 divided into £1 shares. The three directors are each registered with one share, and the remaining ninety-seven are registered to a company called Prince Estates (1986) Limited.

I have further caused a search to be made in relation to Prince Estates (1986) Limited. It is also a company set up to buy and sell residential properties. Its directors in December 1987 were Frederick Costen and Edward Albert Findlay. It has an issued share capital of £100 divided into £1 shares. The two directors each are registered with one share, and the remaining ninety-eight shares are registered to a Harold Robeson.

Signed: Declan Mahoney. Signature witnessed by D.S. West.

Statement of Roger William Duncan
Age: Over 21
Occupation: Banker
Address: c/o Midland Bank, Fleet Street, London EC4

This statement consisting of one page signed by me is true to the best of my knowledge and belief and I make it knowing that, if it is tendered in evidence, I shall be liable to prosecution if I have wilfully stated anything in it which I know to be false or do not believe to be true. I have read this statement.

I am employed by the above bank, and I am authorised to make this statement pursuant to the Bankers' Book Evidence Act 1879. A company named Prince Estates (1986) Limited holds an account at the above branch (number 41081004). On 8th December 1987 the sum of £12,000 was withdrawn from the account. On 9th December 1987 a further sum of £13,500 was withdrawn. The mandate held by the bank only requires one signature of the two authorised signatories on any cheque. The signatory in respect of each of the above withdrawals was Harold Robeson.

I produce herewith the original cheques and copies of the statement of the account for the relevant period marked "RWD 1".

Signed: Roger William Duncan. Signature witnessed by D.S. West.

Charles frowned and put the Notice of Additional Evidence to one side. Sergeant West had certainly been busy. The three statements forged a definite link between Robeson and the property used by the robbers, and showed that immediately before the two getaway cars were purchased he had withdrawn in cash almost exactly the sum required to buy them. For the first time, Charles was faced with evidence connecting Robeson to the crime that did not rely on the word of a police officer or a "grass". He would have to obtain instructions on the new statements, and he was curious to know how Robeson would explain them. Not for the first time, he pondered the strange conference they had had at Brixton, and its purpose.

The telephone rang. That was one of the penalties of working in Chambers; whatever work he started, he was interrupted every ten minutes.

"Yes?"

"Mrs Horowitz, sir," said Barbara.

"Yes, Mum?" said Charles when she was put through. "Is Dad all right?"

"All right? He's fantastic. The hospital's wonderful!"

"Hospital? What hospital? I thought he was at home."

"What hospital, he asks me!" Millie thought he was joking.

"Mum, I'm serious. I haven't a clue what you're talking about."

"Charles, stop kidding. We know it was you who arranged it. Harry told us."

113

"Harry who?"

"Harry Robeson. He's been fantastic, Charles, a real *mensch*. Is he Jewish?"

Despite his confusion, Charles could not resist laughing. A Jew somehow could never quite understand anyone doing them a favour unless their benefactor was also Jewish. Why should anyone else do them favours?

"Look, Mum, start at the beginning please."

His mother sighed, tired of playing what she thought was an elaborate game. "All right. Harry came round, told us you'd arranged a room at the private hospital at Marble Arch, and said you had asked him to give us a lift down. So now we're here. You should see the size of the TV here – colour too. And the menu! It's like a hotel."

"Is Harry still there?"

"Sure."

"Would you put him on, please?"

Charles heard his mother's voice as she held the handset out. "It's Charles. The *meshuggener* wants to talk to you."

"Charles?" asked Harry.

"Yes. What the hell's going on?"

Robeson's voice dropped. Charles could hear his mother and father chattering away in the background. "You told me your father had to have some tests. Well, I had a word with a consultant friend of mine, there was a space here, and I thought, well, we'd better grab it. He'll be out tomorrow or the day after."

"You have no right to interfere, Harry. How the hell are they going to pay for it?"

"Don't worry about that."

"What do you mean 'Don't worry'? I can't possibly pay."

"No one's asking you to. Look at it as a favour from one East End boy made good to another."

"I'm sorry, Harry, this won't do. I'll have to come and get Dad out of there."

"Don't be ridiculous! He needs the tests, right? He'll wait months on the NHS and might die in the meantime. And even if he doesn't, Charles, you'll be worrying yourself sick, and you won't be concentrating on my case. I need your full attention. So, put your pride to one side and let your father have his tests. Look at it as part of your brief fee up front."

Charles paused. It was true, his father's state of health was always at the back of his mind. The attack had shaken them all.

Robeson felt him weaken. "Charles? Listen my boy. Your father needs the treatment; you've got no money. If you must, you can pay me back when things are better. But don't turn me down. *Gey gezinter heit.*"

CHAPTER 11

Harry Robeson sat in his beloved Mercedes in the drive of his Hampstead house, drinking in the car's comfort, listening to Mendelssohn and wondering what he would do if things went wrong. Leave it behind, I suppose, he concluded. He looked at the clock and shook himself out of his reverie. He started the motor, picked up the remote control that operated the gates to the drive and watched them swing open. He drove on to the street, the gates closing silently behind him.

He headed south towards the City. Traffic was light, and he slowed down, realising that he would arrive too early. The blue Ford two cars behind him was forced to drop further back as the cars in between overtook Robeson. Detective Constable North, or as Robeson knew him, Fil, driving the Ford, picked up his radio and reported the fact that he and his quarry had left the Hampstead house and were travelling south, destination unknown. North considered this entire operation to be a waste of time. Jack West hoped that the pressure would cause Robeson to do something foolish, something they could use to augment their case. North doubted it. The wily old solicitor was far too experienced to act rashly.

Robeson turned down the music and picked up his car telephone. He dialled a number and left the handset in position until the ringing stopped. Then he picked it up. He had a "hands-free" facility, but his lifelong habit of secrecy would not permit him to broadcast his conversations, even in the confines of his own car.

"Hi," he said, with a smile.

"Hello there. God, are you on that awful car phone again?"

"Yes, darling."

"Well, I can hardly hear you."

"It's okay, just a quick call to see how things are going."

"Fine."

"Are you enjoying yourself?"

"If you're referring to what I think you're referring, mind your own bloody business."

Robeson grinned. "Just thought I'd ask, that's all."

"Is there anything I can do for you *Mr* Robeson? I have a job to do, you know."

"Oh dear, very professional, aren't we? No, nothing. Just wanted a chat. I'm just . . . a bit worried, you know?"

Her voice softened. "I know. I'm sorry. Look, shall I come over tonight before going home? Or do you want to come down for lunch?"

"Now, that *would* be silly, wouldn't it?"

"Yeh, I suppose so. What about tonight, then?"

"We'll see. I don't know what time I'm going to get in, and you've got to get back. I'll give you a call later."

"Okay. Keep your chin up. I'm sure it'll be all right."

"I wish I was so sure."

"I love you."

"I love you too. Bye."

"Bye."

The follower and the followed were by now in Camden Town. Robeson moved off quickly from a set of traffic lights, almost losing North who got caught behind a bus turning right. North followed the Mercedes down to where it turned into Lincoln's Inn Fields. Robeson circled the square looking for a meter and was lucky to see a car backing out of one on his second lap. He parked the Mercedes and walked into Lincoln's Inn. Cursing, North was forced to leave his car on a yellow line and race after him.

Robeson walked past the manicured lawn and barristers' chambers and ducked under the old wooden door into Chancery Lane where he turned right. It was a bright, but very cold day, and North had left his jacket in the car. His breath came in steamy clouds as he hurried to keep pace with Robeson, who was walking at a remarkable pace for a man of his age. He watched Robeson cross Carey Street, and then run lightly up the steps into the Law Society. North stood on the pavement by the black railings with the gold lions on top, debating what to do next. It was almost lunchtime. Robeson might be hours in there. If North were to wait, he would freeze to death and his car was certain to be clamped. Shrugging, he turned on his heel and retraced his steps.

Robeson poked his head out of the door to the Law Society entrance and watched the policeman's departing back with a smile. Making sure that North had disappeared into Lincoln's Inn, Robeson stepped back on to Chancery Lane and walked north. Near the top of Chancery Lane he entered a small door to his right next to the silver vaults. He walked down a stark empty corridor scanned by cameras. At the end sat a security guard at a desk. Robeson presented a card bearing his photograph to the guard, who inserted it into a machine that rested on his desk. The guard watched a screen before him.

"Thank you, Mr Phipson," he said, returning the card to Robeson.

The guard stood and withdrew from his pocket a bunch of keys on a chain fastened to his belt. He turned to a steel door set in the wall behind him, pressed a button on the wall and looked into the camera. Robeson heard an electrical whirring, and the movement of an automatic lock. The guard then selected a key and unlocked the door, which swung inwards.

"Thank you," said Robeson stepping through. The door closed behind him.

Robeson was in a windowless chamber, although the air was air-conditioned fresh. The room was luxuriously carpeted and the walls above the chairs that surrounded a coffee table were hung with expensive prints. It looked like a basement Harley Street waiting room. Two men, this time wearing blue suits, awaited Robeson at a desk. Robeson handed his card over again.

"Thank you, Mr Phipson. If you would care to sit down for a minute I'll go and get your key. I understand that there is to be another gentleman?"

"Yes."

"We've arranged a room for you to conduct your business."

"Thank you."

The man disappeared through a door opposite the desk and Robeson sat down. There was a sound behind him and Robeson turned to see the door through which he had just entered open slowly. A young fair-haired man stepped into the room. Robeson rose to greet him.

"Mr Phipson," said the other man, extending a hand, "how nice to meet you again."

"Mr Connor," said Robeson, shaking the proffered hand. "I trust you have them?"

"Of course, sir."

The man in the blue suit returned. "If you would care to follow me, Mr Phipson?"

Robeson was taken down a short corridor to a vault, through a set of barred gates, and was shown a wall composed of the fronts of safety deposit boxes. He was taken to a box at the bottom right of the bank and he and the other man each inserted a key into the lock. The door opened and the man pulled out a long thin box and

119

handed it to Robeson. "I will take you and your associate to a private room now," he said.

Robeson and Connor were conducted to a well-appointed room furnished with a desk, two chairs and a telephone. The man closed the soundproofed door and resumed his duties. As he was turning to leave, he just saw Connor out of the corner of his eye tipping something, or somethings, out of a small black velvet bag tied with a drawstring. Whatever it was, it glittered and sparkled. Gems, probably, thought the man. Perhaps Krugerands. One never knew. He was, after all, paid not to know.

Rabbi Glickman paused, pretended to look in the window of a delicatessen and glanced swiftly behind him again. The woman was still there. She had followed him at a distance of fifty yards or so ever since he had emerged from Stamford Hill Station, perhaps earlier than that, although he had not noticed her on the train. He did not feel alarmed, just curious. He guessed from the way in which she would try to catch him up and then lose heart and fall back, that she wanted to talk to him, but could not find the courage. He had not wanted to scare her away and so he had not taken the chance of turning round to look at her. All he could tell was that she was youngish, perhaps in her thirties, poorly dressed, and troubled.

The rabbi was in his late forties, rather fat, with a round red-cheeked face and a full beard which once had been black but now was shot through with grey. He looked like a semitic Father Christmas, with his long whiskers and black clothes. The similarity had been commented on by some of his congregants, and although he pretended to be offended, he secretly enjoyed the comparison. He turned the corner and, on an impulse, stepped nimbly into the doorway of a shop. He waited a few seconds and then heard the sound of footsteps approaching. The woman passed where he stood and then hesitated, scanning the

120

empty street before her. Rabbi Glickman stepped out behind her as she whirled round.

"Now, my dear, perhaps you'll tell me . . ." He broke off, leaning forward and frowning. "Ruth? Ruth Solomons?"

She smiled self-consciously and replied, looking at her worn shoes. "Ruth Goldstein now, Rabbi."

"I haven't seen you in years! What are you doing following me?"

The woman continued to stare at the ground, wringing her hands. The rabbi could not decide if she was distressed or just cold, for although the weather was bitterly cold, she wore a thin cotton dress and a light jacket.

"I saw you on the train, and I was sure it was you. I wanted to talk to you, but I wasn't sure if . . ."

"Are you in trouble?"

"No . . . yes . . . well, not me . . . my husband. Did you hear about him, about us?"

"No. How should I hear? I live in Cardiff now, as you know. I'm only here this week to visit my brother and his family. Look, we can't stand here in the street. Come back to the house. It's just round the corner. The family's there, but we can talk privately."

Ruth Goldstein sat nursing a cup of hot lemon tea, allowing its warmth to take the chill from her fingers.

"I thought everyone would have known," she said.

"Well, I can assure you, I didn't hear anything. If I'd known I would have got in touch to see if there was anything I could do."

He waited. She had told him that her husband was in prison, and what for, but he knew there had to be something more. He took a sip of tea and listened to the ticking of the grandfather clock in the corner of the room. He could smell chicken roasting in the kitchen, and

121

over the sound of the clock came the faint happy noise of children playing upstairs.

"Avraam told me that there was no prospect of parole this year." There was another long pause. "Then, a couple of weeks ago, he told me that things had changed. That he had given a statement to the police and that they were very pleased with him. So pleased that he has been told that he'll be out sooner, much sooner."

"Isn't that good?"

"Yes, but it's what he has said in his statement. They wanted him to tell on someone, and so he did."

"Ruth," said Glickman, confident now that he understood her problem, "there's no need to worry. Your husband is not a criminal, at least not like them. He's not bound by any code of honour among thieves. He needs to be back with you and his family. So he helps another crook get caught— "

"No, you don't understand. I know Avraam. What he did, it made him sick. He hated himself for it. I could see that something was wrong, so I kept on at him and on at him, till he told me. The police wanted him to say he recognised someone, so he said it. But it wasn't true. He just pointed to the man he was supposed to point to." She looked up at him imploringly. "What am I to do, Svi?" she asked, reverting to the name by which she had known her teacher so many years before. "I miss him so badly. God knows, the children need him. He's suffered enough in there. I can't tell you what it's like, it's so terrible. And he's weak, is Avraam. He wants to get out so badly, he'd do anything. But what he's done is a bad thing."

She began to weep silently. Rabbi Glickman patted her hand. "I don't see, Ruth, what *you* can do. He's made a decision, and he's given the statement. You can't alter that."

"But," she said, through sobs, "he has to go to court again. This man he's named, he's being tried soon, and

122

Avraam has still to give evidence. How am I going to feel if Avraam comes home, and I know that another man, an innocent man, is in that prison instead of him? He may have family too. How can I have my husband back by putting another woman through what I've suffered?"

The rabbi studied the woman opposite him. He had last seen Ruth Solomons when she was in her late teens. She had been a quiet, dull girl, quite popular, but not pretty. The idea that she of all people was wrestling with this moral dilemma came as something of a surprise. Many people he knew, even some who considered themselves virtuous, would not have hesitated, particularly if the other man involved was a gentile. Yet here was this unhappy, worn-out woman, struggling with her conscience and showing a strength he found astonishing.

"Would you like me to go and see Avraam?" he asked.

"Oh, no," she said with conviction. "He would kill me if he knew that I was speaking to you."

"Then I don't know what I can do. All I can advise you is that you have to be guided by your own conscience. But the decision is really Avraam's and not yours. You are not in prison; you will not be committing perjury to get out."

She nodded. "I know. Thank you."

"Thank you? Ruth, I have done nothing. I wish I could do more."

"No, Rabbi. I don't know how, but just telling you the situation has helped me. I had no one else to tell. Now I know what I should do. I think I knew all along, really. I just had to listen to myself to realise."

My dearest Avraam,

I am so sorry that I cannot come to see you this month. We are all well, but I feel that I cannot come again until you have thought some more about

your decision. You cannot take back what you have already done, but you can decide to tell the truth later, when it matters. The children are well and look forward to seeing you again. Maybe it will be better anyway if they don't see you until next year, as we originally thought. They have been so unsettled, not knowing when you're likely to be released.
So, until I hear from you, I send all my love.

Your Razel.

CHAPTER 12

The Queen

v.

Harold Joseph Robeson

FURTHER INSTRUCTIONS TO COUNSEL

Enclosures:

1　Proof of Evidence of Terence John Cooper
2　Proof of Evidence of William McCready
3　Defendant's comments on Notice of Further Evidence
4　Contract re: land at Holmbury St Mary, Surrey.
5　Copy bank statements, company searches, and accounts of Prince Estates (1986) Limited.

Counsel will be familiar with this case having advised throughout, and having made a successful bail application on behalf of the Defendant.

Counsel will note from Enclosure 1 that Mr Cooper, an entirely independent witness, does appear to confirm that someone was at the boot of the Defendant's car during the course of the party at the Victory public house, and that person would appear, from the evidence of Mr McCready, to have been someone other than the Defendant himself. There is also a suggestion that the person was a policeman, but

Instructing Solicitors are aware that that evidence is tenuous and may not survive cross-examination.

Counsel requested that we obtain details of any previous convictions recorded against Avraam Goldstein, and we have been informed by the CPS that save for the matter for which he is presently serving, he is of good character.

If counsel requires any further information, a further conference may be arranged.

Robeson & Co.

The tall man sat in his car, and lit another cigarette. The ashtray in front of him was full, and outside the driver's door of his car there was a pyramid of cigarette butts where he had tipped the last full ashtray an hour or so before. He turned off the radio, sick of pop music. He had been listening for over three hours and had the impression that the same dozen records had been played over and over again in sequence. He reached into his pocket again and took out the dog-eared list of names. There were almost thirty on the list, each followed by an address. Most of the addresses were in south London, and half of those had postal districts that indicated that they were in Greenwich. All but three had been crossed through in a smudgy pencil, the same pencil that nestled on top of the tall man's left ear beneath his rather greasy black hair. He had cultivated the affectation when, as a youth, he had worked for a week in the classified ads department of a newspaper. The habit had stuck, though it was incongruous in his present profession.

The three names still to be struck through had something in common: their owners all lived in Leyton. The tall man had therefore left them to last, deciding to do them all in one afternoon.

An old van pulled into the street. The tall man looked

at the name on its side and scanned his list. There! Terry Cooper. Thank God, he breathed. He stubbed his cigarette out, wound up the window and got out of the car.

"Excuse me, sir," he called to a grubby and tired Terry Cooper who was walking up the garden path to number 65 carrying a large bag of plumber's tools. Terry paused. The tall man walked over to him and pulled out a plastic wallet.

"My name's Marlowe," he introduced himself. Improbably apt, but it was in fact his name. The snag was with his first name, which he would have liked to have been Philip, but which was instead Norman. He had tried adopting Philip, but his Mum, with whom he lived, refused to call him anything other than "Norm", and the attempt had failed. Norman Marlowe flashed an identity card bearing his photograph at the young man. "I'm a private detective," he said. Eight years of snooping had not diminished the pride with which he announced his profession.

"Oh yeh?"

At that moment the front door opened and a middle-aged lady in an apron appeared on the threshold.

"What's up, Tel?" she asked.

"Dunno, Mum. This chap says he's a private detective."

"Yes, madam, that's right. May I ask you a few questions, sir? It will only take ten minutes."

"What's he done?" asked Mrs Cooper sharply.

"Nothing, as far as I know. He may have been a witness to something, that's all."

Terry looked at his mother and shrugged.

"You'd better come in, then," said Mrs Cooper, standing back and opening the door wide.

*   *   *

127

PROOF OF EVIDENCE OF TERENCE JOHN COOPER

I live at 65 Drapers Lane, London E10. I am a plumber.

On the evening of 7th June 1991 I went with the rest of the darts team from the Rising Sun public house in Leyton to a public house in Greenwich called the Victory for a darts match with the Victory's ladies' team. The match was at eight o'clock, and we arrived just before.

I went into the public bar where the match was to be held, but I felt ill and left after a few moments to go to the toilet which is outside in a separate building, situated in the corner of the car park. The only cubicle was occupied and I was about to be sick. I vomited just outside the toilet block. While I was still there, recovering, I heard a man approach the car behind which I was crouching. The car was a gold Mercedes. I believe it was a man because of his heavy tread and the fact that I could see beneath the car that he was wearing heavy black shoes, like those worn by a policeman. I noted that his trousers were of heavy dark material, either blue or black in colour. This person came to the very car where I was and opened the boot. There was then a thump, as if something heavy was being placed inside or moved around in the boot. The boot lid was then closed again.

I did not notice where the man came from, but I am reasonably sure that he went towards the pub after closing the boot.

I am prepared to give evidence if requested.

PROOF OF EVIDENCE OF WILLIAM McCREADY

I am the assistant bar manager of the Victory public

house, Greenwich. On the night of 7th June 1991 I was working at the public house. That night there was a private party in the upstairs room and I was the barman on duty.

The party actually began in the late afternoon. At some time in the evening a gentleman came in wearing a suit. He looked quite a lot older than the other guests and was very well-dressed, and I thought at first that he had come upstairs by accident. He was expected, however, and he took a drink and sat at a table. I heard his name mentioned once or twice, and I think it was Robinson, or something like that. I continued to watch him, however, because he seemed so ill at ease and out of place. No one seemed to talk to him much. I can say for certain that he did not leave the bar until about twenty minutes later, when some police officers came in and asked him to go downstairs to the car park to look at his car. I did not see him again after that. The rest of the people came upstairs again and the party continued as before.

I am prepared to give evidence if requested.

COMMENTS OF HAROLD ROBESON ON FURTHER EVIDENCE

I admit that I am the principal shareholder in Prince Estates (1986) Limited which itself is the controlling shareholder in Overbrooke (GB) Limited. Prince Estates (1986) Limited also owns shares in a number of other property companies. In total, Prince Estates (1986) Limited and all of its subsidiary companies own around two hundred residential properties in and around London, most of which are in the Guildford area. Many of the properties are purchased for development or as capital assets, but some are given to agents to let before the company is ready to deal with them. It may well be that the robbers rented premises owned by one of my companies, but that is a pure coincidence. I have no dealings whatsoever with the letting of the premises, and all of the details are dealt with by the agents. Had I been involved as alleged by the police, I would certainly not have been stupid enough to allow the robbers to use a property with which I was connected.

Further, Mr Kenny has been a client of the firm for many years, and in addition to his criminal cases, the firm had conveyed houses for him and dealt with other non-contentious business on his behalf. It is entirely possible that I might have mentioned that one of my companies owns properties in Surrey.

So far as the withdrawal of cash is concerned, as director of Prince Estates (1986) Limited I entered into a contract to purchase some land at Holmbury St Mary, Surrey, from a company called Ross Farm Management Limited. The sale was part of a chain of buyers and sellers, and Prince Estates (1986) Limited entered into a contract race for this land. In an effort to secure the sale, I agreed to pay cash. The contract (herewith) shows that exchange was due to take place on 13th December 1987 and on exchange we were to pay £25,500. I withdrew the two sums of money from the account in the previous week for this purpose. The only reason I made the withdrawal in two parts was because I was nervous at carrying such large quantities of cash around with me.

Withdrawals of large sums of cash are not unusual in the normal course of the company's business, especially when properties are being converted or renovated. Many subcontractors and tradesmen require to be paid in cash. I produce herewith further bank statements relating to the account of Prince Estates (1986) Limited from which it will be seen that other similar withdrawals were made in the six months before this robbery, and one or two were made afterwards also. I also produce a schedule prepared by the accountants of Prince Estates (1986) Limited which shows all the properties under development at that time.

Charles felt something warm and wet moving up his leg. He threw the Robeson papers on the floor, pulled up the bedclothes, and looked down his naked body. Sally had been asleep, curled up like a cat, entirely submerged under the covers.

"Nice snooze?" he asked.

"Hmmmm."

"Feeling more energetic now, are we?"

"Hmmm." Her tongue travelled slowly from his knee to his thigh as she crawled up his body.

"Do I take it that I'm not going to be able to carry on reading?"

"Uh-huh."

"Okay." He pulled the covers over his head, slid down the bed and joined her.

Afterwards, while Sally made coffee and something to eat, Charles turned again to the papers. It was not unheard of for cash to be used to purchase property, but it was quite unusual. Neither the coincidence of the property, nor that of the money, was enough, alone, to convict Robeson. But taken together? He was still looking worried when Sally returned from the kitchen, put a tray on the floor and jumped back into bed.

"Christ, it's cold in there!" she said, cuddling up to him.

"Then put some clothes on."

"I thought you preferred me without any, Charlie. The naked slave girl unable to leave the harem."

"Yes," he said distractedly, turning again to the papers.

"What's so interesting?" she demanded, pulling the Instructions out of his hand. "This again?" She turned to Charles, concerned. "Why are you so worried about this case? You never used to be like this at Chancery Court."

"I know. But he's managed to get under my skin. I don't normally dwell on whether or not my clients are guilty – that's not a decision I have to make. But every now and then you get a case where you're certain that the police have made a mistake and that the man in the dock is innocent, and you do worry more about those. I met him in con. I expected not to like him, and I found I liked him a lot. I listened to him, to what he had to say and I thought, I believe him. He didn't try to persuade me, either. Since then, in only a few weeks, not only has he saved my practice and enabled me to stay in Chambers, but he's been exceptionally kind to my family."

"How's that?"

"Oh, he got Dad into a private hospital for some tests, when he'd have had to have waited for months on the NHS. We're still awaiting the results. Now, not only do I believe what he's told me, but I feel indebted to him."

"So he's innocent. Where's the problem?"

"It's this evidence. This is turning into a grudge match between Robeson and the officer in the case, a chap called West. He's really working hard to get a conviction. And he may succeed – largely because he's not afraid to bend the rules."

"I'm sure you'll do your best."

"That's not it, it's just . . ."

"What?"

"I don't know. Oh, fuck it!" and he threw the papers off the bed and on to the floor. He leaned over her and reached down to the tray she had brought in. "Yum," he declared, coming up again with a bagel in his hand. His

132

shoulder brushed her breasts on the way and he grinned. He leant over to her and caressed the breast nearest to him with his free hand.

"For a nice Jewish boy, heaven is a bagel in one hand, and a *shiksa*'s warm boob in the other," he declared. "You can take me now, God," he said to the ceiling. "Life can't get better than this."

CHAPTER 13

"Are you Harold Joseph Robeson?" asked the clerk of the court.

"I am," replied Robeson in a firm voice.

"You are charged on this indictment with an offence of conspiracy to rob, contrary to section 1 of the Criminal Law Act 1977. Particulars of the offence are that between the first day of June 1987 and the first day of January 1988 you conspired with Anthony Kenny, Peter Simons, Raymond Papier and persons unknown to rob the South African Gem Corporation of a quantity of diamonds worth one million pounds. How do you plead, guilty or not guilty?"

"Not guilty."

"You may sit down."

"Yes, Mr Belloff," said His Honour Judge Pullman QC. Charles knew Pullman well. He had been a successful junior, but when he had taken silk, things had gone rather sour and he had applied for an appointment within a year. He had now been on the bench for ten years and had seen it all, which went some way to explain why he was irritable and impatient with the advocates who appeared in his court. He was also, as Charles had warned Robeson, an utter bastard.

Max Belloff rose to his feet with an audible effort. He was immensely fat, his wing collar flattened and splayed outwards by his multiple chins. He was often to be heard

134

hissing and wheezing as he perambulated his enormous bulk round the corridors of the Old Bailey, where most of his practice was conducted. Charles had met him in the robing room on the fifth floor. Belloff had expressed surprise that Charles was instructed for the defence.

"Didn't think you were a Robeson man, eh, Charles?"

"Nor did I until recently."

"Well, enjoy it. This may be the last case he instructs you on for some considerable time," said Belloff, most of his attention on trying to tie the string of his bands under his chins. He had to tip his head so far back to get access to the area that he ended up looking at the ceiling rather than the mirror.

"Really? I happen to believe the man's innocent."

"Oh, come off it, old chap. He's banged to rights, as they say in the classics. Why don't you offer a plea? There's plenty of mitigation, what with all his good works. He could get as little as five years, and you'll be back in Chambers for tea."

"Thanks, but no thanks, Max. I fully anticipate that Mr Robeson will be triumphantly acquitted."

Belloff laughed good-humouredly. "A bit of professional optimism, that's what I like to see."

Charles shook his head sadly. "If everyone was as certain as you, Max, where would the villains get a decent barrister to represent them?"

"Ah, now, that's the point. Who says they should *have* a decent barrister? If we dispense with the defence altogether, trials would only take half the time, court lists would be cut in a trice, and half the old codgers on the Bench could be retired. Think of the public money saved!"

Charles laughed. "You prosecute too much, you know? Makes a man blinkered."

"I'm sure you're right," said Belloff, smiling. He had succeeded finally in tying a bow round his neck, and pulled his gown round him, although so great was his girth that it looked more like a waistcoat. "You're a credit to the cab-rank principle, old chap." He placed his battered old wig on his head so that it perched there precariously. "See you in court."

"Members of the jury," said Belloff, adjusting his pince-nez, and hooking his pudgy thumbs into the pockets of his waistcoat, "in this case, I appear for the Crown, and the Defendant is represented by my learned friend, Mr Holroyd, who sits nearest to you."

Charles looked up from his papers and smiled generally in the direction of the jury. Now was not the time to establish eye contact with them individually.

"My purpose now," continued Belloff, "is to give you a brief outline of what the Crown's case will be. I hope it will give you a framework into which you can fit the evidence when you hear it. You must not forget, however, that what I say is not evidence. You will decide this case, in accordance with your oaths, on what you hear from the witness box and what is read as agreed evidence to you, and not from what I say."

The problem with Max, thought Charles, is that he is so scrupulously fair a prosecutor and he looks so benign, that juries warm to him immediately. His way of presenting the Crown's case – as if he regretted that he should have to ask the jury to do anything so distasteful as convict – was very attractive. What was more, his appearance was so extraordinary that one was apt to forget the incisive mind that lay behind the piggy eyes.

"The defendant, Mr Harold Robeson, is a solicitor, ladies and gentlemen and, as you will no doubt hear in greater detail from my learned friend in due course, a man of exemplary character. A solicitor of the Supreme Court. A man on numerous charitable boards. A man who has, in the past, been a pillar of the establishment."

Charles looked up at Bellof and thought he caught the

slightest wink directed at him. Bellof continued, his voice theatrically ponderous.

"It is all the more sad therefore that I have to tell you that the Crown say he fell from grace . . . and became involved in a criminal enterprise with one of his own clients, a man named . . . Kenny. You may have read in the newspapers that Mr Kenny was himself tried for a robbery in which one million pounds' worth of diamonds were stolen. And I tell you, with the permission of my learned friend, that he was, in due course, acquitted. That does not concern you. You do not know what evidence the Crown had to offer against that man. You do not know what influenced the jury's minds in that case. You must therefore put it out of your minds entirely. What alone concerns you is whether this man, Harold Robeson, entered an agreement with Kenny and the others to commit the crime. And I shall tell you now, because it is of prime importance, that if you are anything less than sure of Mr Robeson's guilt, you must acquit him, for in all criminal cases the Crown have to prove a man's guilt, and they have to prove it to the highest of standards: so that you are sure. Nothing less will do."

Charles groaned inwardly. The jury were following Belloff's every word. Every now and then a jury member would turn and look at Robeson in the dock, as if examining an exhibit.

"The robbery itself was carried out on 20th December 1987. In it, a man, a security guard, was blown up and crippled for life. It is not suggested that Mr Robeson went on the robbery. That task was reserved for the other men named in the indictment, and others, who have not to this day been caught. It is said, however, that Mr Robeson provided the funds for the robbery to take place. Specifically, he paid for two cars, a BMW and a Jaguar, to be lawfully purchased and unlawfully used, as getaway cars. The Crown also say that he was present

137

at the house that the robbers used before and after the robbery. He was there when the jewels were being valued, in the background, an *éminence grise* watching over the proceedings."

That was a mistake, thought Charles. You do not quote French to a jury composed of honest burghers of Westminster and the City. The common touch is required.

"That house, you will hear, was owned by a company. When you look to see who owned the shares in that company, you find another company. And when you look to see who owned the shares in that second company, you come to the defendant. He interposed a number of 'screens' between himself and the house, but when you strip away those screens, the Crown will without a doubt satisfy you, so you are sure, that the defendant controlled that house.

"Finally, and of the greatest importance, a gun, proved to have been used in the robbery itself, was found later in the back of this defendant's car. So, if you accept the evidence, you will see that he was involved before the robbery in its planning, he has a connection with the weapon used to steal the diamonds, and he was present immediately afterwards in the division of the spoils. The Crown cannot call evidence of the actual making of the conspiracy, the moment of criminal agreement, but they ask you to look at the evidence of what was done in pursuance of the agreement, and to conclude from that, that agreement *there must have been*." He turned to the Judge. "With My Lord's leave, I shall call the evidence."

"Certainly, Mr Belloff."

"My Lord, the first few witnesses are to be read."

"Very well. Members of the jury," said the Judge, turning to the jury benches, "the defence have seen the evidence that the Crown proposes to adduce, and have said in the case of the witnesses who follow, that they agree the evidence and have no questions for the witnesses. Therefore there is no need for them to attend, and their statements will be read to you. The evidence has exactly the same force as if it were given by the witnesses personally."

Charles listened with half of his attention as the clerk of the court read the statements of the two car dealers, the neighbour of the house in Surrey and the security guard. He had no questions for any of them.

"The next witness is to give evidence, my Lord," said Belloff. "Call Peter Millard."

The estate agent entered court and gave the oath.

"Your name is Peter Millard?" asked Belloff.

"Yes."

"At the end of 1987 did you work for an estate agency called Country Estates trading from Windlesham in Surrey?"

"I did."

"What was your job with that firm?"

"I bought and sold properties on behalf of clients. I also acted as a letting agent for some clients."

"Do you know of a property called 'Staplecroft', Orchard Lane, Lower Barnsthorne?"

"I do. We used to let that cottage on behalf of a client called Wilson."

"Did you ever deal with that property for anyone else?"

"Yes. Professor Wilson sold it to a company called Overbrooke Properties, or Overbrooke GB – I can't remember which."

"Do you remember when that sale took place?"

"I think it was before the man with the scar came to rent it."

"Tell us about the man with the scar."

"Well, it was in December 1987, just before Christmas. He telephoned and asked about properties in the village.

139

We only had one on the books actually in that village, that was 'Staplecroft'. He made an appointment to see it and we met at the house. He took it."

"Can you descibe the man?"

"He was tallish, heavy build, with long dark hair and a bad scar running down his forehead and cheek. I can't remember which cheek."

"Did you have any dealings with the man after that?"

"Not really, no. He paid in full before the letting. He dropped off the keys and collected his deposit at the end. That was it."

"Did you see him drop the keys off?"

"Well, no, not actually. I was told by someone in the office that he'd— "

"Stop there Mr Millard," commanded the Judge. "The rules of evidence do not permit you to tell what others told you. Just stick to what you yourself saw or heard."

"Certainly. I'm sorry."

"Thank you, Mr Millard," said Belloff, resuming his seat.

Charles rose. This would be the first time the jury heard him speak. He smiled at the witness.

"The man with the scar did not ask for the house by name, then?"

"No."

"He asked for houses in that village."

"Yes."

"So, had your firm had other houses on its books for that village, he might easily have ended up with a different house altogether?"

"I suppose so."

"One owned by someone else?"

Millard shrugged. "Yes."

"Thank you. Just one other matter, Mr Millard. You said in your evidence that the sale from Professor Wilson

140

to the company had occurred before this man came to rent the cottage."

"Yes?"

"Are you sure about that?"

"Pretty sure."

"Is it possible you have made a mistake?"

"Possible, but I don't think I have."

Wonderful, thought Charles. That's all I need: a reasonable witness. "Do you remember making a statement to the police?"

"I do."

"Would you accept from me that in that statement you told the police officer that you were not certain whether the sale to the company occurred before or after the enquiry from the man with the scar?"

"If that's what my statement says, then I do accept it, yes."

"So it is possible that the enquiry came before the sale to the company?"

"Yes."

"And if that were right, at the time of the letting, the owner of the property would have been Professor Wilson, and not Overbrooke (GB) Limited."

"That is correct."

"Thank you, Mr Millard. I have no further questions, my Lord."

Always be polite to witnesses, thought Charles. The jury likes it, and it is much more effective when you have to get nasty.

There was no re-examination, and the Judge had no questions.

"The next witness, my Lord, is Declan Mahoney. Page three in my Lord's bundle of Additional Evidence," said Belloff, ever helpful.

"Thank you," said the Judge, giving him a friendly smile.

"I have told my learned friend," said Charles, rising to his feet, "that he may lead this witness. There is no dispute about his evidence."

"Thank *you*, Mr Holroyd," said the Judge, smiling at Charles, who could not decide if the smile was a trifle less warm in his case, or whether it was his imagination.

The clerk from Companies House gave evidence exactly in line with his statement, Belloff simply leading him through it and getting him to agree with all he suggested. Belloff sat down five minutes later, curious to hear what questions were to be asked by Charles. Charles rose.

"Your evidence, Mr Mahoney, in a nutshell, is that Mr Robeson controls Overbrooke (GB) Limited and thus, at some time, this property."

"Yes. Through another company called Prince Estates (1986) Limited."

"Would you have a look at these, please?" asked Charles, handing a bundle of papers to the usher. "My Lord, there is a separate bundle for your Lordship, and one here for my learned friend." Charles handed those too to the usher.

"Now, Mr Mahoney, you will see that these are all company searches of the computer which your department keeps at Companies House."

"Yes."

"They are searches in respect of a further eight companies. All seeking information as at 1st December 1987."

The witness counted them. "That's right."

"The Memorandum and Articles of Association of each company have been included, do you see? Am I right in thinking that they are all property companies?"

"They all appear to have been set up to deal in properties, yes."

"Will you look through the register of shareholders in each case? And will you confirm for the jury that Mr Harold Robeson is named as a shareholder in each?"

"That is right."

"The annual accounts of companies have, normally, to be filed at Companies House too, do they not?"

"With some exceptions, yes. All these companies would have to file returns."

"If you look at the photocopied annual returns with each search, you will be able to see what assets each company had."

"Mr Holroyd," interrupted the Judge. "This could take all day. This evidence is not contentious. Why were steps not taken to agree it before the trial so that time could be saved?"

The reason was that Charles wanted this evidence given by a live witness. Evidence given from the box was always far more powerful than a bland admission, or a statement read by the court clerk. Charles was trying to make a point that was of slim value at best; he wanted therefore to make the most he could of it. However, that reason was not one that would appeal to a Judge. On the other hand, he was not allowed to lie or mislead the court.

"The reasons are not straightforward. My Lord will see that the dates on the searches differ— "

"Oh, just get on with it," snapped the Judge testily.

Charles turned back to Mahoney. "Just take the first company, please, D.B.C. Buildings (Surrey) Limited. If you turn to the fourth page of the auditors' report, does it not say that the company owns the freehold of thirty-two residential properties."

"Erm . . . yes, it does."

"Just flick through the others. Did they not also own numerous properties?"

"Fourteen . . . twenty-one . . . forty . . . seventeen . . . do you want me to go through the others?"

"No. I'm sure you'll take my word for it that in December 1987 these eight companies between them owned one hundred and seventy-eight residential properties."

"I accept that, yes."

"And Mr Robeson had as much connection with them as he did with the properties owned by Overbrooke (GB) Limited."

"How can this witness answer that?" demanded the Judge. "You needn't answer that," he directed Mahoney. Charles sat down, satisfied. The point was made, whether Mahoney answered or not.

Belloff rose again. "I have no re-examination, my Lord. Has your Lordship any questions? No? Then I call Roger William Duncan, please," he said, adjusting his spectacles. The banker entered the court, bearing a heavy file of papers.

"Again," said Charles, half-rising, "the witness may be led."

"I'm grateful to my learned friend," replied Belloff.

The witness was sworn, and ran through his evidence regarding Robeson's withdrawals of cash. Charles rose to cross-examine.

"You have produced the bank statement of Prince Estates (1986) Limited for the month of August."

"I have."

"Do you also have in your file the statements for other months?"

"I have the statements from the date the account was opened until the present time."

"Good. Please look at, say, July 1987. There are large cash withdrawals in that month, are there not?"

"There are. They range from two thousand pounds to fifteen thousand pounds."

"Similarly, in August?"

"Yes. There are three withdrawals, from fifteen hundred pounds to six thousand five hundred pounds."

"Let's have a look at the period after the robbery, in January 1988. There is a withdrawal of thirteen thousand one hundred pounds, is there not?"

"Yes, on the 11th. And, to save you the trouble, Mr Holroyd, there are similar withdrawals in February and March."

Charles grinned. "Thank you, Mr Duncan."

To Charles's surprise Belloff rose to re-examine. "Have you looked at any of the other statements, apart from the ones Mr Holroyd has dealt with?"

"Yes, I have done a thorough analysis of the transactions on the account."

"And what have been your findings?"

"Well, there is indeed a substantial number of large withdrawals in the six months before December 1988, and in the three months thereafter. But the account was operated for four years before that, and the pattern did not exist then, nor indeed after March 1989. The withdrawal of large sums of cash seems to have been a short-term phenomenon."

"Thank you. Does my Lord have— "

"There is one further matter," volunteered the banker.

"Yes, Mr Duncan. What is that?"

"I have also analysed the other side of the account, the credits. Although there were a number of large withdrawals in the period, there were also many more smaller deposits. Very nearly the same amount was in fact paid in as went out. The difference is about twenty-five thousand pounds."

Belloff frowned, as if he had not grasped the point. "So are you saying that there was a lot of *apparent* movement, but no *actual* movement of funds— "

Charles leapt to his feet to prevent an answer. "My Lord, the conclusions to be drawn from the evidence are matters for the jury, not for this witness. In any event, this witness can only say that there was a balance of deposits and withdrawals; he cannot say if the money came from the same sources."

"He doesn't say there was a balance, Mr Holroyd; he

says that there was a difference of about twenty-five thousand pounds. In other words, that sum was in fact drawn out and not replaced, isn't that right, Mr Duncan?"

"That is right, my Lord."

"Just pause there and let me make a note of that," said the Judge, making sure the jury had not missed the point. "Now, Mr Holroyd," said the Judge, smiling like a shark, "what was your objection?"

Charles repeated himself. The Judge considered the point for a second and then, grudgingly, agreed. "I think that must be right, mustn't it, Mr Belloff? The conclusions to be drawn from Mr Duncan's evidence are for the jury to decide."

"I don't press the point, my Lord," replied Belloff with an expansive guesture. He hardly had need to. "Does my Lord have any questions?"

"No, thank you."

"Avraam Goldstein, please," said Belloff.

Charles rose. "Before the witness is brought in, my Lord, there is an application I should like to make."

"Do you want the jury to leave?" asked the Judge.

"Well, it is a matter of law, and therefore for your Lordship to decide, but it may be stated in a sentence, and I have no objection to the jury remaining."

"Very well."

"I should like permission for Mr Robeson to come out of the dock and sit beside my Instructing Solicitor behind me. The reason is this: as my Lord knows from reading the papers, this witness's identification is crucial to the Crown's case. It was made in unusual circumstances and my Lord will have to direct the jury in accordance with *The Queen* against *Turnbull* that great care must be taken concerning it."

"Well?"

"If the witness comes into court and sees the man in the dock, when asked to describe the man he saw on the night, he may be tempted, even subconsciously, to describe the man he can see in front of him in the dock. I therefore ask that Mr Robeson may be able to sit behind me for a short period while the description is being given, and cross-examined if necessary. He has been on bail, and the chances of his trying to escape are, my Lord might think, slim."

"What do you say about this, Mr Belloff?" asked the Judge. "It's certainly an unusual application."

"I can see my learned friend's point. The Crown are neutral, my Lord. It's a matter for your discretion."

"Well, Mr Holroyd, I've dealt with hundreds of identification cases, and never heard this application before."

"That may be because I have not appeared before my Lord on this sort of case. It is an application I make quite often."

"I'm not inclined to grant— "

"Please forgive me for interrupting, but what my Lord does not know is the nature of the defence in this case. I am not able to tell my Lord about it at this stage, but in fairness to the defence, if the Crown have no objection, I must ask that your Lordship grant the application."

As he used the words "fairness to the defence" Charles looked at the jury. It was for this reason he wanted the jury in court while the application was made. It was his experience that Judges were often embarrassed into fairness by the presence of the jury. Whether that reasoning was right in this case or not, Pullman relented.

"Yes, very well. I shall rise for five minutes in any event."

The court rose. Charles saw Robeson beckoning him, and slipped back to the dock.

"Why's he risen?" he asked.

"He's a smoker. He probably wants a cigarette."

CHAPTER 14

"You're doing well, Charles," said Robeson.

"Not really. This is just early skirmishing. We're picking up the odd points here and there, but they're insignificant compared with what's to come. I'm irritated about that banker. I should have asked for all the statements before I waded in."

"No, it's not your fault. I left it to the accountant to sort out and I didn't check them myself. I didn't know he'd only picked out the statements that helped."

"What do you say about his point, the balancing entries in the account?"

"Of course there's going to be money going in. What do you think we do with the rents? So far as the last six months are concerned, we took a policy decision to be much more aggressive in property purchasing. The big boys can always beat our offers when it comes to a tasty property, so we decided we'd offer cash instead. That decision was taken in June or July 1988. It didn't really work, so we abandoned the policy in March 1989. There's nothing sinister about it."

"Fine. Let's concentrate on Goldstein. Are they here?"

"Yes."

Robeson signalled to one of his clerks sitting next to the door, and he disappeared outside for a second. The clerk returned with a man, and pointed him towards

148

where Robeson sat. The man was about fifty years old, with greying hair. He sat next to Robeson.

"Charles," said Robeson, "let me introduce Bill Summers. He's an outdoor clerk who work for us." Charles shook his hand. "Are you sure he'll be all right?" asked Robeson. "He doesn't look anything like me."

"No, but he's the about the same age and build. That's all I want. I'm not into pulling stunts. I just want to see how good Goldstein's description is, without him having any help from seeing you alone. If, as we believe, he's been primed to pick you out, they'll have made sure he's seen a recent photograph anyway. Where's Norman?"

"Here he comes now."

Norman Marlowe approched them from the back of the court. He shook hands with Robeson, whom he appeared to know well, and also sat in the same bench. He was in fact thirty years younger than Robeson, and quite different in appearance, but Charles wanted Robeson lost in a crowd. There were now three men sitting behind him on the solicitors' bench, all wearing similar suits.

"The Judge is coming back in, gentlemen," announced the clerk.

There was a knock on the Judge's door, the usher called, "All rise!" and the Judge entered. "Yes, Mr Belloff," he said.

"I call Avraam Goldstein!"

The dock officer moved to one side in the dock, and opened the door that led down to the cells.

"Bring him up," he called.

There was a jangling of metal, and Goldstein was led up into the court, handcuffed between two prison guards. They had allowed him to wear his own clothes while giving evidence, so he was in a suit rather than prison clothing. He wore a skullcap on his head. The three men manoeuvred their way around the narrow dock and filed out. Goldstein was taken to the witness box.

"Religion?" asked the usher, plainly oblivious to the Jew's hair, beard and headcovering.

"Jewish."

"Take this in your right hand and read the words on the card."

Goldstein read the oath, his voice faint and halting. When he had finished, he glanced around the court nervously. Charles noticed that he paid particular attention to the public gallery.

"Your name, please?" asked Belloff.

Goldstein looked round sharply at his interrogator. "Avraam Shimon Goldstein."

"Your occupation?"

"Jeweller. I was a jeweller."

"Where?"

"I had premises in Hatton Garden."

"What is your present address, please?"

He lowered his voice. "Her Majesty's Prison, Camphill."

"You must remember to keep your voice up, Mr Goldstein."

"Her Majesty's Prison, Camphill," repeated Goldstein, unnaturally loud, but staring fixedly at the side of the witness box.

Charles deliberately kept his attention on his notes. He did not want to make eye contact with Goldstein yet or risk him spotting Robeson sitting directly behind him.

"I want to ask you about a night in December 1987. Do you remember any night that month on which someone came into your shop late?"

"I do."

"Who came in?"

"A man called Tony Kenny. It was a couple of days before Christmas. He had been a customer for some time."

"What time of the day was this?"

"Just after six, I suppose."

150

"Keep your voice up, Mr Goldstein. Was he alone?"

"No. He had another man with him."

"What sort of man?"

"Just a man."

"A big man, small man, thin man, fat man?"

"He was big. In his twenties maybe. He didn't speak."

"What did Kenny and this man want?"

"They wanted me to do a valuation."

"Is it usual for customers to come in like that, at that time in the evening, for a valuation?"

"No. He – Kenny – had asked me, some months before, if I would do a valuation for him. I had said yes. It was part of my job."

"Did he tell you what he wanted the valuation for?"

"The first time he mentioned it, he said it was because he was being offered jewellery to pay off an old debt, and he didn't know if it was worth anything." Goldstein's voice was now much firmer. Charles noted that he was now volunteering information, rather than answering as shortly as he could. He was becoming more confident.

"What did he say when he came in on that December night?"

"He wanted me to do the valuation that night."

"Where? In the shop?"

"No. He said the jewels were somewhere else, and that I had to go with them then."

"'Had' to go?"

"He was very insistent. He was offering me more and more money. He got angry when I kept saying no. He said he would hold me responsible if he lost out because of it."

"Did you agree to go?"

"Not for a while. But in the end I went because I was scared. I thought it was easier to go than not to go."

"Where were you taken?"

"I can't tell you. He blindfolded me as soon as we left

151

the centre of London. It felt like a long journey, though, and I think we went on a motorway for a part of it."

"What car did you go in?"

"A Jaguar."

"What, if anything did you notice about your destination?"

"Well, I can't be sure, but I thought that it was in the country, as there was wind in the trees and very little traffic."

"What happened when you arrived?"

"I was guided into a house, and straight up some stairs. The blindfold was taken off. In front of me was a desk and on the desk were diamonds."

"Did you value the diamonds?"

"I did."

"Did you realise that they were stolen?"

"By that time I had guessed that there was something wrong with them."

"You are now serving a prison sentence for assisting Kenny and others in the retention or disposal of the diamonds."

Again Goldstein's voice dropped to almost a whisper. "Yes. Four years."

"Now, Mr Goldstein, did you see anyone in that house?"

"Tony Kenny was there."

The Judge and both counsel glanced sharply at Goldstein. He knew who it was he was there to identify. Was the answer evasive, or just ingenuous?

"Anyone else?" asked Belloff smoothly.

"The driver. I never heard his name."

"Anyone else?"

Goldstein paused. He looked around the court again, as if seeking an escape. A little drop of sweat slid in jerks down his forehead. What the hell is he so worried about? wondered Charles. And who is he looking for?

152

"Yes. A man."

"Can you describe the man?"

"He was never in the light. It's very difficult."

"Well, do your best, Mr Goldstein."

"He was middle-aged. Wearing nice clothes."

"Colour of hair?"

"I'm not sure. Grey, I think."

"Build?"

"Normal. Not thin, not fat."

"Colour of eyes?"

"I don't know. I never saw."

"Can you say anything more about him?"

"No. Not really."

"Did you ever see that man again? After that night?"

Goldstein gulped air like a drowning fish and blurted out his answer. "Yes. When a policeman came to see me on the Isle of Wight. He showed me some photographs and I picked the man out."

"If I were to show you the same photographs, do you think you would be able to pick him out again?"

Charles had no alternative but to jump up to prevent the answer being given. "I object, my Lord. This is in effect a dock identification, which is prohibited. Further, this case has been widely covered in the media, and who knows how many times the defendant's face has appeared in the papers or on television? How do we know that any identification done today is of the man seen that night, as against the man all over the daily papers?"

"Yes. Mr Belloff, in all the circumstances, it would be best not to ask the witness to see the photographs again. The officer will give evidence of who was picked out."

"Yes, my Lord. In that case, I have no further questions."

"It's five to one," said the Judge. "You may cross-examine after the adjournment, Mr Holroyd. Mr Goldstein, you will be taken down in any event, but you are still giving evidence, and I must tell you not to speak to anyone at all about this case until your evidence is completed. Do you understand?"

Goldstein nodded.

"Very well. Members of the jury, we shall adjourn until five past two. I shall give you a direction now that will apply throughout the rest of this trial: do not discuss the case with anyone outside your number. Your families will no doubt be very curious as to what you're doing, but please resist the impulse to tell them anything, as once you start, it's very difficult to stop and to prevent them making some comment. The decision to which you come must be uninfluenced by what others say. Five past two, please. Mr Robeson will be on bail as before until further order."

"All rise!"

The defence sat still until Goldstein had been taken down.

"What are you going to do for lunch, Charles?" asked Robeson.

"I don't know. I've got to make a phone call to find out how Dad is; his test results came in this morning. After that I think I'd just like to have a bite to eat on my own, if you don't mind, Harry. I'd like to have a quiet think about what's coming up next."

"Yes, of course. We'll be in the public canteen if you need us."

Charles made his way up to the robing room, sought a telephone and asked for an outside line. He dialled his parents' number. Millie answered the phone.

"Mum? It's Charles. Well, what do they say?"

"Oh, Charles!" she replied, and burst into tears. Charles could hear her wailing, even though her hand was held over the mouthpiece. The noise grew suddenly louder and another voice spoke.

154

"Charles? It's Sonia. Your Mum's too upset to speak at the present."

"What the hell's going on there?"

"It's your father. He has to have an operation. A heart by-pass operation."

"Why? I thought he just had angina."

"I don't really understand it, but they say he has a blockage in, or near, the left side of his heart. The doctor said he's all furred up like an old radiator."

"Is he in danger?"

"I don't know. The doctor told us, but I can't remember most of what he said. He told us what was involved in the operation. Then he said that there was a risk . . . that your father he might die during it. Your mother went to pieces and I had to look after her. David's spoken to them since on the telephone and he understands what's going on. He'll be here later."

The telephone was taken back by Millie, as she spoke next to Charles. Her voice was a little calmer.

"Oh, Charles, I don't understand it. A month ago he was fit and well, and all of a sudden he's dying."

"Don't talk like that, Mum, he's not dying. Lots of people have this operation, and they live for years after. Do you know when's he got to go in?"

"As soon as there's a space."

"What? You mean he has to wait?"

"Of course. Up to three months." She began to cry again. "He might die before then."

"No he won't. Just calm down, Mum. Everything's going to be fine. I'll sort something out. He won't have to wait three months. Now, I've got to go. I'll come round this evening and we'll talk about it. Okay?"

"Okay." Her voice was no more than a whisper.

"Bye."

Charles no longer felt hungry. He paced about the robing room for twenty minutes and then, because he had nothing better to do, he went down to sit outside the courtroom. He sat there with his eyes closed for a while, feeling a knot in the pit of his stomach and trying to relax. He had been there for a quarter of an hour when he felt a gentle touch on his shoulder.

"Excuse me," said a woman's voice.

Charles opened his eyes. A woman with dark eyes stood before him, a scarf covering her hair. Her face looked drawn and pinched and she had heavy rings under her eyes. She was unmistakeably Jewish.

"Excuse me," she repeated, "but I'm trying to find the right court, but I don't know the name of the case. I told the man on the door and said he thought I should try here."

"What sort of case are you looking for?" asked Charles, conscious that the question sounded odd.

"My husband is giving evidence today for the police."

Mrs Goldstein? he wondered. Was that who Goldstein was searching for in the gallery? "What's your husband's name?"

"Avraam Goldstein."

"Then this is the right court," he said.

"Oh, thank you." She walked away a few paces and then returned. "Am I allowed to go in?"

"Yes, you are. But you will have to go round to the other entrance to get into the public gallery."

"Oh, yes, I know where that is, thank you."

She turned and departed. Robeson, his clerk and the others who had been sitting behind Charles approached.

"You look very pensive," commented Robeson.

"I've had a lot to think of during the adjournment. Come on, let's go in."

156

CHAPTER 15

Charles was already on his feet waiting for Goldstein to be brought up from the cells. Almost the second the jeweller had arrived in the witness box, Charles fired his opening question. He wanted Goldstein's attention on him and on nothing else in the courtroom.

"Do I take it, Mr Goldstein, that you did not want to go with Kenny that night to value his diamonds?"

Goldstein drew a deep breath, as if about to shout, but then answered simply, "I did not want to go."

"You're not saying that you went involuntarily?"

"Well, I didn't want to go. There were two of them in the shop, both big men."

"Did they force you into the car?"

"No."

"Did they actually touch you in any way?"

"No."

"Did they carry any weapons?"

"I don't know; maybe."

"Did you see any weapons?"

"N . . . no."

"Did they tell you they *had* any weapons?"

"No."

"Did they threaten you?"

"Not in so many words."

"Well, in *what* words?"

"Kenny told me that he would be very sorry if I did not

go. That he would hold me responsible if he lost out as a result."

"Did you know that he was a criminal?"

"No. Definitely not."

"So you knew nothing of any reputation he might have had?"

"He was just a customer."

"So, this ordinary customer comes in with a friend and asks you to do a valuation which you do not want to do. He does not coerce you in any way, but just says he will hold you responsible if he loses out. You're saying that that frightened you so much that you went against your will?"

"You don't understand. You had to be there. I felt as if I had no choice."

"You're saying therefore that you acted under duress?"

"Yes."

"Did you plead guilty to handling these diamonds, or were you found guilty after a trial?"

"I was found guilty."

"Did you defend the charge on the basis that you had been forced?"

"Yes."

"And the jury trying your case rejected that defence?"

"I don't know."

"Mr Goldstein, they found you guilty, right?"

"Yes."

"Did you give evidence?"

"Yes."

"On oath?"

"Yes."

"And they didn't believe you." Goldstein stared rigidly at his hands, clasped together on top of the witness box. "They didn't believe you, did they? Are you going to answer me, Mr Goldstein? No?"

Goldstein looked intensely uncomfortable, but did not

respond. The Judge turned and stared at him. "Well," continued Charles, "let's move on. Were you paid anything for the valuation?"

"Yes."

"What did they offer you?"

"At first, £5,000."

"£5,000? To value some jewels?"

"There were a large number, it meant going a long distance and it was out of hours."

"So you thought £5,000 was a fair price?"

"I suppose so. Not unfair."

"Did you accept it?"

"No. I told you, I didn't want to go."

"He then offered you £10,000, did he not?"

"Yes."

"And you accepted?"

"Because, as I said, I was frightened."

"You were frightened at £5,000 too, weren't you? Why did the offer of £10,000 suddenly allay your fears, Mr Goldstein?"

"It didn't. I was still frightened."

"But you thought it might be worth being frightened for £10,000, eh?" There was a sprinkling of laughter in the court.

"No."

"You had the presence of mind to demand £1,500 in advance, did you not?"

"Yes."

"And the balance? What of the balance?"

"At the end, as they dropped me off, Kenny gave me a diamond."

"How much was it worth?"

"I don't know."

"That's a lie, Mr Goldstein. You had just valued them all. In your statement to the police you claimed that it was worth £9,000."

"Maybe."

"Do you want to see your statement?"

"No."

"It was worth, by your own estimate, £9,000."

"Yes," he hissed.

"So you were paid £10,500 for your work."

"Yes."

"What happened to that diamond, by the way?"

"I sold it."

"What did you do with the money?"

"I bought a car."

Charles paused. When he spoke, he lowered his voice and spoke slowly. "Are you still telling this jury that you were forced into going? Or isn't it that you were bought?"

The court fell totally silent, awaiting the answer. Charles looked at the jury with satisfaction. The attention of all of them was riveted to Goldstein. One or two of them looked as if they had bad smells under their noses. They don't trust him, thought Charles.

"I believed at the time that I was forced."

"There was no main light on in the bedroom where you examined the diamonds?"

Goldstein looked perplexed for a moment, unable to comprehend the sudden change of tack. Then he realised that Charles had changed subject, and sighed. The jury also relaxed, shifting in their seats. "That is right," he answered, his voice betraying relief at a simple statement with which he could agree.

"So the only light was from the desk lamp."

"Yes."

"Pointing to the desk."

"Yes."

"So the rest of the room would have been in virtual darkness."

"Well, it was not well lit."

160

"Did you ever speak to the man you later identified?"

"No."

"Did you ever shake his hand?"

"No."

"Were you ever introduced to him?"

"No."

"So did you ever meet him face to face?"

"Not really. I saw him as I stood up and went out of the door. He had been standing behind me watching me work."

"And you then went down the stairs."

"Correct."

"Did you ever see him again?"

"Not in person."

"So how long was he in your sight for?"

"A few seconds. Ten maybe."

"Just imagine you are in the room, about to stand up. Start counting for us in seconds, out loud, please, and stop when you would have gone through the door."

Goldstein shrugged, but did as he was asked. "One . . . two . . . three . . . four . . . five . . . six . . . stop."

"So your identification is based upon a six-second view of someone in shadows?"

"Yes."

"How can you be sure it was the same man as the one you saw in the photograph?"

"I am sure."

Charles whirled round and stared at Goldstein's wife in the gallery. Goldstein's eyes followed Charles's. Charles spun back towards the witness. The effect on Goldstein was as if he had been electrocuted. He was rigid, his eyes and mouth wide open, staring at his wife. I knew it! thought Charles in triumph. It *was* she who he was so anxious about.

"Really sure?" asked Charles.

Goldstein opened his mouth to speak and moved his lips, but no sound emerged.

"Mr Goldstein?"

Goldstein wrenched his eyes from his wife for a second to flash a glance at Charles. His face was a picture of despair.

"Mr Holroyd," interrupted the Judge, "who is that lady in the gallery?"

"I believe it to be this witness's wife, my Lord."

"What is she doing there?" thundered the Judge, suspecting foul play.

"I am not sure, my Lord, other than watching the case."

"Stand up, madam!" commanded the Judge. Up in the public gallery Mrs Goldstein stood. All eyes in the court fastened on her. "Are you here under any sort of pressure?"

"Me? No, sir, not at all," she answered, bewildered.

"Then what is going on? I demand to know what is going on!"

"Nothing, sir . . . my Lord. I came to watch my husband give evidence. I haven't seen him for months. That's all."

Charles watched the Judge's face. Pullman was plainly convinced something *was* going on, and would have loved Charles to have been at the bottom of it, but he seemed to be undecided as to what to do. He stared alternately at Charles and Mrs Goldstein.

"Very well. Carry on, Mr Holroyd."

"I was asking you, Mr Goldstein, if you could be sure."

"I don't know . . . I don't know any more . . . maybe . . . maybe not."

"Is that your wife up there?"

He nodded without looking up at her.

"Your nod cannot be recorded on the transcript, Mr Goldstein. Please answer."

"Yes," he said softly.

"When did you last see her?"

"Two, three months ago."

"And your children? How many do you have?"

"Four." His voice was almost a whisper.

"Do you miss your family?"

"Yes, of course I do," he answered with longing.

"And when are you due for parole?" asked Charles conversationally.

"I don't know."

"Has anyone told you that by giving evidence you might improve your chances of parole?"

"Well . . . I don't know."

"What do you mean, you don't know? Has someone told you or not? You must know if someone's spoken to you about it."

"It has been mentioned."

"Who by?"

"I can't remember."

"Who by?" demanded Charles sharply.

"I tell you I can't remember."

"Was it Sergeant West, the officer who took your statement?"

"I don't know. Maybe. I can't remember."

"Your statement was given to the police long after you were convicted, is that right?"

"Yes. I was in prison."

"How did it come about that you saw the police again?"

"I don't understand."

"Sergeant West is a busy policemen. He doesn't hang about prisons on the off-chance that someone wants to talk to him. So how did you and he make contact?"

"He came to see me."

"At your invitation?"

"No."

"So, what did he say when he came to see you?"

"I don't remember."

"You must have talked about the robbery?"

"I suppose so. He asked if I thought I might be able to identify the man at the house."

"And he showed you a picture of Mr Robeson, didn't he?"

"No. He did not."

"I suggest that's a lie."

Goldstein shook his head and began an answer, and then Charles looked up at Mrs Goldstein. Goldstein also looked up. His voice faltered. He mouthed the word "No" but no sound emerged.

"Speak up!" commanded Charles.

Tears welled in Goldstein's eyes and he silently shook his head.

"Your services were bought by Kenny, Mr Goldstein, and I suggest they've been bought today. You never saw Mr Robeson at that house, did you?"

Goldstein stared at Charles, willing him, pleading with his eyes, for Charles to stop.

"Did you?" repeated Charles.

"I don't know any more."

"The truth is, you can't be sure *who* you saw on that night, can you?"

"No," he conceded, the word coming out like the last breath of a dying man.

Charles looked at the Judge. "May I take brief instructions, my Lord?"

"Yes."

Charles turned and whispered generally to the men sitting behind him. "I don't think it's necessary to take the risk of an identification. He's been so badly damaged, the jury'll never believe him."

"I think you should go ahead with it," whispered Robeson.

164

"My strong advice is not to. It's immensely risky. Why take the risk when there's no need?"

"Charles, I was never there. If he's starting to tell the truth, he can't pick me out! Go for it!"

Charles shrugged and turned back to the court. "Thank you, my Lord. Now, finally, Mr Goldstein, describe for the jury the man you saw that night in the shadows."

Goldstein shook his head. "I can't."

"You can't?"

"No, I can't."

"Do you see any man in court whom you recognise from that night?" asked Charles, crossing his fingers behind his robes.

Goldstein raised his head. His eyes were red and moist and his face glistened with sweat. He looked around the court, at the Judge, at the jury and, finally, at the public gallery. Then, with an almost imperceptible smile, he faced Charles and replied. "No, I do not."

"Thank you. I have no further questions." Charles realised that he too had been sweating while waiting for the answer.

It was as if a ton weight had been lifted from Goldstein's shoulders. He smiled up at his wife and she smiled back at him. Belloff declined to re-examine and Goldstein was led away.

"I shall rise for five minutes," said the Judge. "I should like to see counsel in my room." He stormed out of court.

"What's this all about?" asked Charles of Belloff.

"I don't know, Charles. His Lordship seems to believe that you've been up to skulduggery."

"Well, I haven't."

"I'm sure you haven't, old chap," said Belloff, patting Charles on the shoulder.

"But, as we all know, Charles Holroyd's guilty till proved innocent, right?" said Charles furiously.

Belloff frowned. "Come on, Charles. That's a bit extreme, isn't it?" he chided. "By the way," he continued, as he led the way to the front of the court, "on the subject of innocence, I begin to see why you think Robeson's innocent. That Goldstein fellow was dreadful, wasn't he?"

CHAPTER 16

"Are you ready, gentlemen?" asked the court clerk.

"Yes," replied Charles and Belloff together.

"Follow me, please."

The clerk led the way up the steps beside the Judge's bench and opened a door behind his seat. Charles found himself in a large carpeted corridor with paintings on wood-panelled walls. He followed the clerk and Belloff around a couple of corners and down a short flight of steps. The clerk turned and motioned for the barristers to wait. She knocked on an oak door and waited.

"Yes?"

The clerk put her head into the room. "Counsel to see you, Judge."

"Bring them in."

The clerk opened the door wide and the barristers entered.

Judge Pullman was sitting at his desk still in his robes but with his wig on the desk beside him. He was smoking an untipped cigarette.

"Sit down, gentlemen." Charles and Belloff drew chairs from the walls into the centre of the room and sat facing the Judge.

"Now, Holroyd. Would you mind telling me what the hell's going on?"

Charles smiled and shrugged innocently. "I haven't the faintest idea, Judge."

"Really?" asked Pullman, his tone indicating that he did not believe Charles for a moment. "I don't know about you, Belloff, but it looks to me very much as if that Jew was under some sort of pressure. Extraordinary display. That was a man in fear if ever I saw one."

"Perhaps, Judge," replied Belloff, non-committally.

"No doubt about it. Let me make myself clear, Holroyd," he continued, jabbing a finger in Charles's direction, "I don't like gamesmanship. I will not have my court turned into a circus, is that clear? If I catch even a whiff of any more tricks, I shall report you to your Inn."

"Now just a minute, Judge. I must protest. It was clear to me that Goldstein was very scared of something, but I had no idea what. I'm still not sure. I saw him looking nervously towards the gallery when he started his evidence, but I couldn't understand what was bothering him. At the end of the luncheon adjournment I was approached by a woman outside court who asked if I could tell her where her husband was giving evidence. She told me her husband was Goldstein. I directed her to the public gallery. I have no reason to disbelieve what she told you: she just wanted to see him. I've never seen her before in my life. I just played a hunch. You saw the reaction when he realised she was in the gallery."

Pullman squinted at Charles through his cigarette smoke. "Hmmm," he croaked, evaluating Charles. He was plainly far from convinced.

"What do you say?" he asked of Belloff.

"I've no reason to suppose Charles isn't telling you the truth, Judge. If that's what he says happened, I accept it entirely."

You old darling, thought Charles. Pullman snorted at Belloff's naïvety. "And what do you suppose he found so terrifying about his wife? Unless, of course, she was acting under some sort of threat, and was only there to remind him."

168

"I may be able to suggest something," volunteered Charles.

"Well?"

"He's a *chasid*, a strictly religious Jew. For him to lie on oath would be a very serious matter."

"And what's his wife got to do with that?"

"I'm not sure. A Jewish witness to his perjury, perhaps?"

Pullman snorted again. "I'm not satisfied with that. Belloff, ask the officer in your case to speak to the woman. I want to see a statement from her dealing with her presence here today. I want the officer to speak to you afterwards and tell you if, in his opinion, she is acting under duress." He turned to Charles. "I shall review the position then. Thank you, gentlemen. I shall return to court immediately."

Charles and Belloff filed out. Belloff winked at Charles.

"Thanks, Max," whispered Charles, with gratitude.

Belloff grinned. "No problem."

"Oh, I'm not sure about that. That threat about my Inn could be all it takes to finish me off for good. You know the sort of time I've been having recently."

"Hot air," said Belloff with confidence.

"I wish I was so sure. This isn't the first time I've encountered this sort of thing since . . . well . . . you know. And what if my client *has* been up to no good? Pullman will never believe that I didn't know."

They completed the rest of their journey back into court in silence.

Charles resumed his seat. Robeson beckoned to him, but before Charles could move, the Judge entered. Charles leaned towards Robeson's clerk. "Tell him not to worry, and I'll explain later," he said.

Belloff scanned his papers.

"Yes, Mr Belloff?" asked Pullman.

"Yes, my Lord. The Crown calls Detective Sergeant West."

The sweaty sergeant entered and strode to the witness box. He had finally succumbed to his wife's nagging and, in celebration of Robeson's arrest, had bought himself a new suit, one more commensurate with his increased girth, but the tie around his short, red neck, tightened only the moment he had entered court, still made him look distinctly uncomfortable. He took the Bible firmly in his hand and raised it to shoulder height. He gave the oath in a clear voice without faltering, staring fiercely at the jury, as if daring them to disbelieve that his evidence was anything but the truth, the whole truth and nothing but the truth. He gave his name, rank and number without being asked, turned to the Judge and said: "My Lord."

Belloff addressed the policeman. "I shall be asking you, Sergeant, about events occurring on the evening of 7th June 1991. Will you need to refresh your memory from any notes?"

"I may, my Lord. The notes were made on the same evening, back at the police station immediately after the accused's arrest. That was the first opportunity I had to make them. The matters were fresh in my mind at the time."

"Very good, officer," said the Judge. "You may refesh your memory from the notes if you require." West took a pocket book from his jacket and opened it.

"Where were you at approximately 7 p.m. that evening?"

West consulted his notebook. "At 7.06 p.m., my Lord, I was on duty in plain clothes with Detective Constable North and acting Detective Sergeant Walker in an unmarked police car in Brewers Street, Greenwich."

"What was your purpose there?"

"My Lord, we had been engaged in a surveillance operation on Mr Harold Robeson, who we had reason to

170

believe was involved in the robbery of the South African diamond consignment in December 1987."

Charles realised that West was an accomplished witness. Although being asked questions by Belloff, he turned to direct each answer to the Judge, and he watched Pullman's pen carefully to make sure that he was not going too fast. By the end of the trial, when the Judge summed up, every word of West's evidence would be there to be recited again to the jury.

"What did you do when you arrived there?" asked Belloff.

"We parked the car and entered the Victory public house. Once there we went to the public bar. We waited there for a few minutes, and then as a result of information received we went upstairs to a room where there was a private party in progress."

"What happened upstairs?"

"I identified the accused and asked him to accompany us to his car which was parked in the car park of the public house."

"Did Mr Robeson agree to go with you?"

"He did, my Lord. In the car park I asked him to unlock the boot of his Mercedes car, registration number HJR 8, which he did."

"What happened then?"

"I saw a long dark object in the boot. I reached in and found it to be a shotgun."

Belloff turned to the bench behind him, where a young man was holding out to him a gun wrapped in a plastic sheet. Belloff took it and handed it to an usher.

"Just look at this, please, Sergeant."

West took it and unwrapped the plastic. He looked carefully at the gun and identified the label tied to its stock. "That is the gun, my Lord."

"Let that be exhibit 1," said the Judge.

"I then asked the accused if the gun was his, and he

171

replied 'No it is not. I have never seen it before.' I then arrested the accused at 7.48 p.m. and cautioned him, to which he made no reply."

"What happened to Mr Robeson after that?"

"He was taken to Snow Hill police station."

"Were you involved in this matter any further?"

"Yes, sir. I was present later that evening when, at 10.05 p.m., Mr Robeson was interviewed."

"I think we can take this quickly, Sergeant. Is it correct that Mr Robeson declined to answer any questions at all, as was his right?"

"That is correct, my Lord."

"What did you do with the shotgun?"

"I attached that label to it, and passed it to the forensic science laboratory for examination."

"Thank you, Sergeant. Wait there, please."

Charles rose. "I take it, therefore, Sergeant, that your presence at the Victory public house was not an accident?"

"No sir. As I have explained, we were there as part of an investigation."

"So if I suggest to you that you told Mr Robeson to come downstairs and look at his car because there had been a report of someone tampering with it, you would deny it?"

"No, sir."

"You *did* tell Mr Robeson that someone had been tampering with his car?"

"Yes, sir."

"And who was that?"

"No one, to the best of my knowledge, my Lord." West turned to the Judge and smiled. "There was a very boisterous party in progress upstairs, at which a number of known criminals were attending. I felt that it might be unwise to raise the real nature of our visit in all the circumstances, so I decided to give an innocuous excuse to

172

persuade the accused to come downstairs without causing any alarm."

The Judge smiled. "Yes, Sergeant, I understand. Very sensible."

"Thank you, my Lord." West turned to face the jury and smiled at them, to make sure that they, too, thought that he had been very sensible.

"So," continued Charles, "you deceived Mr Robeson as to the reason he was required downstairs?"

"Yes, sir. An innocent deception, I felt."

"To the best of your knowledge, no one did interfere with Mr Robeson's car?"

"I can tell you for certain, sir, that no one did interfere with it."

"How can you tell us that?"

"Because there was someone observing the vehicle throughout."

"Why was that?"

"Because I didn't want it to be driven away by Mr Robeson, did I?" West looked at the jury again, inviting them to join him in his amazement at such a stupid barrister. One or two of the jury members smiled slightly.

"Yes, Mr Holroyd. That does appear to be obvious, does it not?" asked the Judge.

"If my Lord says so. And who, Sergeant, was conducting the observation?"

"D.C. North, my Lord."

"And Mr North remained outside for the entire period, is that right?"

"That's right. Until we went upstairs to see the accused."

"Why was it necessary for anyone to wait outside? You knew Mr Robeson was upstairs; why not go straight up and get him down? That way, no one had to wait outside to ensure that his car didn't move."

"That's effectively what we did."

"No. That's not so, Sergeant. You arrived at the pub at 7.06 p.m. according to your earlier evidence, but you did not arrest Mr Robeson until 7.48 p.m. You waited for some considerable time."

West grinned mischievously. "Well, to tell you the truth, sir, unprofessional as it may sound, we stopped long enough to have a drink. That was the only reason for the delay."

"You stopped for a drink? Before making an arrest of this importance?"

"I've been a policeman for fifteen years, my Lord. I've arrested many men, and women too, for that matter, on charges every bit as serious as this."

"This wasn't the first time you had had dealings with Mr Robeson, was it?"

"No sir."

"He practises in the field of criminal law, doesn't he?"

"I believe so."

"You *know* so. He's defended in many important criminal trials."

"I expect so, my Lord."

"In particular, he represented Anthony Kenny, the man alleged to have been one of the robbers in this very robbery."

"That is right."

"Mr Kenny was eventually acquitted of that charge."

"Yes."

"And you were not happy about that, were you?"

"It's part of the job, sir. My job is to get the evidence to put before a jury. Then it's up to the jury to decide."

"You thought he was guilty, didn't you?"

"I did, my Lord, or else I wouldn't have charged him with it, but the jury didn't agree."

"And you had to pay back to him eighty-five thousand pounds or so that you had found and seized from his home – money that you thought were the proceeds of the crime."

"That is right, sir. The jury acquitted him, and so that money was his. Or so I was advised."

"That must have been galling. Having to hand back all that money, tenner after tenner?"

"As I said, sir: part of the job."

"That's very reasonable of you, Sergeant," said Charles with heavy sarcasm. "But Tony Kenny was not the first man to be acquitted after you had thought he was guilty."

"Nor the last, I expect, sir."

"Nor was he the first to be represented by Mr Robeson?"

"I expect not."

"Mr Robeson has defended in prosecutions in which you have given evidence on a number of occasions."

"I really wouldn't know, sir. I don't keep tally. Policemen, sir, are generally too busy catching criminals," and here he nodded towards the dock, "to keep scores."

"I suggest to you, Sergeant, that this was one arrest where you would not stop to have a pint before getting your man. This was something of a 'grudge match'."

"You can suggest what you like, sir. It was just another job."

West stood in the box, his hands held behind his back, and rocked slightly on his heels. He was putting on a good performance, and he knew it. "Besides," he added, almost as an afterthought, "at the time, I did not know that the accused was going to be arrested. I didn't know what might be in the boot of his car."

Charles snapped back immediately. "Then what on earth were you doing there?"

West suddenly looked slightly uncomfortable, but he recovered well. "We were there as a result of information received."

Charles paused. If he asked West what that information

175

was, he was certain to get an answer damning to Robeson. West had hardly missed an opportunity to put the boot in, the references to the villains at the party, the nod towards the dock when speaking of 'criminals'. At the same time, the risk of not going into West's "information received" could be as great. The jury would already be wondering what had brought the police to the pub.

"You told us that the interference with the car was a ruse to get Mr Robeson downstairs without any fuss."

"Yes."

"So you must have had a reason to ask him to open his boot?"

"Yes."

"Your 'information received' was that there would be a gun in the boot?"

"Not quite, no."

Charles paused to consider carefully the framing of his next few questions. "I don't propose to ask you the identity of your informant."

"I wouldn't give it to you anyway," replied West, no longer smiling. "Unless, of course, I was ordered to do so by my Lord."

"But it must be right, that the police receive a great deal of information from such people."

"That is right, my Lord."

"Some of it very reliable information, and some of it less so. I expect you've had tips which turned out to be precisely correct, and tips which turned out not to be correct at all."

"Yes, sir."

"Some sources can be relied on, others cannot."

"All sources are variable, sir. Some are more variable than others."

"And you have to be very careful about how you act on these sources."

"Indeed."

176

"They may have their own motives for informing."

"They all do. Money, mostly." There was some laughter at that. West had recovered his lost confidence.

"They may perhaps want to settle scores."

"That's possible."

"Those working in the criminal courts, policemen, barristers, judges, they can easily make enemies in the course of their work."

"I suppose so."

"As can solicitors."

West's expression changed as he realised Charles's direction.

"If you're trying to say that this information was unreliable because it was given by someone with a grudge against Mr Robeson, sir, you're wrong. I don't know if the person has a grudge or not. But the information was right. The shotgun from the robbery *was* in the boot."

"So that *was* your information? That the shotgun was in the boot?"

"Not quite. We were told to be there by a certain time, and that the accused would be there and that we should look in the boot."

"Just be there and look in the boot?"

"Yes."

"That was pretty slim information on which to mount an operation involving so many police officers. Why did you go?"

"Because I thought the information was reliable."

"Did you pay for it?"

"No."

"Did you know who it came from?"

"I didn't take the message."

"That's not what I asked you. Did you know the name of the alleged informant?"

"No."

"Why then did you think it would be reliable?"

West began to look more uncomfortable. The jury were watching him closely now. "I . . . don't know, sir . . . a hunch, I suppose."

Charles laughed. He spoke with as much derision as he could command. "You had a hunch that a respected solicitor might just be carrying round in the boot of his car the shotgun used in a robbery committed by an ex-client of his a year and a half before? Is that what you're saying?"

"Yes. Well, I had a hunch that the tip might be worth following up."

"A police officer – not you – receives an unsolicited message from an unknown source, that this respected solicitor will be at a certain public house at a certain time, and that you should go and look in his boot. And that was enough for you?"

"Yes."

Charles shook his head in disbelief. "And, based upon this *hunch* of yours, how many busy officers did you involve in this operation, Sergeant?"

"Four or five."

"Four or five people, on the basis of that tip?" asked Charles incredulously.

"Yes."

"Then, I'll ask you again, Sergeant: isn't the truth of the matter that this was indeed a very important 'collar' for you? You *wanted* Mr Robeson."

West answered angrily. "A bent solicitor is a dangerous animal. It's far more important to catch him than the criminals he helps!"

"So, now we're getting there, Sergeant West. Now we see some of your true feelings about Harold Robeson."

"Please save your speeches for the right time, Mr Holroyd," interrupted the Judge.

"I apologise, my Lord. It is right, is it not, that your

178

feelings about catching Mr Robeson were not exactly indifferent?"

"I was not indifferent, no. I think he's a very dangerous and clever criminal—"

Charles interrupted him. "Less of what you think, please, Sergeant! Speeches for the Crown are made at the end, and then by counsel. As you have already said: it's for the jury, and not for you or I to decide."

"Mr Holroyd!" protested the Judge.

"My Lord?"

"I will tell witnesses what they can and cannot answer! How dare you!"

"I apologise to my Lord.

Charles took a deep breath and started again. "Sergeant West: you have told us that you were engaged in surveillance of Mr Robeson. May I take it that that surveillance began before the tip about the car boot?"

"We were keeping an eye on him, yes."

"When did that start?"

"I cannot remember exactly. Before that evening anyway."

"And what happened to prompt such surveillance?" It was a dangerous question, as Charles only suspected, and did not know, the answer.

"We received some evidence."

"The evidence of Avraam Goldstein?"

"That's right," replied West, frowning.

"You took Mr Goldstein's statement from him in prison on 4th June 1991."

"If you say so, sir."

"So, the position is that Mr Robeson first becomes a suspect when you see the statement of Avraam Goldstein."

"That's correct."

"By that time, Goldstein had been serving a prison sentence for over two years."

"Yes?"

"Why did you suddenly decide to see him then?"

"I went with another officer who was to show him some photographs."

"You're being evasive. Why did you decide to see Goldstein then and not some time during the previous years?"

"Because I accompanied the inspector. The rules require that someone showing photographs should not be part of the investigation. He had nothing to do with the case"

"You're still not answering my question. This inspector would not have decided to go and see a serving prisoner for no good reason. Someone had to ask him to go. That someone was you, was it not?"

"I don't remember, my Lord. It may have been."

For the first time, His Honour Judge Pullman's patience with West showed a frayed edge. "The point being made, Sergeant, is that you, or another officer, made the decision to go and see Goldstein. You're being asked why."

West now looked distinctly uncomfortable. "I really can't remember, my Lord."

"Between Goldstein's conviction and 4th June 1991 Kenny was tried twice."

"Yes, that would be right."

"You didn't think of calling Goldstein to help the prosecution convict Kenny?"

Belloff rose to interrupt. "That is not a matter that can be commented on by this witness. The decision of who to call, and who not to call, would have been made by the CPS in consultation with counsel."

"I shall rephrase the question, my Lord," conceded Charles. "Did Mr Goldstein give evidence in either of the two trials against Kenny?"

"No. I don't believe he did."

"Do you remember speaking to Mr Goldstein between the time of his conviction, and the time you went there with another officer to show him photographs?"

180

West did not answer, but stared at the ceiling, apparently deep in concentration. Charles persisted.

"It's simple enough, Sergeant: did you visit Goldstein at the prison before this occasion?"

"I can't remember," concluded West, with a shrug. "I don't think so."

"Surely you would remember if you had visited the man in prison at the Isle of Wight. That's not exactly part of your 'patch' is it? It would mean a special trip, wouldn't it?"

"Yes, it would, my Lord."

"Well then, did you go to the Isle of Wight before this occasion to obtain from Goldstein a statement regarding Kenny's involvement?"

"I don't think so, but other officers may have done. I'm part of a large team."

"Have you ever seen any other statement made by Goldstein?"

Charles bent and whispered to Belloff. "Is there one?"

Belloff shook his head. "If there is, *I*'ve never seen it."

West saw the whispered conversation and guessed what had been said.

"I cannot remember ever seeing one," he answered.

"Very well. So, for many months, during the course of which the police brought two unsuccessful prosecutions against Kenny, you did not think to speak to Goldstein, who, without any doubt at all, would have been able to identify Kenny. Correct?"

"Yes, sir."

"Nonetheless, within a day, of Kenny's final acquittal, there you are, digging away at Mr Goldstein, looking for evidence against *Mr Robeson*, Kenny's lawyer."

"I did interview Goldstein, yes."

"You've already admitted that you weren't indifferent to Mr Robeson. I suggest that it went much further than that. This was something of a crusade, wasn't it?"

"If you mean that I wanted to catch a dangerous and clever criminal, then yes. I did. 'Crusade' is your word."

"You thought he was a criminal because of the outcome of Kenny's trial!" shouted Charles.

"Yes! If you want to know the truth, I think he fixed that jury!"

"Is that right? Well, I'll come back to that in a moment. But you're not quite so indifferent to the verdicts of juries as you pretend, are you? You weren't satisfied with their verdicts in Kenny's case, so you decided to put the matter right?"

"I decided to make a further investigation."

"To right what you considered to have been an injustice?"

"It's always an injustice when a crime is committed and a criminal escapes."

"Indeed. From your point of view, Sergeant West, you felt that the system had failed in the case of Kenny, and you were going to try to ensure that it didn't happen again."

"Yes – no! I started an investigation, that is all. As a result of that investigation I came to a conclusion. Not the other way around."

"Let us summarise your evidence so far, please, Sergeant. At first you tell us that Kenny's acquittal did not affect you. "Part of the job," you said. Now you admit that you felt an injustice had been done, by Mr Robeson, and you decided to see if you could get evidence on him. Why did you feign indifference at the outset of your evidence?"

"I suppose because I thought it was irrelevant to this case."

"What was irrelevant?"

"My suspicions that Robeson fixed the jury."

"All right, let's deal with that now, shall we? Have

you a single shred of evidence that the jury was fixed by anyone?"

"Well, Kenny was acquitted."

The moment he said it, West realised that he had made a dreadful error. His face flushed, and his eyes darted around the court.

"I beg your pardon?" asked Charles, incredulously. "A man is acquitted, so the trial must have been fixed? You have scant regard for what the twelve men and women of the jury thought," said Charles, pointing to the jury. "I suppose you'll say that *this* jury has been fixed too, if they have to gall to acquit Mr Robeson."

The members of the jury stared in open hostility at West. The Judge turned again to look at him.

"I'm sorry, my Lord. That didn't come out the way I meant it. I felt that he was acquitted against the weight of the evidence. Many of us thought it."

"Perhaps, Sergeant, the jury did not accept some of the police evidence," suggested Pullman wryly.

Charles raised an eyebrow. Even Pullman was beginning to have his doubts about West.

"The fact is," resumed Charles softly, and with regret in his voice, "you were so incensed at the result of the earlier trials, that you went straight to the prison and you put pressure on Goldstein to give evidence against Mr Robeson. Isn't that right?"

"It is not. He signed that statement of his own free will."

"We have seen him give evidence this morning. Can you think of any reason why he might have felt under pressure?"

The Judge again looked up from taking his notes and scrutinised West.

"No. None."

"Did you mention parole to him when you saw him?"

"Not at all. That would have been improper."

"I'm not suggesting that it would have been correct to do it; I'm suggesting that you knew it was improper, but did it none the less."

"Well, you're wrong, sir, my Lord. I would not do such a thing."

"Did you see Goldstein before he was shown the photographs?"

"I had to. I had to tell him what we were there for and introduce the other officer."

"So you told him you were about to show him some photographs including that of Robeson?"

"Certainly not. I told him that the officer was helping our enquiries into the robbery and that he would explain the procedure. I did not mention the photographs at all."

"And that's all you said?"

"That's all."

"So it would have taken a minute at most."

"Probably."

"Where was the other officer during that minute?"

"I can't remember. He was probably with us. I can see no reason why he would not have been."

"You told Goldstein precisely who he was supposed to pick out, didn't you?"

"I most certainly did not."

Charles looked down at his papers and paused. He felt everyone in court waiting for him to speak. When he did, he did not look at West, but at the jury. It was an old trick, and one he found cheap, but he had to make them think about his next point.

"When did you receive your alleged tip-off? On that Friday?"

"It was not an 'alleged' tip-off. It did occur. And I received it on the Thursday. It may have been received at the station a day or so before then."

"Did you not think it an extraordinary coincidence that

184

within as little as forty-eight hours of seeing Goldstein in prison, someone contacted you with information about Robeson's car?"

"I did, yes. I thought someone might have been told that I'd been to Camphill, and decided to give me a hand."

"I suggest to you, Sergeant, that this entire story of a tip-off is complete nonsense. You never received any such thing."

"I did, sir. At least, I didn't, but I was informed that a message had been left."

"I suggest, Sergeant West, that so incensed were you by the acquittal of Kenny, that you decided to take matters into your own hands. To that end you went and saw the hapless Goldstein and bullied him into concocting a false identification of Mr Robeson. With that in your hand, you planted the gun in Mr Robeson's car and arrived with five other officers, already certain of what you'd find."

"That is an outrageous suggestion, my Lord. I never put any pressure on Goldstein, and I'd never seen that gun in my life until I found it in the back of that Mercedes."

"I have no further questions," said Charles, resuming his seat.

The Judge closed his notebook. "It's five minutes to four, Mr Belloff. You may re-examine tomorrow morning. Sergeant: you are in the course of your evidence. Please do not speak to anyone about the case in the meantime."

"I'm sorry to interrupt, my Lord, but I have no re-examination for Sergeant West, and it would assist me greatly if I could speak to him over the adjournment."

"So be it. You may stand down, Sergeant. Members of the jury: remember the warning I gave you about discussing this case with anyone outside your number."

"Court rise!"

185

CHAPTER 17

Robeson was required to stay in the dock until the jury had departed. Finally the dock officer opened the gate and allowed him to descend into the court. Charles had remained in his place while the court emptied, collecting his papers.

"Well done, Charles," said Robeson, coming up behind him.

"No. If you think about it, we didn't get very far with him. Oh, yes, he looked shifty. But all we obtained from him was his conviction that you're guilty."

"Who's being called first tomorrow?"

"Either D.C. North or D.S. Walker. Then the identification inspector, followed by the ballistics man. Then you."

"Do you think I'll be giving evidence tomorrow?"

"Probably."

Charles felt Robeson's hand on his arm. "What's up, Charles? You look very down."

"Oh, it's nothing. Bad news about my father." He continued tying the pink ribbon round his case papers.

"Tell me."

"I discovered at lunchtime that he's got to have a heart by-pass operation. The sooner the better."

"No need to worry. It's almost a standard operation nowadays."

"It's not the risk that's worrying me – although that's

186

bad enough. It's just that there's a long waiting list."

"Ah, I see."

"And this time, the cost to have it done privately is thousands, not hundreds."

Robeson turned Charles round to face him. Charles looked at the solicitor's face for the first time, and saw genuine concern.

"That needn't be a problem, you know, Charles."

Charles drew a deep breath. "I can't ask it of you, Harry. When I was at the hospital with Dad last time, I asked the anaesthetist. He said £9,000, assuming no untoward problems."

"Two years ago, Charles, I have no doubt that you could have written a cheque out for that without even speaking to your bank. Believe me, I'm better heeled than you ever were! That sort of sum won't break me."

"Yes, but— "

"But nothing. You're halfway through the most important case of *my* life. I need to be confident that you're relaxed and on your toes. So, leaving aside the fact that I like you, and your parents for that matter, it's in my own interests to help you out. I may even be able to set it off against tax as a business expense," he joked. He put his hand up to stop any argument. "Nothing you can say will change my mind, so don't waste your breath. I'll speak to Kenneth tonight."

Charles looked at Robeson, took his hand and gripped it for a moment. He felt his eyes sting with tears and he had to wait a moment before he could rely on his voice. "You're under more stress than most people ever have to cope with, and I'm coming to *you* for help." He shrugged awkwardly. "I just don't know how to thank you."

Robeson held Charles's gaze, and his hand. "Win the case, my boy. Now," he said breezily, clapping Charles on the back, "I could do with a drink. Have you time?"

"No, thank you. I've work to do for tomorrow and I've

187

got to go to Mum and Dad's."

"Fair enough." Robeson picked up his briefcase. "See you tomorrow. And cheer up. You're going to win. I have faith in you." He waved and left.

Charles hefted his case papers and all three volumes of Archbold's *Criminal Pleadings, Evidence and Practice* and turned to leave.

"Hang on, Charlie," came a woman's voice from the back of the court.

Charles spun round. "Sally? What on earth are you doing here?"

She came up to him. Charles had a quick look around and kissed her on the lips.

"I was here for a 'tea party' with a load of other clerks, trying to fix a couple of cases, and I thought I'd pop in and listen for a few minutes. How's it going? Here, let me get that," she said, reaching for the door handle.

"Oh, all right, I suppose."

"He looked awful to me."

"Who?"

"That sergeant."

"Yes, but you're not on the jury."

"Don't worry, Charlie. I was watching them. They were interested."

"Interested isn't convinced."

"Patience. You ain't even halfway through the case yet."

Charles halted. "Erm . . . Sally?"

"Yes?" she said with a smile, anticipating him.

"I've got to my parents' for a while, and then I've an hour or so's preparation for tomorrow, but, after that— "

"Yes. The answer's yes. Mum went to Wales to visit her cousin yesterday. Just had a hysterectomy, and needs a hand round the house. There's nothing like someone even more ill than she is to buck up my mum. So, if you give me the keys, I'll warm the bed up."

"Wonderful. I'm in love."

"No you ain't. But it's nice of you to think so. Now, I've gotta run. See you later."

She stood on tip-toes, kissed him on the nose and ran off.

"Take a seat, gentlemen."

Sergeant West took the armchair in the corner of the room. The CPS solicitor sat at the desk facing that of Max Belloff so that he could take notes. Belloff squeezed into his leather seat, which groaned slightly under the assault. There was a knock at the door and a man's head appeared. "Oh, sorry, sir, I didn't realise you were back," apologised Belloff's clerk.

"That's okay, Henry. We've got to have a short con about today's case. Any chance of some teas?"

"I'll try, sir, but Bob's checking the list and the phones are going like mad."

"Well, don't worry about it, then."

"May I just get a brief from your desk, sir?"

"Yes. Which one?"

"The buggery at Chelmsford, *Saddler*. I'm afraid it's in tomorrow."

"Shit. Who's going to deal with it?"

"I don't know yet. Things are very busy tomorrow. It may have to go out of Chambers, I'm afraid. Anyway," he said, picking up the brief, "I'll leave you to it."

The door closed behind him.

"Now," said Belloff. "I'm not saying we're in bad shape, but things are not going as well as I'd have liked. Holroyd's substantially watered down the connection between Robeson and the house, and the evidence relating to the bank account is not as clear as I would have liked, even at this stage, before Robeson starts putting in his documents, as he's bound to do, to explain his withdrawals. He'll certainly be able to muddy the waters

189

enough to render the evidence neutral. Goldstein's next to useless– " and he glanced at West, who looked studiously at the pattern in the carpet " – and that really only leaves the gun."

He paused. "Now, Sergeant, with the exception of a couple of completely daft answers, you didn't do *too* badly under cross-examination. Holroyd has a bloody good point though. Why you went to Goldstein for help in your case against Robeson, but *not* in two cases against Kenny, God only knows."

"Well," began West.

"It's too late now to explain," interrupted Belloff. "Anyway, I'm not happy to leave the evidence as it is. I want to come back to what we were discussing last time. Richard," he said, addressing the solicitor, "do you have that bundle of company documents Holroyd produced?"

"Yes," replied the other, handing it across.

"Hmmm," said Belloff as he leafed through it.

"If you're thinking what I think you're thinking, sir, it would be impossible in the time available."

"I'm not so sure about that, Sergeant. Look: finding a residential property to work from is easy. They really didn't need it at all – it just tied up a loose end. But they *had* to have somewhere to do the painting. You can't paint two vans in British Gas livery in the middle of the street. Someone would be bound to ask questions. So, they had to have a garage. Somewhere they knew they wouldn't be disturbed. Where the landlord's friendly. If Robeson is guilty– "

"He's guilty," interrupted West.

"Then somewhere in these 178 properties, I'll bet there's one with a garage, or stables, or an outhouse of some description that was used as paint shop. We've just got to find it. The task's been made a lot easier with Holroyd's list here."

"In a day?" asked Richard.

"Yes. Maybe two, if we're lucky."

"Like I said, it's impossible," repeated West.

"No. Difficult, yes, but not impossible. Work on a radius of, say, five miles of 'Staplecroft'. I can't believe they would have gone much further afield than that – would have caused too many logistical problems. That will probably cut out seventy-five per cent of the properties. Then get an Ordnance Survey map and have a look at the ones that remain. If they're terraced, mews or suburban semis, you can forget them – too small. We're looking for a farm, or warehouse, something like that."

"Right," said West, standing up and holding out his hand for the bundle of documents. "I'll get cracking."

"Fine. And, Sergeant," added Belloff, "if you find it, I'll want further statements from you and from the Scenes of Crime chap, for service on the defence."

"Sally?"

"Yes. Where the hell are you, Charlie? What time is it? Jesus, it's almost eleven. I fell asleep."

"I'm sorry. I'm still in Chambers. I got back from Hendon about an hour ago. Look, I'm going to be a while yet. There's some papers here that I've got to sort out tonight. Do you want to give it miss?"

"You don't learn, do you, Charlie? Why do you think Henrietta was so bloody unhappy? 'Cos you work too bloody hard!"

"Look, I said I was sorry. If you want to go home, I'll understand. I haven't been working. I told you, there were things I had to discuss with my family. My Dad's quite ill."

"All right, forget it. But I'm going home. I might as well sleep in me own bed and have a clean blouse to put on in the morning. Oh, no! Me knickers are still soaking. I washed them out and put them on the radiator to dry."

"The radiator's broken."

191

"Oh really? I'd never have guessed. You're a pain, Charlie Holroyd. I'll see you tomorrow."

She hung up. Charles laughed to himself, and got on with his work.

About twenty minutes later, he heard the outer door to Chambers creak open. He had left the hall in darkness and he listened for the light switch, but heard nothing. It was obviously not a member of Chambers. He held his breath and then heard the light pad, pad of footsteps coming down the corridor. He turned his own lamp off and stood up, tip-toeing to the door of his room. The footfalls got closer, reached the door and went past.

"Can I help you?" Charles asked, turning on the light as he spoke.

"Jesus Christ, Charlie, you scared me half to death!"

"Sally, what on earth are you doing creeping about my chambers in the pitch black?"

"Trying to get these back to you!" she hissed, holding up his front-door keys. "Or would you have preferred to sleep here tonight? I couldn't find the bloody lightswitch," she explained.

"Oh, thank you. Come in a second."

He led the way into his room.

"Ooh, this is cosy," she said, putting her bag down and perching on his desk. "Curtains and all. Do you share?"

"Yes, with Peter Bateman, remember?"

"Oh, yeah? Look, you'd better take these before I forget," she said, offering him the keys. He went up to her and put his arms round her neck. He kissed her on the lips. She dropped the keys by her side and put her hands round the back of his neck.

"Sorry I couldn't make it," he said softly.

"Yeah, well, you don't know what you've missed."

"I do," he said, kissing her neck. "That's why I'm so sorry. What did you do about your knickers?"

She took her arms from him and reached behind her to

192

her bag. She delved in, coming up with a plastic freezer bag. "I borrowed this from your kitchen," she said, holding it up. They was too wet to put in me pocket. The bra too." Charles could see her damp underwear folded up inside the bag.

"Which presumably means . . ." he said, sliding his hand up her thigh to be met with soft warm fuzziness.

Sally sighed deeply. "Oh, Charlie . . ." she said, putting her arms back round him and letting her legs move apart.

She let him touch her for a few seconds, her face nuzzling his neck. Then she gripped his wrist firmly and extracted his hand.

"That's enough of that," she said firmly. "Don't start what you can't finish."

"Who said I can't finish it?" he whispered in her ear.

"What, here?" she asked, incredulous. "On your blotter?"

He stepped back from her. "Don't move!" he ordered. "Just don't move!"

She heard him run down the corridor, and then the two doors slammed. He ran back into the room, closing the door behind him. He approached her again, putting his arms round her.

"God, are you serious?"

"Why not?"

"But this is silly, Charlie. You've got a perfectly good flat and a nice double bed three hundred yards from here."

"I know," he said, licking her neck, his tongue travelling up to her left ear. He felt her shiver. He slid her skirt up her thighs with one hand until it was bunched around her waist.

"But what if someone comes in?" she said, putting her arms round his back.

"They won't." His hand moved to her left breast and,

through the cotton of her blouse, found her nipple. He caressed it through the material and felt it harden under his touch.

"But what if they do?" she asked quietly, reaching down with both hands to his fly.

"I'll think of something," he whispered, taking her earlobe in his mouth.

She undid his trousers and they fell to his ankles. Like a ferret, her warm hand snaked past his underpants and went straight to him.

"Oh God," he moaned.

"You ever done this before, darling?" she asked. "In Chambers, I mean."

"No."

She shifted her weight so that she was sitting right on the edge of the desk, and opened her legs wide, hooking her ankles behind him. With one hand on his erection, and another on his buttocks, she pulled him into her.

"I bet you look quite a sight from behind," she giggled.

"Frankly, my dear . . . oh God . . . I don't . . . give a damn."

CHAPTER 18

"Detective Constable North, please."

The detective entered court. He was tall and slim, with thinning sandy hair. He was about ten years younger than West. He took the oath and gave his name, rank and number in a quieter voice than had his sergeant. It turned out that he had not made up any notes of his own concerning Robeson's arrest. He had instead read Sergeant West's notes and signed them as correct. He was given permission to use the same notes if he needed them, although he did not appear to want them, as they were left unopened on the lectern in front of him.

He answered questions simply, without elaboration, and his evidence in chief was almost identical to that of West. Charles did not bother to take a note of his evidence, but simply watched him. In the fifteen or more years that Charles had been in practice, he had developed a keen eye for untruth. Like everyone, he could be taken in by a good liar, but he had begun to trust his sixth sense. That sense told him now that North was, by and large, more honest and less evasive than Sergeant West had been. Charles looked at the jury. They were following his quiet voice carefully. And they liked him.

Belloff sat down.

"Yes, Mr Holroyd," said the Judge.

Charles rose.

"The 'Compass Team'. Isn't that what you're called?"

North grinned and looked slightly embarrassed. Oh, yes, thought Charles. They'll like you. This will have to be done carefully.

"That's right, my Lord. We're called that sometimes."

"Why?" asked the Judge.

"Well, Officers West and North, you see, my Lord."

"Oh, I follow. Yes, carry on."

"Have you been part of the same team for long, Officer?" asked Charles.

"Two years."

"And you get on well?"

"Very well, sir."

"I guess you have to trust one another implicitly."

"Of course. There are times when your life depends on that."

"Do you trust Sergeant West's intuition?"

"Yes, I would say so. He's an experienced policeman."

"Even when his orders are a bit of a pain?"

"I'm sorry, but I don't follow you."

"Well, there must have been times when he thought he was on to something – relying on his intuition – and you've wondered if it was all a bit of a waste of time."

North grinned. "Occasionally, perhaps."

Charles smiled at him conspiratorially. "Perhaps when he had you following Mr Robeson all over London, it felt a bit like that."

"A bit," conceded North, still smiling.

"Did you by any chance accompany Sergeant West on his visit to the Isle of Wight to see Mr Goldstein?"

"No, I didn't."

"But I assume that you would have seen the statement that resulted from that trip?"

"Yes. Or I would have been told about it."

"It would have been a major break in the case?"

"It would have been important."

"And before that, what evidence was there against Mr Robeson?"

"I don't think I'm qualified to answer that, my Lord."

"You were part of the team investigating Mr Robeson, were you not? You'd have had to have known what evidence there was against him to be able to do your job, surely?"

"In broad terms, yes, but Sergeant West had the file most of the time. If there were any briefings, I would have been there. For the most part, I did as I was told."

"Let me ask it in this way: are you aware of any evidence that you, the police, had against Mr Robeson before Goldstein's statement was obtained?"

"Not specifically."

"What was your understanding of what the 'Compass Team' was doing at the Victory that night?"

"We were going to arrest Mr Robeson," he said, nodding towards the dock.

"To arrest him?"

"That's how I understood it."

"Not just to question him and see if there were grounds for an arrest?"

North hesitated. "No, at least not as far as I was aware. I understood that it was certain that he would be arrested. That's why we had all the entrances and exits covered."

"Was there a briefing before the police left the police station?"

"Yes, there was."

"And who gave that briefing?"

"Detective Inspector Wilkinson partly. Mostly Sergeant West."

"And who was it who said that the purpose of the visit was to arrest Mr Robeson?

"I can't remember. I would guess it was Sergeant West, but I may be wrong."

"Thank you." Charles pause to look at the jury. One or

two of them returned his glance. They had not missed the discrepancy with West's evidence. "Now, then, we have heard something of some information that was received and which prompted the arrest. Were you the officer who received it?"

"No."

"Were you told of it?"

"Yes, I was."

"And what were you told?"

Belloff raised his huge bulk from the bench. "I object to that question, my Lord. The answer is hearsay."

"Isn't that right, Mr Holroyd?" asked Pullman.

"No, my Lord. With respect to my learned friend, it is not. I do not solicit the answer so as to prove that the words allegedly spoken were true – just the contrary; my case is that they weren't in fact spoken at all, and in any event they would have been false. It is the officer's state of mind that I am concerned with, and for that I need to know what information he had."

"Yes, very well."

"What were you told?"

"Just that we were to be there and look in the boot of Mr Robeson's car."

"Do you know who took this message?"

"I don't. Sergeant West told me about it."

"Do you know of any officer who claims to have heard of this message from any source *other* than from Sergeant West?"

"No."

Charles changed his tone and smiled as he asked the next question. "I gather you were the odd man out, the one not invited inside for a drink?"

"I don't know what you mean, sir."

"Oh," said Charles, feigning surprise, "didn't the other officers go into the pub for a drink, while you waited outside?"

"I certainly waited outside, my Lord, but I'd be very surprised if the others had a drink."

"Why? That would be unlike Mr West, would it?"

"Most unlike him," replied North vehemently. "Particularly on such an important operation."

"I see. This was an important arrest, then?"

"Of course. A man was crippled on that robbery."

"Not the sort of arrest to be taken lightly?"

"No."

"Not the sort of arrest that could be deferred for a quick pint?"

"With five men and two cars tied up? The arrest of a well-known solicitor?"

"Well then, can *you* explain to me what the delay was for? The delay between arriving at the pub and actually speaking to Mr Robeson?"

"I don't know. I was told to wait outside and keep an eye on his car, that's all. You'd have to ask Sergeant West."

"I did. He said he stopped for a pint."

North frowned, thought about the information and then shrugged.

"Did you watch the car throughout?"

"Either I or other officers did, yes."

"You mean that you were not outside for the entire time?"

"No. I came inside to report once. And once Sergeant West relieved me, so I could . . . relieve myself, if you see what I mean. It was quite a chilly night in that car park."

The jury laughed and the tension broke. Charles waited for silence before continuing.

"So, there was a period during which Sergeant West was guarding the Mercedes?"

"Yes. Only for about five minutes, though."

"And he would have been on his own out there in the car park?"

"I guess so."

"And after you returned?"

"Well, it was then that we went upstairs to find Mr Robeson."

"The waiting ended then?"

"Yes."

"After Sergeant West's period guarding the car?"

"Yes."

"Thank you, Officer. I have no further questions."

"I have one or two further questions for you, Officer," said Belloff. I guessed you might, thought Charles to himself. "Where was the Mercedes parked in relation to the road?"

"It was in the far corner of the car park. I'd say about forty yards from the road."

"I assume you arrived at the pub in a vehicle?"

"Yes."

"And where was that parked?"

"In the road."

"How far from the Mercedes was it parked?"

"Sixty to eighty yards, I suppose."

"Whose car was it?"

"It was an unmarked police car."

"I'm sorry, it's my fault. Who used the car normally?"

"I did. With Sergeant West."

"How long were you away from the Mercedes, when you went to the lavatory?"

"No more than three minutes."

"In that time, would it have been possible for someone to have gone from the Mercedes to the police car and back again?"

North considered this, and nodded. "Probably. It would depend on whether they knew where they were going, I suppose. The car park was quite dark, and the Mercedes was away from the road."

"Thank you, Officer. Does my Lord have any questions?"

"No, thank you."

Charles watched the jury as North walked out. It was notoriously difficult to anticipate a jury's views, but Charles was confident that they had taken the point. West had known that he was going to arrest Robeson even before he left the police station, which could only mean that, despite his denials, he *had* to have known what would be in the boot of the Mercedes before he even looked. Further, and this was an unexpected bonus, he had clearly had the opportunity to plant the gun there while he was on guard at the car. It was always much easier to allege impropriety against one officer than a conspiracy involving several. Charles was relieved that he had not had to suggest that North planted the shotgun; the jury would never have believed it. When North's evidence was added to West's obvious anxiety to even the score with Robeson, the Crown's case began to look decidedly shaky.

Charles felt something tug at his gown from behind. He turned to see Robeson's clerk holding out a piece of paper to him. Charles opened it and read: "There's a Mr Cooper outside. He's been waiting all day and wants to know when he's going to be needed."

Charles whispered to the clerk. "What's he doing here? He won't be needed until tomorrow at the earliest."

"Mr Robeson organised the witnesses. He told Cooper to be here today."

"Okay. Tell him I'm very sorry, but he won't be required until tomorrow, at, say two p.m.

"Okay. But he's not going to be very happy about it. Apparently his father's not well. He wants to go to the hospital."

Charles thought for a moment, pondering the coincidence. Then he stood.

"My Lord, a matter has arisen which requires my

attendance outside court. I wonder would your Lordship consider rising for five minutes to enable me to sort out the problem?"

"Very well, My Holroyd. I should think that the jury would enjoy a short break. Five minutes."

The Judge rose and Charles went outside with the clerk. Sitting facing the door of the court was a young man in a suit. He looked worried, and the pile of cigarette butts by his feet bore testament to a long wait.

"Mr Cooper?" asked Charles.

"Yeah?" replied Terry, getting to his feet and grinding out his current cigarette.

"My name's Charles Holroyd," said Charles, offering his hand, which Terry shook. "I'm the defence barrister, and I'm afraid it's my fault you've been called to give evidence. Look, I gather you've got a problem which means you need to be somewhere else."

"Yeah, I'm sorry an' all that, but me Dad's been taken poorly. He's got emphysema and it's suddenly got worse. I'd really like to be with me mum at the hospital."

"I really do understand, because, funnily enough, my father's very ill at the moment too. I'm very sorry you've been brought here today, but things have taken rather longer than was anticipated. If you were to be released now, do you think you could come back at two o'clock tomorrow afternoon? I'll do my best to ensure that you're away within a couple of hours."

"Can you guarantee it?"

"No, I'm afraid I can't, as it's not within my sole control. Normally the defendant gives evidence before his witnesses, but I shall ask for special permission to call you first so that you can get away. How does that sound?"

"All right. As long as I don't have to come back again. I don't want to be difficult, you understand – I want to help if I can – but it's me dad, y'know?"

202

"I understand perfectly. I'll see you again tomorrow at two."

"Righto. Bye, then."

Terry Cooper rushed off towards the exit, anxious to get to the hospital as soon as possible. He did not see the man that had been standing behind one of the statues discard his newspaper and hurry after him. Nor did he see that man signal to another waiting just outside the main entrance. So preoccupied was he, that he failed to notice the two of them follow him all the way to St Paul's Underground station, and thence to the London Hospital.

"I'll be back in a tick!" called Terry from the door of his van.

Mrs Cooper waved from the front door of their terraced house and stepped wearily inside. She had spent the whole day at her husband's bedside and she was exhausted. She had had no time to make tea, and so Terry had offered to pop down to the chippie and get some fish and chips for them both. She went straight to the kitchen and put the kettle on.

Terry drove the mile and a half to the fish and chip shop, named the Peking Dragon Fish Shop since the Ho family took over a few months back. The additon of Chinese food to the menu did not seem to have affected the quality of the cod and chips. Indeed, as far as Terry could tell, they were rather better than they had been when Mr Tibbs had been the owner.

He came out of the shop, juggling the two bags of food, two cans of shandy, a packet of cigarettes and his car keys, and did not see the two men that waited for him, leaning arrogantly against his van. They walked straight up to him and grabbed him by each arm, propelling him backwards.

"Hey!" protested Terry, but a sudden hard blow struck him in the stomach, completely taking the wind out of his lungs. Terry dropped his purchases, gasping for breath, as the men dragged him backwards around to the far side of the van and into the shadows. He felt himself slammed up against the side of the van.

"Now, sonny," said the man to his right, still gripping him by the upper arm, "you listen to me and you listen carefully. You do *not*," and the man cuffed him hard across the face with the back of his free hand, "want to give evidence, right?"

Terry was still gasping for air, although with rather more drama than his state required. He allowed his arms to sag slightly.

"Are you listening to me?" asked the man. He repeated his previous sentence, punctuating each word with a slap. "You . . . do . . . not . . . want . . . to . . . give . . . evidence."

Terry heaved his arms apart, throwing the man to his left off balance. For a second the grip on his left arm slackened and he wrenched it free. He swung it hard at the man to his right. Terry was right-handed and it was a ham-fisted blow, but he was a strong young man, used to heavy work, and it connected hard with the other's chest and pushed him away. Terry's other arm came free and he threw one good punch at the man who had done the talking. It landed with a satisfying crunch on the other's nose, and blood spurted onto Terry's jacket. Terry turned to locate his other attacker just in time to see an arm rise and fall. He felt an excruciating pain in his temple as a cosh landed on his head. The ground rushed up to meet him.

He was conscious of blows and kicks to his body and head, but they seemed to come from miles away and did not hurt him. After a while they too stopped and Terry remembered no more.

CHAPTER 19

"Call Inspector Bathington."

It was shortly after lunchtime on the following day. The statement of the ballistics expert had been read as agreed evidence; Charles did not dispute the fact that the shotgun found in Robeson's boot was the same one as used on the robbery. Detective Constable Brian Walker (who, for reasons Charles did not comprehend, Robeson insisted on referring to as "Denis") had also given evidence, but to little effect. He had been the third member of the police team inside the Victory, but he had remained inside the pub throughout until the group descended from the party, at which time he came to the car park but said, and apparently heard, nothing. He claimed that he not known of the purpose of the visit because he had missed most of the briefing. He had maintained that he had been "volunteered" as he entered the police station, and told to come along and make up numbers. Robeson was convinced that he was lying, but if so, Charles had made no impression on him. The one essential piece of evidence that Charles had been able to get out of him was that Robeson had not left the upper room of the pub from the moment at which the police officers entered, until he went out to the car park in their company.

Inspector Bathington was to be the last prosecution witness. He was the officer who had shown Avraam Goldstein the album of photographs including that of

Robeson. He strode into court, a big, upright man in uniform, indeed, the first uniformed witness the jury had seen.

Charles had given permission to Belloff to lead him through his evidence, and it thus only took five minutes until Charles rose to cross-examine.

"I understand from your evidence, Inspector, that you had nothing whatsoever to do with this case until the day on which you showed Mr Goldstein that album of photos?" asked Charles, pointing to the album.

"That's right, my Lord."

"Who was responsible for making up the album?"

"I was, my Lord."

"How did you go about that?"

"I keep a large number of photographs as part of my duties, and I went through them to find eleven others of similar types of men."

"Eleven others?"

"Yes. Sergeant West provided me with a photograph of the accused, and I had to find eleven others to go with that one to form this album. I try to find others of a similar type so that the suspect does not stand out."

"When did you do this?"

"I can't tell you exactly. A couple of days before we saw Mr Goldstein in prison."

"You had never met Mr Goldstein before?"

"That is correct."

"Did you have any idea what the case was about?"

"A brief outline. I didn't concern myself with it very much. I had other duties at the time."

"And when you arrived at Camphill Prison, what happened?"

"We were shown in, and I went through the formal procedure according to this form."

"Yes, you've already been through that with us. So you

206

just walked in, plonked the album in front of Goldstein and started with your first question?"

"No, of course not. Sergeant West went in and explained the purpose of our visit, and then I started the process."

"You waited outside?"

"Yes, I think so. But not for long."

"Twenty minutes?"

"Good heavens, no. Nearer ten."

"So Sergeant West had a ten-minute private conversation with Mr Goldstein?"

"It was a few minutes. I wouldn't like to be precise about its length."

"Did Sergeant West tell you that he would speak to Goldstein alone first?"

"Yes, my Lord, he did."

"Did he tell you what he wanted to say to Goldstein?"

"Yes. He wanted to tell the man that I was there with an album of photographs, and to tell him that I would conduct the identification."

"And that took ten minutes?"

"Five, ten. Something like that."

"Thank you, Inspector. I have no further questions."

"Unless my Lord has any questions for Inspector Bathington, that is the case for the Crown," said Belloff.

"I have no questions, thank you. Yes, Mr Holroyd."

"I have an application, my Lord, to call a witness out of turn. A Mr Terence Cooper has been waiting to give his evidence for two days now, and his father is quite seriously ill in hospital. He naturally wants to get away as soon as he can. I have asked my learned friend if he would have any objection to Mr Cooper giving his evidence before that of Mr Robeson, and he has agreed. Would my Lord permit me to call Mr Cooper first?"

"You have no objections, Mr Belloff? Have you seen a medical certificate?"

"I have not, my Lord. But if Mr Holroyd tells me that

Mr Cooper's father is ill, I have no reason to doubt it. I have no objections to my learned friend's application."

"Very well, Mr Holroyd. You may call your witness first."

"Thank you, my Lord. Mr Terence Cooper please."

There was a pause while the usher went outside and called Terry's name. He returned and said, "No answer, my Lord."

Charles whipped round to Robeson's clerk. "Where the fuck is he?" he hissed.

The clerk shrugged. "I don't know. He wasn't there at two o'clock after lunch, but I assumed he was just a couple of minutes late. I've not been out since."

"Mr Holroyd?" asked Pullman.

"My Lord?"

"If he's not here, I suggest you call your client in the normal manner. That will give your instructing solicitor time to make enquires."

"Yes, my Lord. In that case— "

Charles was cut short by the door behind him opening, followed by a sharp intake of breath from the jury, who, unlike counsel, could see the door from their seats. Charles turned around again. Terry Cooper walked up the aisle towards the front of the court. His head was bandaged so that only a small part of his scalp was visible. His face was swollen, both eyes blackened, the right one completely closed. His lower lip was split, and the black string of sutures trailed over his chin. So astonishing was his appearance that Judge, jury and counsel watched open-mouthed as he made his slow way to the witness box. He climbed the two steps in obvious discomfort and waited there patiently.

The Judge found his voice first. "Mr Cooper?"

"Yes," replied Terry, his voice muffled and his articulation impaired by his swollen jaw and stitched mouth.

"I can't believe, Mr Cooper, that you are fit to give

evidence. I thought that it was a relation of yours who was ill."

"It is. My dad."

"But then— "

"This happened last night. I want to give evidence."

He said it with such grim determination that the Judge, who had been ready to refuse to proceed, was taken aback. "Why? Surely you should be in hospital?"

"Maybe, but *after* I've given evidence."

"Mr Holroyd?" asked the Judge, seeking assistance.

"I knew nothing of this, my Lord. And I agree, Mr Cooper does not look fit, and I wouldn't dream of calling him in this state . . . but if he insists . . .?"

The Judge shrugged. "Very well. Usher, get him a chair so he can sit— "

"I don't want a chair, thank you."

The Judge sighed. "Then proceed with the oath."

Terry gave the oath in a quiet, muffled voice. Belloff leaned over to Charles and whispered to him. "I'll tell you, old chap, my heart's gone right out of this prosecution. If *that* was done by anyone on the Force, I swear, heads'll roll." Charles nodded, and turned to address Terry.

"Could you give us your name and address, please?"

Terry did so.

"And you are a plumber, is that right?"

"Yes. I have me own business," he replied, a measure of pride apparent through the muffled speech.

"Mr Cooper, what on earth has happened to you?"

"Last night, two men. They beat me up. Told me not to give evidence."

"They did *that* to you?" asked the Judge.

"Yeah. I reckon, well, if they'd do this to stop me from giving my evidence, it must be pretty important. So I thought I'd better come along. There was a right barney at the hospital, I can tell you, but I discharged meself –

209

for the minute anyway. I'll get a taxi back to hospital when I'm done."

"Can you tell me who these men were?" asked the Judge.

"No, sir, I can't. I'd never seen them before. The police have shown me some pictures, but I ain't identified them yet."

"I see. Well, Mr Holroyd, you'd better get on with it, and let Mr Cooper get back to hospital. I shall require a full investigation into this matter, Mr Belloff."

"Of course, my Lord."

Charles drew a deep breath. "Mr Cooper, do you know the Victory public house in Greenwich."

"Not well, but I know it."

"Have you ever been there?"

"Once."

"Do you remember when that was?"

"It was a Friday night in June. That's all I can tell you. Quite a chilly night, I remember."

"What were you doing at the pub?"

"I was there for a darts match. I was the captain of the darts team from my local in Leyton."

"What time did you get there?"

"The match was from eight o'clock. We got there about ten to fifteen minutes before that."

"Did you actually play darts?"

"In the end, yes."

"Why do you say, in the end?"

"Well, I was taken ill and the match was delayed."

"How were you taken ill?"

"The match was about to start, I suppose it was about five to eight." He paused. Speaking was obviously difficult. "I suddenly felt sick. Well, actually, it wasn't sudden, 'cos I'd been feeling a bit dickie for most the afternoon. But it suddenly got worse, and I had to make a dash for it."

"A dash where?"

210

"To the toilet."

"Where is the toilet in the Victory?"

"In an outhouse in the corner of the car park."

"So you went outside?"

"Yeah. But there was only one cubicle."

"And?"

"And there was someone inside."

"So what did you do?"

"Well, it was pretty urgent. There was a sink, but it was bunged up, paper towels floating in it, you know. So I looked around for somewhere else to be sick. I got as far as the doorway, but knew I wasn't going to be able to hang on, so I just made it behind some car."

"Were you sick?"

"Yeah. Very."

"Do you know by what car it was you were sick?"

"Not at that time. It was just big and shiny. Gold, I thought. But later on I saw that it was a Mercedes."

"I'd like to deal with it in order, so we'll come back to what happened later in a moment. Did you actually throw up on or near the car?"

"On, I'm afraid. I'm very sorry," he said, looking at the Judge. "I would never have done it if I'd had any choice, but I couldn't help meself."

"And how long were you by the car?"

"Five or ten minutes. I felt really ill. Me legs went, and me 'ead was spinning."

"While you were there, did anything happen?"

"What do you mean? About the bloke?"

"Tell us about the bloke."

"Someone came up to the car while I was beside it. I thought it was the owner, and I was pretty worried, 'cos I'd made a good mess of his wheel. Wheel arch too, I reckon. I was still retching, like, so I just kept me head down."

"What did this man do?"

211

"He came up to the car and opened the boot."

"What then?"

"I heard a thump. As if something heavy was being put in, or moved around in the boot. Then the boot closed and the man went away."

Charles risked a quick glance at the jury. They were riveted to Cooper's evidence.

"Could you tell which direction he went in?"

"I thought that he went back to the pub. He certainly didn't go towards the road, or else he'd have gone the opposite way. He might even have tripped over me."

"Did you see anything about what this person looked like or what he was wearing?"

"No, not really. He had quite a heavy tread, so I'm sure it was a man. I don't remember seeing any clothes except a pair of shoes."

"And what were they like?"

"Dark, quite sturdy. I can't say any more than that."

"What happened then?"

"I felt a bit better after a while. The air was cool, so I stayed out for a couple more minutes to make sure I wouldn't throw up again and then I went back into the darts match."

"Did you play darts?"

"Not immediately. I was waiting to play, when there was a bit of a commotion outside in the car park, and people began going to the windows and the door. I went to have a look too. There was a crowd of people exactly at the spot where I'd been ill. I thought there was going to be trouble about me damaging the car."

"Did you see then what sort of car it was?"

"Yeah. A Merc – Mercedes."

"Did you see what happened then, outside, I mean?"

"No. I was called back to the board for my throw."

"What did you do after that?"

"Nothing. Except get beaten at darts."

The jury laughed, and even Judge Pullman permitted himself a smile.

"Thank you, Mr Cooper. Please remain there for a while."

Max Belloff rose.

"So it was just chance that you happened to vomit over that particular car?"

"Yeah."

"Why didn't you use the lavatory?"

"I've already explained. It was occupied."

"Are you sure?"

"Positive. The locks on them often don't work or are broken off, right? So I never like to push at the door in case you . . . you know . . . barge in on someone. So I had a quick dekko under the door first, to make sure."

"Why didn't you wait for a few seconds to see if the occupant came out?"

"Well, for one thing, I was desperate, and for another, he weren't going to come out in a hurry."

"How on earth do you know that?" asked Bellof with some irritation. "Did you ask him?"

"'Cos I could see. His boots were, like, pointing towards me and his trousers were round his ankles. I guessed he'd be there a while."

"Boots?"

"Yes, boots, or heavy shoes. Black, they were."

Charles cursed under his breath. According to Terry's proof of evidence the black boots had been worn not by the occupant of the toilet, but by the man approaching the car. He'd mixed them up! Then a thought occurred to Charles. He turned back to the point in Terry's statement where the occupant of the toilet was dealt with. There was no mention of any of this. It did not appear that anyone had thought to ask about the occupant of the toilet or his footwear. Maybe he was *not* wrong. Hadn't North said he'd gone to the toilet? There

213

might have been police shoes under the door *and* under the car!

Belloff decided to change tack. "Forgive me for asking, Mr Cooper, but what had you had to drink that night by the time you went out to the lavatory?"

"Nothing. I'd had a pint bought for me, but only had a sip of it before I went out."

"Nothing at all?"

"No."

"What about at lunchtime? Have a couple of pints at the pub?"

"No," replied Terry, clearly aggrieved at the suggestion. "I never drink when I'm working."

"Well, you might like to help us as to the reason for your sudden illness."

"I can't tell you. Maybe what I had for lunch. I got something from the shop next door to where I was working."

"Are you often ill like that?"

"Never before, at least as far as I can remember, and never since."

"I understand from what you said before that you were quite doubled up."

"I was."

"In pain?"

"Yeah."

"We all no doubt know how unpleasant it can be when we're sick. It makes your eyes water, your belly hurt?"

"Yeah."

"And that's what happened to you?"

"Yes."

"And in the middle of this someone approaches where you are crouching?"

"Yes."

"Someone by whom you would rather not be seen?"

"Yes."

"So you get your head down."

"Yes."

"The car park was dark, was it not?"

"It was, yes."

"It would be fair, would it not, to say that your ability to see accurately what was happening in the car park was quite limited, by your position, your discomfort and your wish not to be seen?"

"Yes, it would be fair. But the light was behind this person as they came from the pub, and I am certain that they came to the car I was by."

"How?"

"Because the car moved slightly as the boot was slammed shut. So I know that it was the same car as I was by."

"Very well. But what about that car? At the time, you thought just that it was a gold car?"

"Yes."

"Did you count the number of gold cars in the car park?"

"No, of course not."

"It is possible that there were several?"

"I suppose so."

"Indeed, there might have been more than one in that part of the car park?"

"Maybe."

"All you can say is that you vomited on, or near, a gold car?"

"Well . . ."

"And that after a few minutes, a crowd gathered in the same area of the car park, around a gold Mercedes."

"They did— "

"But you can't be sure that they were the one and the same, can you?"

"I can."

"But how? You didn't take the number of either car. If

215

there had been two similar cars in that area of the car park, you may have been ill by one, and the crowd gathered by the other."

"I don't think so. The crowd was exactly where I'd been."

"You didn't go outside though."

"No, but— "

"And you were watching from a brightly lit pub, through a crowd of interested people, all looking out into a dark car park."

Terry looked concerned. His swollen face contorted into a frown, and he looked at Charles sorrowfully, as if to apologise for being unable to disagree. Charles avoided his eye. He did not want the jury thinking that he had been coaching the witness. He was, in any event, thoroughly depressed, and he did not want Terry to see that and be tempted to alter his evidence. The truth was that Belloff was doing a good job of discrediting Charles's star witness.

"Isn't is possible that, after all, you vomit over Car One, and see people crowd round Car Two? That would mean that whatever was put in the boot of Car One had nothing to do with this case. Isn't that right?"

"I suppose so. It's possible, but I don't think it's likely. I was certain, at the time, that it was at the exact same spot."

"But now you're not so sure?"

"Well, the way you go on, I begin to wonder."

"Thank you, Mr Cooper— "

"But then, what I want to know is this: if I saw nothing to do with this case, why did anyone bother to do *this* to me? Eh? Someone obviously thought I'd seen something."

Charles looked up at that, and saw several members of the jury nodding their heads in vigorous agreement. You little darlings! he thought. They believe him.

At that moment, for the second time that afternoon, the

door burst unexpectedly open. Sergeant West appeared in the doorway. He almost ran down to Belloff, a crumpled piece of paper clasped in his hand. He was hot and sweating, and his face bright red, but the look of triumph on his pudgy features was unmistakeable. He thrust the paper under Belloff's nose and whispered to him. The entire court had watched his entrance and there was an uncomfortable silence. Belloff became aware of it after a few seconds. He halted West's furious flow with a raised hand and looked up at Judge Pullman, and Charles saw that his face too was altered. His earlier expression of grudging acceptance that Robeson might be innocent had given way to a barely suppressed grin.

"I do apologise to your Lordship for this hiatus. A matter has just been brought to my attention that is of the greatest importance in this case. I shall have an application to make, which would best be done in the absence of the jury."

CHAPTER 20

Statement of Jonathan Peter West
Age: Over 21
Occupation: Detective Sergeant
Address: Snow Hill Police Station.

This statement consisting of two pages each signed by me is true to the best of my knowledge and belief and I make it knowing that, if it is tendered in evidence, I shall be liable to prosecution if I have wilfully stated anything in it which I know to be false or do not believe to be true. I have read this statement.

I make this statement further to my earlier statement of 7th June 1991. Yesterday, during the course of this trial I took receipt of a list of properties owned by Overbrooke (GB) Limited and Prince Estates (1986) Limited in December 1987, which had been prepared by the Defence in this case. Of the properties listed there, fifteen fell within a radius of five miles of "Staplecroft", the property used by the robbers before and after the robbery. Of those, eight were, or included, premises large enough for large vehicles to be stored. I commenced a search of those eight properties in the company of S.O.C.O. Leavis from the Surrey Constabulary who had been one of the S.O.C.O.s originally to investigate the robbery. The third such property, called "The Ridings", is a farm in the village of Lower Barnsthorne. I produce an Ordnance Survey map of the area from which it may be seen that although no roads connect "The Ridings" to "Staplecroft", there is a path which leads from the farm to an alleyway that runs along the back of the terrace of cottages of which "Staplecroft" is one. I investigated the path and found that it is in the position indicated on the plan.

"The Ridings" includes several outbuildings, in one of which Mr Leavis and I found markings of paint on the walls and floor.

Signed D.S. West. Signature witnessed by D.C. Walker.

Statement of Frederick Leavis
Age: Over 21
Occupation: Scenes of Crime Officer
Address: Guildford Police Station

This statement consisting of two pages each signed by me is true to the best of my knowledge and belief and I make it knowing that, if it is tendered in evidence, I shall be liable to prosecution if I have wilfully stated anything in it which I know to be false or do not believe to be true. I have read this statement.

On the 21st December 1987 I was one of a team of Scenes of Crimes Officers attached to the Robbery Squad investigating the robbery of a quantity of diamonds from the South African Gem Corporation at Brighton Road, Coulsdon, Surrey. At the scene of the robbery I found abandoned two vans painted in the livery of British Gas. I examined the vans and came to the conclusion that they had been spray-painted recently. I took samples of the paint on each van and placed them in separate containers which I labelled "FL 1" and "FL 2" respectively.

Yesterday, I was requested by Detective Sergeant West to accompany him while he examined certain properties in Surrey. One such property was "The Ridings", Lower Barnsthorne, Surrey, which is a small farm with a number of outbuildings. One such building appears to have been constructed for use as stables, but is used now to store agricultural machinery. At the far end of this building I found evidence of paint spraying. The walls and floor had marks indicating that a spray gun had been used in close proximity to them, and in the north-east corner of the building I found four empty paint cannisters, which I produce as exhibit "FL 3".

I took scrapings of paint from the walls, and have been able to extract small quantities of paint from the empty cannisters. A full analysis of the paint is awaited from the forensic science laboratory, but from my examination of it, it appears to be indistinguishable from the retained paint flakes "FL 1" and "FL 2".

It is my opinion based on this evidence that the two mock British Gas vans were painted in the outbuilding at "The Ridings", Lower Barnsthorne, Surrey.

Signed Frederick Leavis Signature witnessed by D.S. West.

"What the fuck are we going to do?"

It was the first time Charles had seen Robeson look really frightened. He paced up and down the cell that doubled as an interview room, his brow contracted into a frown. Ominously, the Judge had directed that he remain in custody for the duration of the short adjournment while the new evidence was considered. He threw himself on to the wooden bench and stared morosely at the cell wall. It may have been the dim light of the cell which emphasised the lines and creases in Robeson's face, but Charles thought for the first time that he looked his years.

"Well, firstly, Belloff has to obtain leave to re-open his case. It seems also that this evidence is not definite; it's a provisional conclusion. That presumably means that he'll want an adjournment. I suggest I deal with those applications first. If and when he's successful, we'll consider what we should do."

Robeson did not appear to be listening. He launched himself from the bench and resumed pacing. Charles reached out and touched his arm.

"Harry? Harry? Listen, I know this is worrying, but you've been amazingly resilient so far. Don't go to pieces now. You're almost home and dry. Harry? What on earth's wrong with you?"

The solicitor sighed deeply. "Nothing. Just coming to terms with it."

"Coming to terms with what?"

"Charles, I reckon if this evidence goes in, I'm sunk."
"Nonsense— "

Robeson held up his hand. "Don't tell me 'nonsense'!" he interrupted furiously.

"Why? asked Charles, perplexed.

Robeson smiled grimly, and shook his head. "Let's just wait for the Judge's decision, eh?"

"That's better."

Charles squeeze the other's arm in affection. "Come on," he said gently. "Terry Cooper was a winner. The whole thing's falling into place. We've established that West had the motive and the opportunity to plant the shotgun, and put pressure on Goldstein. Terry's evidence – and the state of the poor bloke – they sew it up. You must have seen the jury; they loved him."

"Do you think so?"

"Sure of it. *This*," said Charles, holding up the two new statements, "is hardly proof that you entered into an agreement to rob."

Charles looked at the older man, wishing he could dispel his worries. He realised then how much Harry Robeson had come to mean to him in the last few weeks. He was no longer a client, indeed he had ceased to be that within a very short time of their meeting; he was a friend. Charles cared for him far more than would have thought possible a month before.

"Come on. Let's see what Belloff has to say about this."

Belloff had much to say.

"My application, my Lord, is to re-open the Crown's case so as to lead this evidence. I accept that the proper time for calling it would have been during the course of the Crown's case. But the task of finding all the companies with which Mr Robeson had a connection in December 1987, and isolating those companies which owned property in Surrey, would have been virtually impossible. I do not say 'impossible', but almost so. In my submission this was not evidence that the Crown could reasonably have called before now.

"Since we were provided with the list, every effort has been made to investigate the properties on it as quickly as possible. As a result, the Crown has discovered yet another link between Mr Robeson and the vehicles used in the robbery. The force of the evidence, should the jury accept it, is great. Whereas it may be contended that the connection with the other property was mere coincidence, a link with two properties cannot be. It now appears that Mr Robeson controlled not only the property used by the robbers before and after the robbery, but also the property used by them to disguise the vehicles."

222

"I see. Tell me, I have a discretion, do I not, as to whether or not to permit the evidence to be given?" asked Pullman.

"You do, my Lord."

"Do you agree with that, Mr Holroyd?"

"Yes, I do, but I do not accept that your Lordship's discretion should be exercised in favour of the Crown."

"I will hear you in a minute. Is there anything else you would like to say, Mr Belloff?"

"Yes, my Lord. The new evidence falls within a very narrow compass and can be considered in a matter of minutes. Although I should not oppose a Defence application for a short adjournment – say, overnight – to consider their position, the late reception of this evidence will, in my submission, cause no prejudice. It is of course of the greatest importance to the case, and this is a very serious charge. The interests of justice must require that all relevant evidence be placed before the jury if at all possible."

Belloff sat down.

"Mr Holroyd?"

"Firstly, I rely on the general rule that all evidence that the Crown wishes to adduce should be given before the close of their case. This is a very old case. It has been the subject of investigation since 1987. I do not accept that the Crown could not have discovered the alleged link with this property in all that time. It is only a hundred yards from 'Staplecroft'! I understood that policemen did house-to-house enquires as a matter of course. Such enquiries would certainly have revealed this information without the necessity for the 'virtually impossible' investigations at Companies House.

"Further, my friend is not only seeking to re-open his case, but it is he who is, in reality, forced to seek an adjournment. The evidence of Mr Leavis is only provisional. He will need, as I understand it, to send the paint to the Home Office laboratories for full analysis."

"Mr Belloff?" interrupted Pullman. "Is this right?"

"If my Lord grants the application, I shall need to take instructions to find out if Mr Leavis has the expertise required to undertake any further tests. I suspect, however, that he hasn't. If that is right, I shall apply for further time for a full chemical analysis." He turned and saw West nodding reluctantly. "Yes, my Lord. That appears to be the case." He resumed his seat.

"And," continued Charles, "who knows how long that will take? Once that has been done and the final results given to the Defence, it must then be open for me to have an expert instructed on behalf of the Defence to verify or challenge the findings. That will certainly take days, if not weeks."

"Weeks, more likely," commented the Judge.

"As my Lord says, weeks, more likely. What is to happen to the jury in that time? They have heard all the evidence in this case save that of the defendant. They have heard it all within the last two days. It is hardly fair to require them to keep it in mind for days or even weeks while the case is adjourned.

"Finally, there is the prejudice to Mr Robeson. He is a man of exemplary character, facing trial on a most serious criminal charge. His personal and professional lives are in tatters already, but they face complete destruction if he is convicted. The strain of this case has been immense, as I'm sure my Lord can imagine. Is he to be required to wait for an indefinite period while the Crown get their tackle in order for a second bite at the cherry? I would submit that that would be most unfair.

"The Crown obviously considered that the evidence they had at the outset of this trial was enough to secure a conviction, or they would not have proceeded. They should be required to take their stand on that evidence. In all the circumstances, I submit that the application would cause substantial injustice to Mr Robeson, and ought not be granted."

Judge Pullman looked at Belloff again. "Anything else, Mr Belloff?"

"No, my Lord."

"Then, in my view, it would not be proper for me to permit the Crown to re-open their case at this stage."

Charles turned round and winked at Robeson. The solicitor smiled broadly at him.

"I think," continued the Judge, "that Mr Holroyd's submissions are well founded – particularly with respect to the necessity for the trial to be adjourned for an indefinite period. If the evidence regarding the paint was said to be conclusive, that is, if it showed that the paint was definitely the same, I might be of a different view. But it is conjecture only. It looks the same, but it might not be – and we shall not know until after a full analysis; maybe not even then. I am not prepared to interrupt this trial on that uncertain ground. Now . . ."

Pullman was interrupted by his clerk, who turned and spoke quietly to him.

"It appears, gentlemen, that there is an urgent application to be made in another case, and as our jury is out, I've been asked if I will deal with it. I am told that it will only take five minutes. Will you forgive me, please? Mr Robeson can go down for the present."

CHAPTER 21

"Charles, that was brilliant!" Robeson's face had altered completely since the last time he was in the room. His cheeks were flushed and his eyes shone. He was elated. He clapped Charles on the back. "Brilliant!" he repeated.

"No it wasn't."

"Well, you've saved my skin, Charles, that's for sure!"

"I did nothing of the kind, Harry. Even had they been given leave to put the evidence in, I'm sure we'd have come up with something."

"Are you? What would you have done, eh?"

"Well, the paint on analysis might have been quite different. Even if it wasn't, for all we know it might be very common . . ."

Charles stopped in mid-sentence. Robeson was lighting up a cigar, grinning from ear to ear, shaking his head.

"Why are you shaking your head?"

Robeson winked at him. Then his attitude changed, and he became serious. "Forget it, Charles. Who are you calling next? Me, I suppose."

"No, just hold on, Harry. What are you saying to me?"

"Forget it, Charles." He sat on the bench and crossed his legs, wreathed in cigar smoke. "I meant to ask you about young Cooper."

"Harry! Don't treat me like a idiot. I want to know what you meant."

"No, you don't. Believe me, Charles, you don't."

Then, only then, did Charles appreciate what was being said to him. He stood in the tiny converted cell and stared at Robeson, his mouth slightly open.

"You did it?" Charles spoke softly, the words a question, but one to which he suddenly knew the answer. "You're saying you did it." He tried to assimilate the information. "I don't believe it. I just don't believe it."

Charles paced up and down the cell, oblivious to his client. Robeson watched him warily. Charles suddenly stopped and spun on his heel, his finger pointing at Robeson.

"But wait a minute! What about the shotgun. Terry Cooper wasn't lying, I'd stake my life on it."

"No, he wasn't."

"So the gun *was* planted?"

"Of course it was. What the hell would I be doing driving around with that gun in the back of my car two years after the job?"

"Well, then?" asked Charles, uncomprehending.

"I have been wondering when one of you two clever barristers would work it out," replied Robeson with ineffable smugness. "If the police had had possession of that shotgun, don't you think they'd have used it against Kenny? Come on, Charles, think about it. The *police* never recovered the shotgun."

"Then who . . . wait a minute . . . if the police never had it, then the robbers would . . . Kenny! Kenny planted it there?"

"Either he or one of his chums, that's my guess. I suspect it was his lads who did Terry over, too. Funny," he mused, "I'm surprised he had the nerve."

"But . . . but . . ." Charles stared at Robeson, lost for words. "But why? Why should he do that? If you and he were in on it together?"

"Hah! Why do you think? We fell out, over the money.

227

There's no honour among thieves, Charles. Of course, he had his way in the end. I'm no hard man."

"Then I still don't understand. Why go to all this trouble?"

Robeson took a deep breath and looked hard at Charles, weighing him carefully.

"Look, something happened during the job—" Robeson waved his hand dismissively – "you know nothing about it, but something happened, you see?" He saw Charles was still frowning. "Someone died, Charles. Yes, I know, there's nothing about it in the case papers. The police obviously never tied it up with the robbery. But I found out about it from one of the others. I thought it gave me a cast-iron insurance policy. I couldn't believe that Kenny would ever involve me – I could've sent him away for life so easily, understand? Apparently I was wrong. I guess he couldn't resist the temptation to get rid of someone with a hold over him. All he had to do was contact West, tell him to be at the Victory at the right time and wait for me to fall into his lap. And I'd never have known he had been responsible. That's presumably why the police had to wait until eight o'clock before arresting me. They had to wait for the gun to be put in the boot. Quite an unholy alliance that."

"So you *did* do it," repeated Charles. "You bastard."

"Come on, Charles," said Robeson, no longer smiling, "don't get upset. You've done a first rate job – I knew you would." He stood and approached Charles. "With a bit of luck my evidence will be completed by—" Charles pushed him violently in the chest, throwing him back to the bench on to which he fell with a thump. He stared up at Charles, shocked.

"How could you? How could you, Harry? You lied to me."

Robeson looked up from where he sat, taken aback by Charles's violence. He tucked his silk tie back inside his jacket. "Don't be a child, Charles. Of course I lied to you.

Don't most of your clients? You're not fussy, are you? You just put forward their stories and leave it up to the jury. And very often you know bloody well that they're guilty."

"I do not!"

"All right," he conceded, "then you suspect it. It comes to the same thing." Robeson sneered at him. "You barristers give yourselves such airs and graces! You stand there in court, robed in your professional ethics, as if the dirt you deal with every day, day in, day out, never touches you. You think you all have such clean hands! I swear to God, there may not be many bent briefs, but I prefer the company of those few. At least they're not hypocrites!"

He got to his feet again and came so close that Charles could feel his spittle on his face as he spoke. "How many times have you been a willing party to miscarriages of justice, eh? That's how you boys make your reputations, isn't it?" He turned his back on Charles and sat down again. "You sicken me. You're like a whore complaining of being raped."

The anger seemed to desert him momentarily and when he spoke again his tone was one of persuasion. "Try and understand, Charles, this isn't some clean, professional chess match for me. I'm fighting for my life here! How long do you suppose I'll last inside? I'm facing fifteen years; I'll never live to see the end of it."

"But all that crap you gave me at Brixton, why bother with that, eh? I would've represented you without any of it!"

"Yes, maybe, but how well? You believed in me and you fought for me as if I was innocent."

Charles shook his head in amazement. "You really are a calculating bastard."

Robeson threw back his head and laughed heartily. "Thank you."

"I mean it, Harry. You used me. You used me to practise a deception. I thought we were friends."

"Oh dear, Charles. You're sounding like a schoolboy. I hope we are friends. I know Sally does, too."

"What?"

Before he could answer, there was a knock on the door and a prison officer put his head round the door. "You're wanted back in court, gentlemen. The Judge is waiting to continue."

"We'll be right there," said Robeson breezily.

"Wait a minute!" commanded Charles. "Tell His Lordship that something has arisen and we have to have a further five minutes. Tell him I'll explain then."

"Well, he's waiting in court, sir, so I think you'd better come and ask him yourself if you need some time."

"Tell him!" shrieked Charles. "I shall not be up for five minutes, d'you hear?"

The prison officer's eyes widened in astonishment. He hesitated for a second and then disappeared. Charles turned on Robeson.

"Sally? What are you talking about?"

"Sally. Your ex-junior clerk? The one you've been . . . seeing, for want of a better word."

"Sally?"

"Yes, Charles, *Sally*. My daughter."

Charles felt as if he were in a dream. "Sally's your daughter?"

"Yes. She didn't tell you, then? I'm surprised; I thought she had."

Charles shook his head slowly, his eyes wide. "You are breathtaking, Harry. You even had your daughter screw me, just in case I needed further persuasion. Oh, God!" Charles slapped his forehead as he remembered. "And Dad's hospital fees. My God, you're unbelievable!"

"Insurance. But, now, don't give me too much credit, Charles," Robeson said with a smile, "Sally may well have something to say about– "

He got no further, as Charles punched him hard, with

230

all the considerable weight of his body, full on the jaw. Robeson collapsed like a stack of cards onto the floor of the cell. He lay still for a moment and then stirred. He looked up at Charles, feeling his chin. Charles stood over him, fists ready.

"Take it easy, Charles, I'm not getting up again. I'm not sure how many of those I can take."

There was movement at the door and two prison officers stood there.

"What the hell's going on?" asked one of them. He looked from Charles to Robeson and back again.

"Nothing, Officer," replied Robeson. "Just a little dispute about tactics," he said with a smile. "Do you think I might stand up now, Charles?"

Charles relaxed his fighting stance and stood back. Robeson stood up and brushed off his jacket.

"The Judge has given you five minutes, sir," said the other officer. "Although he was not best pleased and wants an explanation."

"Thank you," said Charles. "Will you leave us for a minute, please?"

The two men walked back up the corridor.

"Well, Harry. What now?"

"I'll tell you. I'm going upstairs to give evidence. Then I'll listen to your storming speech for the Defence and, with a little luck, I shall be acquitted. Then I shall get on a plane with a few belongings and a little nest-egg that I've converted into universal currency and I shall disappear. London may not be terribly conducive to my health for a while. Tony Kenny is a vindictive man. Not to mention Sergeant West."

"No," replied Charles softly.

"No, what? You think Tony Kenny is *not* a vindictive man?"

"I mean 'No' to all of it. You're not giving evidence, Harry. I'm not calling you."

231

"You can't stop me, Charles. Look," he said, placatingly, "you can square your conscience. You never knew until now, right? You did your job with clean hands and an unsullied heart. Not a soul can blame you."

"You're right: I can't stop you. But I'll have no part in it. You may have contempt for barristers generally, and me in particular, but *I* have certain standards, things that *I* believe in, that *I* live my life by. And it may be naïve, childish, even meaningless for someone like you, but I believe in justice. That's why I took the job. Because I feel I'm doing something worthwhile, something that's decent, that will last. And I won't allow myself to be used to pervert it; not for you, not for Sally," and here he paused, "and not even for Dad."

"What are you going to do?"

"Well, the first thing will be to tell the Judge that I'm professionally embarrassed. I can't call you to give evidence which I know will be perjured."

"That's tantamount to telling him that I've confessed."

Charles looked him straight in the eye. "Yes."

"You can't do that, Charles."

"I can and I will. You know as well as I what my professional rules dictate. I cannot knowingly allow myself to be used as an instrument of your perjury."

"But the jury will know. You must at least make a speech. If I agree not to give evidence, you can do at least that, surely?"

"No. On your instructions I have made the most scurrilous of attacks on the police. I've even suggested that a particular officer planted that gun, when you knew full well that he did nothing of the sort. How can I make any speech now, when I know that the entire basis of the case I've run was a lie?"

"But if you suddenly disappear, the jury will guess what's happened. Barristers don't leave their clients halfway through trials . . ."

"Indeed. That's a risk you should have considered first."

"This must be in breach of your professional rules."

"It isn't. It's my professional rules which give me no choice in the matter. And if you disagree, then report me."

"You fucking hypocrite!" spat Robeson. "You weren't so concerned with professional ethics when *you* were up against it! From what I read, you broke into buildings, deceived people, even assaulted one or two! Well, my life is no less at risk than yours was then."

"Yes, but there's a difference: I was trying to clear my name when I was innocent. *You're* as guilty as sin. What's more, I asked no one else to do my dirty work. You want to deceive the court: fair enough, you do it. But not with me."

Charles glared at Robeson, willing him to do something that would allow Charles to knock him down again. Instead, Robeson stepped back and sat heavily on the bench.

"Jesus Christ, what am I supposed to do?" he asked plaintively.

"That's no longer my problem, Harry. You may be able to persuade the Judge to give you a retrial. I doubt it, though. My advice is to plead guilty. Tell the Judge that you simply couldn't bring yourself to lie on oath. Say anything you like. I no longer care."

Charles made to go. Robeson grabbed him by the upper arm. "What about Sally? Don't you care about her?"

Charles eyed him icily. "Let go of me or I shall beat the living daylights out of you here and now."

Robeson let go. Charles stared at him for a further moment, and then swept out.

CHAPTER 22

Charles marched into court and demanded to see Pullman in Chambers. Belloff raised an interrogative eyebrow at him, but before Charles could answer the clerk came out to take them into Pullman's room.

"I apologise, Judge, if I've appeared rude, or if my behaviour has seemed bizarre, but . . . extraordinary as it may seem this late in the case, while in the cells my client has put me in the position that . . . I cannot continue to represent him."

Pullman stared at Charles in surprise. "Good heavens," he exclaimed. "At this stage? The man must be mad. I thought he had every chance of getting off."

"So did I."

"Then what's he playing at? Is he hoping for a retrial?"

"No, that's certainly not it. I'm sorry, but I really can't explain it, Judge."

"I understand."

In fact Pullman had misunderstood. Charles's inability to explain was not due to any professional constraints, but because he still could not believe that Robeson had committed forensic suicide. Charles did not think the point worth clarifying.

"And you are quite sure that you cannot continue to represent him?" asked Pullman.

"Quite sure."

"Well, Belloff, what are we to do?"

"I think that's a matter for you, Judge. We can either proceed without Charles, or we could discharge this jury and start again with different counsel."

"Very well. I shall come into court, and you, Holroyd, had better make your application to be relieved of further conduct. I'll then hear what Robeson has to say and make a decision."

Charles and Belloff returned to court. Judge Pullman entered a moment later.

"I am grateful to the time given to me, my Lord. I regret, however, that as a result of what has been said to me during the time I spent in conference with my client, I find myself professionally embarrassed. It is with the greatest reluctance that I must therefore ask to be discharged from further representing Mr Robeson."

There was a sudden muttering in court which grew, like the rumblings of a storm. Newspaper men began scribbling furiously and the people packed into the public gallery shifted restlessly.

"Silence in court!"

"Are you quite sure, Mr Holroyd?"

"I regret, my Lord, that I am."

"Then of course I must discharge you. However, would you please remain in court for the moment."

"Of course."

"Now, Mr Robeson," said Pullman. "Do you have anything to say about this?"

Robeson stood upright in the dock. He smiled at the Judge. "Yes, my Lord. May I ask for the indictment to be put again?"

"I beg your pardon?"

"I want the indictment to be put again."

Pullman looked staggered. "Mr Holroyd, did you anticipate this course?"

"Not at all, my Lord."

"Mr Robeson, you are unrepresented at present, and I am reluctant to allow you to take such a course without proper legal advice. Do you wish to apply for a short adjournment?"

"No, thank you. I know what I am doing, my Lord."

"Be that as it may, I'm not happy with what's occurred. You are under no obligation to alter your plea because of Mr Holroyd's difficulties."

"I appreciate that. My Lord, I have been a solicitor for longer than I care to remember – longer than your Lordship has been at the Bar or Bench, I daresay. There is nothing that any counsel could tell or advise me that would change my mind. I do not wish to be represented further. I have decided to alter my plea."

"Well, if that is what you want."

"It is, my Lord."

"Very well. Let the indictment be put again."

The clerk of the court rose. "Harold Joseph Robeson, you stand charged with an offence of conspiracy to rob, in that between the 1st day of June 1987 and the 1st day of January 1988 you conspired with Anthony Kenny, Peter Simons, Raymond Papier and persons unknown to rob the South African Gem Corporation of a quantity of diamonds worth one million pounds. How do you plead, guilty or not guilty?"

"Guilty."

"Well, I'll be damned," muttered Pullman to himself. He peered over his bench to the shorthand writer. "Did you catch that?" he asked in a stage whisper.

"Yes, my Lord, but I didn't record it."

"Good. I mean, thank you."

"Harold Joseph Robeson, you have decided, albeit late in the day, to plead guilty to this offence. Notwithstanding your wish not to be represented further, I appointed Mr Holroyd to act as *amicus* so as to assist the court, and I have been greatly helped by what he has said. You owe him a debt of gratitude. I take into account the fact that, as Mr Holroyd rightly says, you had every chance of acquittal, and that to plead guilty at this stage of the trial took much courage. I also take into account the fact that it was your reluctance to commit perjury that persuaded you, at the last, to change your plea. For those reasons I think I am, unusually, entitled to give you credit for pleading guilty as if you had done so at a much earlier stage.

"I also take into account that you had an unimpeachable record that spanned sixty years before this matter, and that however long a period you serve, your career as a solicitor of the Supreme Court is finished. None the less, this was a professional robbery, made all the more so by your assistance. In the course of the robbery, one man was disabled for life and, even though you took no part in the execution of it, you knew that firearms were to be used and you allied yourself to the plan to use violence to steal those diamonds.

"In all the circumstances, the very least sentence I can pass, bearing in mind the fact that the case is now over four years old, and your age, is one of eight years' imprisonment. Take him down."

Robeson was led away. "Mr Holroyd," said Pullman, smiling like a shark, but with a genuine attempt at warmth, "I would like to thank you for the extremely professional and able way in which you have conducted this matter. The court is grateful." Charles bowed low to the Judge. "I shall rise now."

There was the usual scuffle and hubbub as those in the press bench fought to get out and those in the public gallery stood to leave. In the well of the court, the CPS solicitor congratulated Belloff on securing the conviction and the police officers busied themselves with slapping one another on the back. Belloff leant towards Charles and spoke confidentially to him.

"Bad luck, Charles, old chap. Still, look at it this way: you couldn't have proved more effectively that you're honest."

Belloff was only half-serious, but Charles did not find the comment amusing. "So people thought I was bent, did they?"

"Well, you know what the Temple's like. Some people have nothing better to do than gossip and slander."

"I see. So I've saved my reputation, at the cost of Robeson's eight years and my father's life. Wonderful."

"Your father's life? What are you on about, old chap?"

"Nothing," replied Charles bitterly. "Forget it."

He picked up his papers and turned to leave. He heard someone call his name and turned round. Sally stood in the aisle next to him. Her eyes were red and her mascara smudged.

"Did you hear?" asked Charles.

"I heard," she answered calmly.

"I'm sorry, Sally. I don't know what to say."

Belloff pushed past Charles and diplomatically herded out of court the police officers who were still standing around congratulating one another.

"You don't have to say anything. It's me who has to talk to you, Charlie, if you'll let me."

He shrugged. "I don't know what there is to say. Perhaps it would be better if we just left it there."

"No. I have to speak to you, just a for a while. I know what you're thinking, and you're wrong."

"Am I?" he asked, derisively. "You and your father make quite a team."

"No," she said, shaking her head violently like a little girl, "it's not true. Please let me explain."

Charles looked hard at her. She returned his gaze, her eyes pleading, her lower lip trembling. "Well," he replied finally, "I'm going down to see Robes— your father. You can wait for me if you want. I shan't be long."

She nodded silently and bit her lip, on the verge of more tears. "Do you think they'll let me see him?" she asked.

"I don't know. Maybe. I'll ask if you like. Perhaps you'd better come down to the cells with me."

"No, I couldn't speak to him with you there."

"I didn't mean that. I should think they'll let you see him when I've finished."

"Okay. Then I'll come."

They went together to the basement and Charles rang the bell. When the door was opened Charles asked if Sally could see Robeson after he was finished.

"No, sir, I'm sorry. No social visits."

"Look, no one expected him to change his plea, and we weren't anticipating a verdict today. He's now got eight years. Can't you allow her even two minutes? She's his daughter."

"I'm really sorry– "

"But she's a barrister's clerk. Can't you put her down as a professional visit? She can come in with me and wait by your desk until I've finished. Then I'll wait for her and take her back up again."

The prison officer wavered. "Please?" begged Sally.

"All right. Come on, then. But you'll have to be signed in together."

He took their names, left Sally by his desk and escorted Charles to an interview room. Robeson joined him a few minutes later. He entered without speaking and sat at the tiny table, his hands clasped before him. As a convicted prisoner, he had had his cigars taken away from him and he fiddled with his fingers nervously.

"Well, Charles. What can I do for you?"

"Nothing. I came down to see how you were and if there's anything I can do for you. Anyone I can contact, anything like that."

"Still the conscientious professional man, eh?" He said it without bitterness.

"Harry, I'm sorry. Believe me, I'm very sorry. I didn't want things to turn out this way, particularly as it's hurt Sally so much. But you left me no choice."

"I know. I only have myself to blame. I misjudged you. You're a damn good barrister, Charles, but a bit too straight for my taste. Funnily enough, although you fear the worst, now it's actually happened, it doesn't feel so bad. It's a relief in a way."

"I hope that feeling lasts," said Charles, doubting that it would. Robeson was still in shock. It would take some weeks before he realised what had happened to him. "Eight years is not that– "

"Please, Charles," he interrupted, "don't tell me I've had a good result. That really would be too much. And I don't want to hear about remission and parole either."

Charles shrugged. "I understand. If there's nothing you'd like me to do, I'll go now. Sally's here to see you."

Robeson nodded.

Charles transferred his books and papers to his left hand, and held out his right. Robeson did not take it. Instead, he reached into his trouser pocket and pulled out a piece of paper. He stood up and handed it to Charles. "Give my regards to your parents," he said.

Charles turned the paper over in his hands. It was a cheque for £9,000. He looked at Robeson, his head shaking slightly, speechless.

"Take it in good health." Robeson grinned, and shrugged. "What am I going to do with it? Better that you and your family should get the benefit from it. Now, Charles, my boy, bugger off and let me see my daughter."

Robeson took Charles's hand which was still out-stretched, the cheque clasped in it, and squeezed it with both of his. Then he turned away and leaned against the wall, his back to the room. Charles turned and, without a word, departed.

Sally was no more than five minutes and when she returned, Charles was surprised to see that she was composed. As the outer door banged shut after them, she faced Charles. "I need to wash my face and tidy myself up a bit. You've got to get changed. There's a wine bar almost opposite, down that little side street, under the arch. Can I meet you there in fifteen minutes?"

"Yes, I know it. I'll see you there."

Charles went back to the top of the building to get out of his wig and gown. It was not quite four o'clock and the robing room was almost empty, most cases still being in progress. He fixed his day collar to his shirt and knotted his tie. As he stood looking in the mirror someone came up behind him.

"Hello, Charles. I gather you've had quite an afternoon."

It was Sebastian Campbell-Smythe, a member of Charles's old Chambers. Charles had not spoken to him once in the year since he had left. His first reaction was to tell him to piss off, but then, he thought, what the hell? So he smiled with as much sincerity as he could command, and replied.

"Yes. Things have been a little hectic."

"I gather Pullman gave you a public acknowledgment. We must have a drink some time and you can tell me all about it. I'm dying to hear the inside story of Harry Robeson."

Charles turned and looked at the barrister.

"Rehabilitated, am I?" He smiled bitterly. "Sure, we'll have a drink some time."

Campbell-Smythe patted Charles on the shoulder as he left. "See you soon, then."

Charles took the lift to the ground floor and left the building. He crossed the road and began to walk towards the wine bar, but the nearer he got, the slower and more hesitant were his footsteps. He stood before the door, reached up to push it open and stopped. Then, with a deep sigh, he turned and walked off towards Chambers.

CHAPTER 23

During the following weeks Charles found himself suddenly much more popular. He did not know whether it was the publicity of the Robeson case, or just the long-awaited upturn in his practice, but the diary filled up well into the New Year and the pile of briefs on his desk grew. Christmas celebrations began, the Temple began to feel like the friendly place it once had been. Rachel was still in America, but Charles was busy most evenings, catching up with people he had not seen for some time.

He was not looking forward to Christmas, however. His father had come out of hospital a week before, the surgery successful, and David had driven him and Millie to the home of friends in Bournemouth where he was to recuperate. They would not be back until the New Year. David and Sonia had invited him to spend the holiday with them, but sincere as the invitation was, Charles knew that the newlyweds would rather be alone.

He thought often about Sally, her urchin smile and soft skin, but he could not bring himself to telephone her. One Friday night, however, a couple of days before Christmas, he was about to go home after a few drinks with colleagues in the Witness Box when he saw a familiar figure at a table at the other end of the bar. Charles excused himself and went over, pushing through the crowd.

"Hello Sally."

She sat alone at a small table, almost surrounded by a

large and boisterous group of drinkers all of whom were standing. There was an empty glass before her. She did not look up, but her cheeks flushed.

"Do you mind if I sit down?" he asked, looking about for a second chair.

"I've been watching you and wondering if you'd see me," she said. "I'm surprised you want to talk to me at all."

"I wouldn't have come over otherwise."

She neither answered nor looked up. Charles waited for a while. Then he shrugged. "Perhaps you're right," he said. "I'll go. I just . . . felt I owed you an apology. For not meeting you in the wine bar after the case. I . . . I just couldn't face it. I'm sorry."

He took a step back. Sally looked up and Charles saw tears in her eyes. He pulled a chair from an adjoining table and sat down. Sally bent over the table again, her hands clasped tightly in front of her. Charles could see her nails digging into the back of her hands, and, hesitantly, he reached across and placed his hand on hers.

"I wouldn't do that," she said, her voice catching in her throat, "people will see."

He left his hand where it was, and she made no attempt to remove it. Two tears ran down her cheeks and plopped on the shiny surface in front of her. Charles reached into his pocket with his other hand and pulled out what was, thankfully, a clean handkerchief. He offered it to her and she took it from him with her free hand and dabbed at her eyes.

"I didn't expect you to understand," she said, still sobbing, "but I thought at least that you'd have the decency to listen."

"I didn't feel there was anything to say. You did what you thought was right, that's all."

"You're wrong."

"Am I?" he asked, disbelieving.

She reached into her handbag and drew out a plastic season ticket holder. Slipped into the back, behind her ticket, was a piece of card. She handed it to Charles. He frowned, and turned it over. It was a photograph.

"I was three. Michelle must have been a few months old. Tracey hadn't been born yet."

Charles had to hold up the dog-eared photograph to examine it in the dim light. It was in black and white and showed a couple on a windswept pier. In the woman's arms, entirely swathed in a shawl, was an infant. The man stood beside her, squinting slightly into the sun. He held a child by the hand. She was small and dark and was frowning, also perhaps because of the light that shone in her eyes. The family stood in front of an amusement arcade behind which Charles could make out a huge expanse of grey sand and, in the distance, the sea.

"It was taken at Southend. The little girl's me. And that's Dad," she said, pointing to the man. It was unmistakeably Robeson, then, Charles guessed, in his late thirties. Charles studied the slice of life he held in his hand. He peered into the grainy photograph, trying to see into Robeson's eyes, looking for any glimpse of the man he would become or the fate that awaited him twenty-five years hence.

"He left about a year and a half after that. Mum never remarried. When she took up with Frank – I was about twelve – she changed all our names to his, but only to stop the neighbours talking really. I don't know if she ever loved 'im, but they stayed together long enough. I'd forgotten almost everything about Dad by then anyway. I kept the photo, though, and I would look at it and try to picture what had happened before it and after it. It was my one bit of certainty, d'you understand? At least I had proof that I had had a father, even if only for that day, at that very moment."

Charles nodded.

"And from that I would extend it outwards, like I was reclaiming land, until I could imagine the whole day, all of it, like I had a video of it. Then the whole week, then a month, until I could imagine him as part of my life. Like he was there. I'd guess what he'd have thought or said in any given situation. I even used to have imaginary conversations with him in bed.

"Then, after, when I'd left college and I was looking for a job, I saw an advert in the *Standard* for a barrister's clerk. I went for the interview and I didn't get it, but the idea stuck. I tried for months, and then Mum said that she knew someone who might be able to help. She never said who he was or nothing, just an old friend. I didn't meet him. Mum just told me that an interview had been set up and I should go. That was at Chancery Court. I got the job. It wasn't until a couple of months after that Stanley mentioned that a Mr Robeson had got me the interview."

"'Course, I knew immediately who it must have been. I looked Dad up in the Solicitors' List and got in touch. I never told Mum, I suppose because I thought she'd be hurt. And it was just as I'd imagined it for all those years. He spoke to me just as he did in my head. It was . . . fantastic."

"Why are you telling me all this, Sally?"

"Well . . . because I want you to understand."

"This isn't helping me understand."

"I love him."

"Yes. So what? What're you saying? Because you love him, you agreed to sleep with me? Okay, I understand now." He shrugged. "What I *don't* understand is what effect you thought it would have on me? Did you seriously believe that it would affect how I represented him?"

"No, that's the point. Dad may have, but I knew you, before your trouble over Henrietta. I knew it wouldn't make any difference to you."

"I might have been prepared to believe that, if it weren't

246

for the timing, Sally. I saw you in the pub, that first time, remember? And two days later – it may even have been the next day – I start getting Robeson and Co. briefs in. I find that difficult to swallow, I'm afraid."

"I'm not saying that that was coincidence. I *did* speak to Dad to see if he could help out. I was worried about you, Charlie, you were going to leave the Bar. I weren't even sure you'd take the work – I knew it would look odd. But I asked. And I was delighted he tried to help. That's all there was to it, Charlie, I swear."

"Then why didn't you tell me? Why didn't you say: 'My father's Harry Robeson, and he's agreed to send you some work'?"

She stared into her empty glass. "Because I was afraid you'd stop seeing me. Or stop taking the work. I didn't want either. And so what if he decided to instruct you in his own case? I mean, he might have had his own motives, but from my point of view, I knew you'd do a good job, so why not?"

"And you had no idea he would use our relationship as a lever if he had to?" he asked sarcastically.

Sally hung her head and nodded. "Oh, yeah. I knew what he might do. I've got no illusions. He might've instructed you 'cos I asked him; on the other hand, it wouldn't have surprised me if he'd had his own motives. But what was I supposed to do? Deprive me father of his best chance of acquittal? Or stop seeing you?" She looked away from him again.

"Oh, come on, Sally, we'd only been seeing one another for a couple of weeks. Don't try to tell me . . ."

Charles stopped in mid-sentence. Her head was bent low and tears now rolled one after another down her cheeks and splashed on to the table, leaving two small puddles.

"I knew it, you see?" she sobbed. "Whatever I did, I was gonna lose both of you."

"I can understand why you're so upset over your father," Charles said gently, "but I don't see— "

"No, you don't see, do you? Why are you so fuckin' blind?" She almost shouted the last words, causing some of the people standing about them to look down at the two of them and grin at one another. She did not appear to care, but stared up at Charles, almost defiantly, her mascara smudged, her eyes red and her cheeks wet. He felt a wave of tenderness for her sweep over him.

"I'm in love with you," she said softly, still staring into his eyes. "I've been in love with you for years. Since long before you were my knight in shining armour. I never thought for one minute anything'd come of it. I was just the junior clerk and you was married to the daughter of the head of Chambers. And then it happened . . . and . . . it was wonderful. Sort of, like my father, y'know? No, don't laugh. I'd imagined what he was like, and when I got to know him, I was right. So, just the same, I'd imagined what it'd be like with you. I had run that first time over in my mind a thousand times before it actually happened. And when it did . . . it was fantastic." She paused, and spoke quietly, more to herself than to him. "Like coming home."

"Oh, Sally." He reached out and took her hand.

"You do believe me, don't you, Charlie? I saw all this coming . . . I just didn't know how to get out of it. Please say you believe me."

"I do. I believe you."

Her nose was running, and she sniffed, to little effect. She laughed, embarrassed. "Sorry," she apologised. She disengaged her hand and blew her nose noisily.

"Well?" she asked, her voice muffled.

"Well, what?"

"I dunno. Just . . . well . . . now what?" She tried to wipe the black tracks that coursed down her face.

"You look a state," he said with a grin.

248

"I bet."

"Look, the flat's just over the road. Do you want to come over and tidy up? I think you even left some makeup there."

"There's a mirror in the loo here," she pointed out. "I wouldn't want to disrupt your evening."

"You won't. I had nothing planned. I was going to watch TV and have an early night."

"On your own?"

"Not necessarily," he said, as he took her hand in his again.